PRAISE FOR EMILY SCHULTZ

Praise for *Sleeping with Friends*

"This propulsive thriller will have you on the edge of your seat as old friends reunite to solve a mystery that implicates them all. Schultz raises questions of art and artifice, memory and trust, all while telling a page-turning, unputdownable story."

—Anna North, *New York Times* bestselling author of *Outlawed*

Praise for *Little Threats*

Apple Books Best of November 2020 pick

"Fans of Tana French, Kimberly Belle, and *Orange Is the New Black* will fall under this book's spell . . . Terse and tense, *Little Threats* investigates righteous anger, teenage angst, and the enormity of setting the record straight."

—*Booklist*

"A taut psychological thriller . . . Schultz knows how to keep the reader engrossed."

—*Publishers Weekly*

"Brilliantly structured and gorgeously written, *Little Threats* is a captivating mystery about a young woman accused of a brutal murder—one she isn't sure she's committed. It's a story of love and loss, the power of guilt, and the savagely delicate fabric of family."

—Kimberly McCreight, *New York Times* bestselling author of *Reconstructing Amelia* and *A Good Marriage*

"Emily Schultz unfolds her story with masterful precision and restraint, delivering a novel that is pure emotional dynamite."
—Wendy Walker, bestselling author of *The Night Before*

"A pulsating mystery, where small details enlighten and illuminate."
—Lori Lansens, author of *The Girls* and *This Little Light*

"Emily Schultz's *Little Threats* is a complex, powerful, emotionally wrenching thriller with a deceptively simple premise: What if you agreed to serve fifteen years in prison for a murder you have no memory of committing? Intense, twisty, and compelling—once you begin reading, you won't be able to stop!"
—Karen Dionne, author of the #1 internationally bestselling *The Marsh King's Daughter*

"At its heart, *Little Threats* is a devastating and elegiac novel about teenage friendships, sexuality, drug use, and, ultimately, betrayal. Emily Schultz is unflinching in revealing the way prison isn't merely a place but a feeling that can haunt a girl who grew into a woman behind bars. Freedom isn't absolution, and the answers are as painful as the questions in this heart-stopping, powerful story."
—Bryn Greenwood, author of *The Reckless Oath We Made* and *All the Ugly and Wonderful Things*

"*Little Threats* hooked me from the first line. A gripping, haunting story about family, memory, and, most of all, grief—this book is difficult to put down and more difficult to stop thinking about."
—Rob Hart, author of *The Warehouse*

"Emily Schultz's *Little Threats* is an exquisitely written and thrilling novel about growing up and breaking apart, about the past refusing to loosen its grip on us, and about the impossibility of going back and righting the wrongs that send us spiraling out of control. And, of course, it's a whale of a whodunit. This is a riveting and powerful novel about friendship and fate, youth and time, and the toll these things take on all of us. Don't miss it!"

—David Bell, *USA Today* bestselling author of *The Request*

Praise for *The Blondes*

Best Book of 2015 by NPR, BookPage, and *Kirkus Reviews*

"*The Blondes* is scary and deeply, bitingly funny—a satire about gender that kept me reading until four in the morning—and a fine addition to the all-too-small genre of feminist horror."

—NPR (Also a Great Reads 2015 selection)

"*The Blondes* is intelligent, mesmerizing, and fearless. An entirely original and beautifully twisted satire with a heart of darkness."

—Emily St. John Mandel, author of *Station Eleven*

"A nail-biter that is equal parts suspense, science fiction, and a funny, dark send-up of the stranglehold of gender."

—*Kirkus Reviews*, Best Books of 2015

"Funny, horrific, and frighteningly realistic, Schultz's second novel is a must read."

—*The Library Journal* (starred)

SLEEPING
WITH
FRIENDS

OTHER TITLES BY EMILY SCHULTZ

SLEEPING
WITH
FRIENDS

EMILY
SCHULTZ

THOMAS & MERCER

Published by Thomas & Mercer, Seattle

www.apub.com

Amazon, the Amazon logo, and Thomas & Mercer are trademarks of Amazon.com, Inc., or its affiliates.

ISBN-13: 9781662513480 (paperback)
ISBN-13: 9781662513473 (digital)

Cover design by Sarah Horgan
Cover image: © durantelallera, © cybermagician / Shutterstock

Printed in the United States of America

To Betty and Dawn,
my unshakable, wild lovelies

Cinema is the most beautiful fraud in the world.
—Jean-Luc Godard

Prologue

Save the Date

At first, Mia thought the blood in her eyes was an Instagram filter. Above her, the trees had gone red. The morning fog, auburn. But then, Mia couldn't tell if she was dreaming or watching a film where a woman, alone, winds her way slowly down a country lane. Blumhouse or art house? Was she a strong female character? No matter—the scene needed more light. Too flat. Whoever was making this film should have waited for magic hour. Mia squinted, placed bare feet against stone, left, right, as if every step mattered, looking down, seeing her movements more than feeling them.

Her ears rang, and her head felt thick, as though she were carrying a sandbag across her shoulders. Yet as she advanced toward the road, it occurred to her she wasn't carrying anything but the weight of pain. When she blinked hard, her ears would pop, and she could hear the sound of morning—birds twittering overhead—for a few seconds before the ringing again blotted out everything real.

She knew the moment the stone driveway turned to gravel. It meant she had gone through the gate, reached the road. Whose gate, which road, she didn't know, but something inside said, *A little farther.* She could see squares of light ahead, peeking through branches: another house. How far—a half mile? More? She didn't know. She didn't look back, but she thought, *Whoever did this, they'll come for me again.* It became a song in her mind and drove each step. She gripped her white robe tighter around her, closing it with one hand at her throat. There was burgundy all down one sleeve, like a tumble of cherry blossoms. But it wasn't a pattern, just more blood.

The pitted road cut into her bare feet, so she loped toward a ditch and cold, dewy grass. Then, a slight embankment. She felt the smooth cement of another driveway, and she sank to her knees, grateful. Her feet and legs were numb. This was safety, as close as she could get. Her hands wrapped around the bars of the neighbor's gate. She shook it as hard as she could, screaming.

Chapter One

Prep Time

Mia was everyone's wife. When you were with Mia, she was more than present. She was yours—there for you in a way no one else was. She looked into your eyes the whole time you were talking. She heard you and knew just what you needed, even when you didn't. In Agnes's opinion, Mia Sinclair was the most sincere and generous person she'd ever met—so smart, so beautiful, with a sense of humor that could wilt anyone who underestimated her. It was that bond that happens only when you're in your early twenties, when you meet a friend and know: *This is the girl I would die for. This is the person I'm meant to know forever.* That's why it was a shock when Mia actually did get married, as if the vows of friendship meant nothing anymore.

She'd abandoned not just Agnes but everyone—Victor, Ethan, Zoey—the whole five-way marriage that had grown around Mia and her friend circle during college.

That time now counted as "years ago," but Agnes still instinctively grabbed her phone to call Mia anytime something "big" happened—whether it was a disaster like her car stalling in the middle of the Williamsburg Bridge or a thrill like seeing the French actress Marion Cotillard outside a McDonald's in the East Village. But the last time Agnes had phoned Mia, she'd had to leave a message. Mia couldn't have picked up because she had already been taken to the hospital and put into a coma, her slightly open eyes fluttering inside a fractured skull no one could explain how she'd gotten.

Now she was out of the hospital, and it was time to help her heal. Agnes drove fast, eager to get to Mia's house in Connecticut, with Zoey in the passenger seat. They zipped past red maples that were pink with buds and serviceberry trees emerging in blossom. Beyond the highway they shifted in the breeze like delicate white ghosts.

Over the last few weeks, Agnes had dropped everything and acted as a conduit between the friends and Mia's family, forwarding updates from doctors, researching medical terms: *stents, aphasia, visual memory loss.* When it had first happened, Agnes had emailed a pediatrician cousin and asked why they would put Mia into an induced coma for a head injury.

It's pressing pause on the patient's life, she'd written back. Because they don't know what else to do.

In some ways, Mia had already done that by moving out here. Although she'd spent some time in Brooklyn, it seemed like more and more over the last year, when Agnes would phone her, she'd be "in the country."

Agnes peered at the road signs, and Zoey shifted uncomfortably in the passenger seat. Agnes could tell that Zoey wished she were the one driving instead. "I was invited up here a few more times," Zoey said, casually declaring the old status wars of who had the most Mia Time. "Probably because Ethan and I are a couple."

Couple or not, on the count of Mia Time, Martin had clearly won over everyone else.

After being weaned out of the fourteen-day coma and the subsequent recovery time, Mia had been under her husband's constant supervision. When Agnes had visited Mia in the hospital, she could tell Mia hadn't remembered her. Whenever Agnes smiled at her, Mia's bloodshot eyes just glanced away. She hadn't been herself. A roughly shaved spot on the back of Mia's head showed the stitches that closed up the wound caused, Martin had said (often and loudly), by the corner of their marble kitchen island at the country house. Agnes could see the nursing staff thinking *Husband did it* as they rotely adjusted IV drips and charts. Martin had told her he was at their brownstone in Brooklyn when it had happened.

No one would ever think that two weeks of sleep could erase so many wide-awake years. The number of concerts they'd been to together in the early days, the art and writing projects, the joints passed back and forth, the blouses or jeans lent and never returned. Still, Agnes had a hard time believing it—the entire inventory erased.

Then, as Agnes had been leaving the hospital that first day, Mia had said a name—*Thora*—in such a thin, plaintive tone that Agnes set down her purse again.

"We were friends, weren't we? Like in *Ghost World?*" Mia asked.

Taking her hand, Agnes had told her yes. Yes. *How in the hell does she remember Thora Birch but not me?* Agnes had wondered. Was the implication that Mia was Scarlett Johansson?

———

It was Agnes who convinced Martin to let them hold a "remembering party" once Mia was allowed to go home. Let her be surrounded by faces she'd known for years. Agnes and Zoey would bring photos and videos. Her favorite foods. Mia's sister, Stephanie, would come, too, fly in from Chicago. Martin had seemed more drained than convinced. "It's more a remembering *game*, isn't it?" he'd asked. "Deciding what she remembers. People change."

What Agnes heard was a man worried that there was more of Mia's friends left inside her head than him.

———

"I'm not sure where our exit is. Were you mapping this for us?" Agnes asked.

Zoey picked a phone up from the console. "Oh wait. This is *your* phone."

Agnes ducked her head. "I have that model now. Because you said you liked yours. And I could pay on a monthly plan."

Zoey laughed. "Ah, rose gold too." She peered down at the phone screen and said, "You've got a notification. It's an email from your bank."

"Oh, they can wait. Give me that."

Agnes took the phone back as Zoey dug through her purse for her own. She woke it up and held the map up for Agnes. Zoey glanced at the road ahead, looking for the exit to Kettlebury, Connecticut, the closest town. It would be on the right in two miles.

Agnes snapped on her turn signal early and moved into the right lane. "When was the last time you came up here?"

"We were invited a lot." Zoey always found a way to one-up. "But since the show took off, it's been tough getting away."

Zoey Wilder and her boyfriend, Ethan Sharp, produced a YouTube show called *Movie Fail* against a green sheet in their apartment, in which they counted continuity errors in hit films. Things like whether the room in *Pulp Fiction* had already had bullet holes on the wall before the shoot-out began. Or how Don Cheadle could open a stereo store at the end of *Boogie Nights* with only a hundred dollars taken from a doughnut-shop robbery. Ethan and Zoey's show had gone viral after the director of a Marvel movie had gotten mad and tweeted death threats at them.

"Same here," Agnes said. "I was dealing with that breakup."

"Right, your Aussie. Charlie. How'd you mess that up? God, she was gorgeous."

"Too blonde and too tall. It put me on edge. They all look like elves from *Lord of the Rings* down there."

"What happened with her?"

"Two months in she said she was having visa problems. She basically proposed by handing me paperwork to fill out."

Zoey argued, "It might have been worth it. A hot Australian with 'visa problems.' It's a rom-com."

Agnes shook her head. "A day after breaking up with her, I was walking past the Cubbyhole, and she was making out with someone else already."

Until then, Agnes had always been the friend who agreed to everything. *Yes, I will pick up the phone every time you call. I will answer each text. I will tell you he was so wrong for you—but only after you've broken up with him. I will attend your hastily planned wedding and never complain about not being maid of honor. And yes (finally), when you get out of the hospital, I will be the one to organize and host the remembering party to help you find your way again. I will make sure everyone who should be there is there.*

But she hadn't said yes to her girlfriend. Maybe because there had been no one else there to tell her that she should say yes.

Maybe Mia had always stood halfway between Agnes and Zoey. Maybe that was why the friendship had worked for so many years. There was always an anchor.

Back in the day, Agnes would drink too much with Mia at hip hotel bars on payday and try not to be sick on the subway home, or they would buy designer clothes to go to restaurants, then return the outfits the next day. (Mia's favorite hustle.) Sometimes Mia had called their adventures *networking*, but mostly they'd done it just to be out in the city and take photos of each other, talk about everything they would do one day. They'd done many things but, in the end, very little of what they'd planned. Instead of writing her own book, Agnes worked at the literary agent's office and then moved on to an indie publisher just large enough to have health coverage. Mia had strolled from one internship to another but never made anything permanent.

Agnes took the exit slowly. Zoey pulled up Spotify on her phone and waved it back and forth. "I made a playlist to help her remember. You know, songs from *the days*."

Agnes had noticed that Zoey always referred to their friendship as if it were far in the past. Agnes still considered Mia her best friend. Never mind that they saw each other less and less after she married Martin. She wondered why Zoey didn't think of it that way, as something that continued inevitably and always. She noticed she hadn't offered to plug in the playlist during the drive. Perhaps she'd been content with the Tegan and Sara CD warbling out of Agnes's old car stereo.

The car was her mother's pass-down. After retiring, her parents decided they didn't need two cars. The Nielsens considered it extravagance. For a long time, she'd been the only friend in their circle with a car, parking and reparking the Ford Focus on the filthy streets of Brooklyn, picking up war wounds on the bumper as bad parallel parkers chipped away at the white paint. She was secretly proud of the one thing she owned. Then one day, she hadn't been the only one. Zoey had bought a Honda Accord, while Mia married, then suddenly had two cars and a summer house. Even Ethan had begun buying expensive camera equipment—his conversations consisting entirely of grumbles about having to track down the right BNC cords. Agnes had kept the same car, although the Ford Focus needed more repairs now. The morning mirror showed Agnes some of the war wounds she'd picked up over the years too.

She realized during the hour drive from New York, neither she nor Zoey had mentioned Mia's actual accident. They had talked about Mia and the old days, of course—how they'd met in Adaptation Studies and how Mia had always been the center of any room—but nothing about her health. The accident had been a shock for all of them. Martin had written a long Facebook post, tagging all the old friends and explaining how Mia had been found by a neighbor, bloody on a country road near their weekend house, semiconscious.

"I hate to do this on social media . . . ," the post had begun, and at the time Agnes had the immediate thought that really what he hated was to have to include them in his life, in Mia's tragedy.

Weeks later, it still made Agnes feel shaky to think of Mia alone, hurt in the dark countryside, and all her friends finding out that way. Martin had said she must have slipped on some water in their kitchen and then, confused, left her phone and wandered outside and down the road. No shoes. That was the detail that haunted Agnes. Her version of Mia had always been put together—impulsive sometimes, but ready for anything.

"Can you imagine that walk?" Agnes had asked Zoey over the phone back when they first heard, but Zoey had cut her off.

"Where is Mia? Which hospital, which room?!"

Agnes had understood Zoey had been upset, but the fact that she hadn't been listening and dismissed Agnes's concerns outright bothered her. It felt as though over the years, all Zoey's strength and patience had shifted, getting hoovered up by Ethan until there was none left for anyone else. That was the thing with couples—they became one entity after a while. It was eerie, like when dogs start looking like their owners.

"Okay, where are we? Guide me," Agnes said as the car moved into Kettlebury, a commuter town between Stamford and Norwalk. As she drove, she thought about how the sky had been winter gray when Mia had her accident, and now it was waking with her: the yards flashed with tiny purple bruises of crocus. There were daffodil stalks but no showy yellow heads yet. Those would come soon.

A reminder alarm went off on Zoey's phone. She swore under her breath. "My Ovidrel shot. I need to find a bathroom." Zoey pointed out a coffee shop up the road.

"Getting knocked up in a Dunkin' Donuts bathroom?" Agnes joked.

Zoey laughed and said it was just a "trigger shot," to stimulate ovulation. Then she added, "Maybe you're right. A Starbucks would feel better." She wasn't joking, and in twenty seconds, Zoey had located a Starbucks on her phone. The Starbucks was five miles farther. Agnes would have been happy with Dunkin', but that was Zoey. She was willing to wait in line at a sample sale or go five miles for a better coffee; the little moments of luxury mattered to her. She believed she deserved good things.

"It's so exciting you and Ethan are trying to have a baby," Agnes said. They'd been together since just after college graduation, so it made sense they would go that route.

"I know," Zoey said, looking at her phone. "This baby is going to energize my social feeds."

"That's . . . true," Agnes hedged.

Zoey turned in the passenger seat to face her. She bit her lip. "Don't tell anyone, but the sperm in the cooler bag is not Ethan's."

Agnes shot her a look. "Whose junk is in my trunk?"

"Don't worry. He's totally on board."

Reading Zoey's expression, Agnes suspected he might not be. "Is getting pregnant the right thing to do? I mean, right now?"

Zoey sighed. "I figure, you don't get to choose where your car breaks down. If you hit thirty-six and you want a baby, you have it with the person you're with, wherever you are, or it's not going to happen."

Agnes nodded. "I can totally see that on a Hallmark card. Watercolor of a car broken down on the New Jersey Turnpike."

Zoey laughed. "And in a nice script font, the words 'Because you decided to accept things as they are . . .'"

Agnes began laughing and couldn't stop. "Oh shit, I think I just peed myself a little."

There was a sudden *thwack*, and Agnes felt herself rise for a second off the seat. She skidded hard. Out the side window, she saw a raccoon crawl from the shoulder into the woods beyond.

"Oh no. That's not good." Agnes slowed the car.

"It's fine. Don't stop."

Agnes braked anyway.

"This is serious! I have to take my shot!" Zoey insisted.

In the rearview, Agnes could see something dark far back on the shoulder. There'd been two of them, but only one had made it across. "I can't leave it to suffer."

Zoey turned and looked back over her shoulder at the receding road. "I can't see anything. The bump had to be a pothole."

Agnes shivered. She had never hurt an animal before. "They're so much like us . . . little human hands. I feel horrible."

"There was only one. You didn't hit anything, babe," Zoey reassured her. "It's fine." Agnes wondered if this was how her friend would deal with the chaos of a baby—middle-of-the-night crying jags, spit-up, fevers, and tantrums—coolly, efficiently, unflinchingly.

Maybe it was the more logical approach to the things life threw at you. Agnes girded herself and picked up speed again. But the gnawing feeling in her stomach didn't subside, and she found herself glancing left and right at the fields beside them, hoping nothing else bolted into her path.

———

In the Starbucks lot, Agnes watched Zoey unfold from the compact car. She was tall, with a dancer's body. She had worn her hair the same way for as long as Agnes had known her, parted this way or that but always cascading down in a waterfall, curling just at the ends. Unlike Mia or Agnes, she'd never tried out different dyes or cut it short. How would she deal with the constant change of a child?

But Agnes had to admit that all around her, priorities were shifting. All the friends were on track for goals that she herself hadn't even thought about yet: 401(k) plans, second degrees, houses or condos, weddings or babies. The most viable goals on Agnes's list were *Say hello to the coffee barista* and *Buy a whole month's stock of food and litter for Major Tom*. The real ones were so huge they felt out of reach. *Become famous, somehow. Pay down mountain of student debt. New apartment big enough for a dog.* To this impossible list, she added one more daunting but vital thing. *Make Mia well.* As if she could somehow magically heal her.

Who would have thought that by her midthirties, Mia would wind up with Martin, who ran his own investment fund. This was a girl who had once shot spitballs to try to get Thurston Moore's attention during a packed and sweaty night at Southpaw. Agnes remembered it well: Mia dressed in a lace cami, a miniskirt, and a wide belt, her short honey-brown hair bobbed and slicked across her forehead as she grinned and tore little pieces of paper from a napkin, wadding them into a straw and shooting them at the guitarist of Sonic Youth. Yet that wild girl was gone, and she was now the attractive younger second wife in immaculate tailored clothing, creative but unemployed, playing babysitter to Martin's teenage son and picking up her husband's shirts from the dry cleaner. Getting gossip in the bakery line was the major moment of her day. Mia had once interned at *Vanity Fair* and published her stories in small literary magazines that only Agnes was impressed by. Yet Mia had given herself entirely to the marriage: the brownstone in the city, the house out in the country, a gently used vagina, a child that looked like another woman, and a black cat that Martin allowed to avoid the dog Mia really wanted. To fill her time, she volunteered as a literacy tutor. She took real estate courses but never went for her license. Despite the little disappointments of the day, she had everything.

As Agnes ordered two coffees inside the Starbucks, she felt her phone vibrate and chirp. When she pulled it out of her pocket, she saw a text from Mia's older sister, Steph, whom she had met only twice before. For a few years Agnes had followed her posts online, making her feel like they knew each other better than they maybe really did. Steph said she was en route now but that there was one slight hitch in the plan: apparently Martin's teenage son, Cameron, was planning to stay at the house in Connecticut.

It was supposed to be just us? Agnes texted back with a question mark, as if she didn't want to pass judgment on the new development.

Don't worry about it, Steph texted. *He'll probably just play video games in his room.*

Agnes had assumed the boy would be with his mother or at the very least with Martin at their brownstone in Brooklyn. Rich people had so many options but never seemed to make the right choices.

"Decaf latte with oat milk," Agnes said with a half smile as Zoey came out of the bathroom.

"Aw, you remembered my lactose sensitivity! How do you remember everything?" Zoey grinned.

Agnes had forgotten this, though: the warm, special feeling she could get around her friends. There was a time not that long ago—before Mia's wedding, before they all drifted—when it had even felt golden. One day they might even laugh about Zoey shooting up hormones in a Starbucks.

Agnes thought about the sperm Zoey would inject in a day and a half. She wondered if it was the same consistency as during sex or if it was different after being thawed, the way spinach was. Having slept with a total count of one guy many years ago, she had only a vague understanding of regular sperm and no idea how store-bought sperm worked. Her friend was tougher than she thought if she was able to just walk around giving herself needles. She imagined Zoey's ovaries like little pincushions, but you didn't inject directly into them, right? It was probably the buttocks or the thigh. Agnes shuddered. She must have really wanted this. Where did that desire come from, and so suddenly? Agnes understood wanting a small human in your life, but she felt surprisingly squeamish thinking about all the rest of it.

"Cameron's at the house and apparently not leaving," she informed Zoey.

"Seventeen-year-olds. They waste all that sperm." Zoey waved a hand like she was trying to shoo away the image. Then she took a long sip from the latte as they both settled into the car again.

"You know, I'm just so glad Mia's going to be okay!" Zoey said.

None of them really knew if Mia would be okay, but it felt good to say she would. They had been saying it to each other for a week now, since it became clear she wouldn't succumb to her injury. They'd said it by text, by email, and over the phone. Agnes nodded her head and sipped her coffee.

"When Ethan went to see her at the hospital, she kept calling him Duckie. He thought it was cute, but it made me worried," Zoey confided.

"Duckie?"

"From *Pretty in Pink*."

Mia had definitely caught the boyishness of Ethan, Agnes thought. He had expressive dark eyebrows that twitched and lifted at the slightest thing he disagreed with, a sulky bottom lip that pushed out a little more than the top one, and ears that stuck out slightly on either side of his tortoiseshell glasses. But despite staying slim into his thirties, he lacked both the style and substance of the '80s character, Agnes reflected.

"You didn't go too? I thought you went," Agnes said.

"I wanted to, but I was on deadline for our show."

"You said you were going!" Agnes felt a hot shot of anger, her forehead beading instantly with sweat.

"You know how Ethan is. Him and Mia. He wanted to see her by himself. I try not to make a big deal of that whole vibe they have. I just let him have that."

Agnes started the car and aimed it toward the town's grocery store. Ethan and Mia had dated / not dated in the early days, long before he was with Zoey. Which meant that according to Ethan they had, and according to Mia they'd watched Werner Herzog's *Grizzly Man* and shared a bag of peach candies. She made a mental note to get some if the store had them. Maybe it could stir a memory.

She was surprised Zoey hadn't gone to the hospital, though. She thought Zoey would have yearned to be the first one of them for Mia to remember. Agnes considered her the third friend in the trio—the one who constantly tried too hard because she wanted to be part of the partnership. Agnes wasn't sure why she was irritated by Ethan being there instead of Zoey—she just wanted Zoey to be a better friend, maybe. Mia deserved that. But Zoey was here now and would help with the groceries. In fact, Zoey was already brainstorming: typing ingredients on a list in her phone.

"What I want," Agnes explained once they were inside the Stop & Shop, "is to stimulate her sense memories. That's really important for the party to work. Look for the foods that are associated with our times together."

This was their job, she told Zoey: to help Mia. To help her back from this, help her remember who she was, the good times.

"Yes, got it! Sense memories." Zoey nodded as they strolled through the deli section.

The two of them parted ways. Agnes watched her stride off on those long legs, thinking about how in two days, she might be conceiving new life and how weird that was. It felt the same as when Mia got married—a ritual of adulthood that Agnes had never fully understood.

She hadn't really considered it with Charlie the Aussie when it was being offered to her. Agnes was thirty-seven, and her mom back in Michigan was leaning on her hard to move home, forget about making rent (which Agnes hadn't; it *was* becoming a problem as costs rose), and embrace a quieter life. "What are you really doing there?" her mother asked on every phone call, her voice older than it sounded when Agnes saw her in person. "Building a career," Agnes always said, but the Nielsens didn't believe in careers—careers were for people who didn't need paychecks—and in truth, unless someone above her was #MeToo'd into early retirement, there was not a next pay level to achieve at the book publisher where Agnes worked. Slipping into debt had become surprisingly easy, even with autopays and a fairly lean lifestyle. It was hard to put into words, but New York had become Agnes's identity, her nervous system. It wasn't an option to just leave it behind, no matter how expensive it got.

At a large cooler, Agnes's hand hesitated, hovering over hummus, contemplating. After Mia had married Martin, there hadn't been many gatherings, and if there were, they were catered. Hard cheeses were easy—they were always about good times. Repulsive challenges like Roquefort or Camembert reminded Agnes of their differences. Agnes's feral roots were small town. Mia was born confident in Manhattan. Agnes added both the hummus container and a farmhouse cheddar to the cart.

Zoey returned with chocolate chips, baking soda and powder, and flour. "I can bake," she said. She looked down at the hummus tub. "Are you sure about that? Mia stopped eating hummus a long time ago."

"Let's test the waters."

"Oh. Okay then." Zoey's expression was unreadable; then she shrugged.

"You know, she called me Thora at the hospital," Agnes told her, picking up on the *Duckie* part of the conversation they'd had earlier. Zoey seemed to know exactly what she was talking about. That was the beauty of old friends—you could circle back to a topic and pick up again in the same place without having to explain yourself. Like knitting a sweater, the needles were always waiting in the stitches, exactly where you'd left off.

"Thora?"

"Like Thora Birch." Agnes didn't think she really looked like Thora Birch. They were a similar height, and both had dark hair, but Agnes's was curly. And she wore her reading glasses only at the office.

"Right. From *Ghost World*." Zoey nodded. "And that means she's ScarJo? Well, I can see that," Zoey said, placing the chocolate chips and flour in the cart.

"I was thinking maybe it's because we met in Adaptation Studies."

"That was just one class so long ago." Zoey was driving the cart up another aisle now.

"Seventeen years." They were both silent for a second, considering the number. Had it really been that long? Neither of them felt old—not yet! Then Agnes pressed on: "But it's an adapted film. She's confusing characters for us."

"Friend characters. So she *recognizes* we're her friends. That's something."

They added other things they hoped would stimulate their friend's sense memories. Limes because Mia had always pulled them from the rims of bar glasses and obliterated their pulp with her teeth, an ecstatic smile on her face as if she craved the acidity. Bananas because they had eaten them every morning during the trip they'd taken to Costa Rica the year they'd all turned thirty. Vegan hot dogs because Mia had flirted with vegetarianism for several years.

"We probably have enough. I remember there's a big pantry, and Martin has people who take care of those things for him." Agnes turned the cart toward the tills. She didn't want to say she knew the precise amount her credit card would take.

"God, I love Mia, but I hope this isn't going to be as traumatic as the fake wedding," Zoey said.

Fake wasn't exactly accurate. Traumatic was. There had been a dress and flowers, cake and caterers—all the usual things one might expect of a wedding. Except that no one had been happy with it. Not Agnes or any of the friends in their gang. And it didn't help that Martin had never been comfortable with their tightly woven little group. *Confused art-school weirdos*—Mia had once let slip his words. He'd been happier picking Mia up and ferrying her away into his world: his Peloton-owning friends, his two-acre weekend house, his overtanned family, his first-class business trips. Even Mia's Upper West Side, *Harper's*-subscribing upbringing didn't seem enough for him. It shouldn't have been a surprise that he would want to do the wedding his way too.

There had been an emailed invite with barely time to shop for a gift, but Agnes had wanted to be there for Mia's moment and truly hoped it would last longer than so many of the weddings they'd attended together after college. The last time she'd seen Victor, though he'd been one of their group, had been at one of those, maybe in 2014. There had been no mention of bridesmaids or registries for Mia's. When they'd been young, no one had talked about getting married—it seemed like such an old-fashioned concept. Agnes had always assumed they'd find people and live together. Or even stay roommates through the strings of short-lived loves.

Agnes had asked if she could do anything to help Mia prepare for the wedding, bring anything, but Mia had said, "Oh, it's taken care of. Just show up."

Agnes hadn't understood why Mia had been so casual until she and all their friends arrived on the date to Martin's wooded yard in Connecticut and saw the professional photographs dry mounted and propped up on easels: a bouquet toss frozen in midair; Mia showing off her hourglass figure in a clinging white crepe high-neck dress; Mia in silhouette in a dance with her father against a Tuscan sunset; Martin and Mia saying their vows underneath a two-thousand-year-old olive tree. They had already gotten married in Italy and never told any of Mia's friends. Instead they'd been cast in the shitty American remake.

Agnes had been hurt, but Zoey had been furious—she'd sent Agnes almost a hundred texts before the restaged wedding was over. Agnes had muted her phone and made a cut-it-out signal with her hand to Zoey across the aisle. Zoey had sat on Martin's side as if she were done with Mia forever. Agnes had worried they would be bounced from their best friend's wedding. It had been an opulent party, even for one that had been put together hastily. Martin, Agnes had thought, had the money, and that meant he got things the way he wanted, even for *her day*.

So Mia had made some mistakes, rushed into a life without consulting. That was part of the impulsiveness Agnes and all of them loved about Mia, wasn't it? The fact that she craved excitement.

"Who's paying for all this?" Zoey wondered as Agnes turned the cart into a lineup. "Are we going halfsies?"

But before she could accept the offer, Agnes saw Martin far off in the pharmacy area of the store. Zoey followed her gaze.

"Is that—" Agnes started to ask, but she knew the answer before the words formed.

Martin was tall with broad shoulders, as if he did something physical for a living instead of managing wealth portfolios. Mia had always said he spent more time working out than he did talking. He turned and walked toward them, and as he came closer, they saw he had a box of Tampax in his hand.

While he was still several aisles away, Zoey dropped her voice. "Wasn't it so classy, the Facebook post? In an emergency, I mean, you pick up the phone."

Agnes agreed, but she smiled as Martin came closer. It was only a moment, and then he recognized them. It probably wasn't difficult to pick them out. They looked like hip Brooklynites in a small country town: Zoey in a pair of strappy shoes from Free People, and Agnes in her Warby Parkers.

Martin was unshaven, a rugged knit sweater covering his rower's physique. There was no fat on his body, as if he simply didn't have time for it. Agnes had always felt the rich knew style in a way most people didn't, that it came to them as easy as breathing. The folds of his hair were expertly ruffled, though she was sure he hadn't styled them. She could admit he was attractive. For a second she wondered if all the friends were jealous of Mia for snagging Martin and having an effortless life full of the best things. Was this why they didn't embrace him warmly, even after several years? Maybe it was the real reason they got together once every six months instead of every Friday night like they once had.

"I was just—for Mia, you know." Martin looked sheepish and embarrassed about the tampons. "I guess I don't have to run this back to the house now," he said and added it to their cart.

Zoey gave Agnes a mortified glance, but Agnes said, "No problem. Are you heading back into the city, then?"

"Sure. I mean, that's what you want, right?"

Agnes felt her shoulders stiffen. She couldn't tell if his tone was derisive. Zoey made no niceties, which Agnes felt only stranded her with the duty. She inquired how his work was going, then, when he grunted a reply, switched topics to ask how Mia was doing. Martin glanced at the cheese, bundles of pasta, and boxes of butter. He winced and said, "She lost some weight in the hospital. Maybe it's better if she stays fit."

"Do you think bread caused her memory loss?" Agnes asked. She wondered for a second if she had actually said that aloud. It was unlike her to be so blunt. Calling people on their shit was usually Zoey's job.

Zoey finally contributed. She glanced down at the Tampax box and said, "No person has a 'regular-size' vagina. You need Super—at least Super, if I know Mia. It's the green box."

Martin's casual misogyny was silenced, but Zoey went for the kill, as she could. "Unless they're for a preteen? If it's a preteen vagina, you're all set."

"Maybe you could pick them up."

"Yeah. I'll go back." Zoey snagged the product out of the cart and made an escape, suppressing a laugh.

Martin glanced around, then took the moment to speak to Agnes alone. "Actually it's good we ran into each other. Did any police contact you?"

Agnes felt a sharp pang below her diaphragm and shook her head.

"No one talked to you? At the hospital last week?" His handsome face suddenly looked pinched. "They said they were done searching the house. But if they show up, give me a call, okay?"

Behind him, Zoey approached with the better category of menstrual products. Agnes began to steer the cart toward the till.

"Well, at least the insurance company can't say we're milking them. That's the one upside." As they stood there, Martin seemed to realize he should pay for the Tampax. He took out his wallet and flipped through some bills before handing them to Agnes. It was enough to cover everything they'd put in the cart. "No drinking for Mia. Her medication and everything."

He left them to it without a goodbye except a nod of his head.

"He was a tall drink of disturbing," Agnes said as she and Zoey loaded the full paper bags into the cart. She was about to mention the police investigation, but Zoey didn't give her a chance.

"You know, he's never once called me by my name."

Up until four weeks prior, Martin had barely spoken to Agnes when they were in the same room. Mia had always said he was secretly shy, but Agnes thought maybe he didn't see a point to speaking to women unless an HR director ordered him to. Agnes stopped partway across the parking lot, the dumb realization hitting her. It was why he had her number but couldn't call it. He hadn't known her name, and too much time had passed to ask again. He'd forgotten who Mia's friends were because it didn't matter enough to him to know. So he'd made a post online.

What Agnes wondered as she and Zoey loaded the haul into the back of the car was, Did Mia matter to him at all, then?

"He just told me the police questioned him about the accident."

"If it wasn't an accident . . ." Zoey trailed off. She ran her hands up and down her arms like she'd gotten a chill. "Have you ever seen a crime documentary where the husband didn't do it?"

Chapter Two

Mimotional Wrecks

Mia stared at the gate. There was something about it that she didn't like. She had been standing there looking out the front windows of the house since Martin left, waiting for either him to return or the women who were supposed to be her friends to arrive. The remembering party had been one of their ideas, though she wasn't sure whose. Martin had insisted the country house was better for it—more restful for her. He was still concerned about her doing anything much. He'd made that clear. Her bare feet felt rooted to the floorboards, as if she'd been dipped in wax and had hardened in place. From the basement she could hear the teenage boy, Cameron, cursing as he carjacked senior citizens on the PlayStation. Or maybe it was the kickboxing game. It was hard to say. Although he had his own car and had driven out to the estate, he seemed younger to her than seventeen. Even his Jeep was purple and childlike, a toy that had rolled away from a LEGO set. She wondered what kind of person she'd been at seventeen that made her feel that way? But she couldn't remember who she'd been last month, let alone a couple of decades ago. Since being released from the hospital, Mia tried to say as little as possible to anyone, but the teenager had skulked around her just like that black cat in the city apartment, a thing that always wanted to be in the same room even if it barely glanced at you.

He had sat nearby and texted his friends, and they texted him, *ding, ding, ding,* but he said very little aloud.

At the hospital, no one had made any demands of her. There had been a wide metal door to the hospital room, and when the night nurse closed it, she'd always asked Mia if she wanted the light turned out too. Every night Mia had said yes, and after the fluorescent above the bed had darkened, the nurse would shut the door quietly, taking all light from the room with her. Mia had lain there those first couple of nights, breathing in the dim room. She'd felt like the black strip of celluloid that snaps through a projector in a darkened room before the image appears. The emptiness of it had been strange and lovely, and feeling that way about it terrified her. Shouldn't she want the picture? The memories, images in flashing color? Was there something awful about her life that made her not want to remember it?

A plainclothes detective, Officer Yang, had come and sat beside her hospital bed one morning before Martin arrived. Which morning had it been? Mia couldn't say. The officer had worn a brown blazer and asked Mia questions in a low, confidential tone. At one point she had said, "If there's anything at all you want to tell me, I can help you. If there's anything that makes you afraid . . . ?"

But all Mia could recall from the accident was that she hadn't been able to find her phone. She remembered being on the floor—in water or blood, she wasn't sure which—and getting up, and her hand searching the counter, looking at the table, the phone not there either. Then leaving. Each step taking too long. She remembered that old-fashioned iron gate was open, and she'd walked through it down the road.

"Do you remember why you didn't take your shoes?" the officer, who had kind eyes and short hair, had asked.

Mia had shaken her head.

"Was someone else there with you?" When Mia hadn't responded, the cop had asked, "Did you feel you needed to leave quickly?"

Mia had searched for it in her mind, but it was like staring at the screen of a TV that wouldn't turn on. She had told Officer Yang she didn't know.

The interview had been interrupted by a bushy-eyebrowed lawyer who'd come through the hospital room door with his hand already out to shake. "Rich Smiarowski," he'd said, and when he'd seen Yang already had her notebook out, he'd spelled it: "S-M-I-A . . ."

He was Mia's lawyer, apparently. "She's not competent to answer questions in her current state," Smiarowski had said. "We ask that you direct all questions to myself and Mr. Kroner."

It had taken a few minutes for Mia to understand "Mr. Kroner" was her husband. Martin. She'd met him a couple of days before, through a haze.

"This is standard procedure for the hospital and an injury like this," Officer Yang had told the lawyer.

"Well, I'm standard procedure for Connecticut."

Mia had noticed the officer looked thrown off. She'd written down his name on her pad; she'd also taken his card. She hadn't ceased her questioning of Mia, but the man had stayed for the rest, saying to Mia "You don't have to answer that" to every question until the interview concluded.

After they'd both gone, Mia had texted her sister, Stephanie. She'd remembered her phone number but not her name. Mia had thought about texting that woman, Agnes, but she seemed so sad when she visited, Mia wasn't sure she was the strongest friend she had. She sensed a hesitancy. She could tell that Agnes expected her to know her, but everyone expected her to know them. Still, she'd seemed more hurt than the others. She had to assume a sister was more trustworthy. *Jo, Meg, Amy, Beth* came to mind as possible names for her sister. Mia had realized even then how bizarre it was to have a flash of actors' faces at the ready—Saoirse Ronan, Florence Pugh—when the photo on her phone with her sister's name under it looked unfamiliar to her.

Mia had gone into the hospital bathroom, pulled up her gown, and looked at her body in the mirror. She turned around and around, craning her neck. What's my biggest mole? she'd texted the sister she'd not yet met, as if knowing something personal like that would confirm their familial relationship. Martin had told her that Steph had been there during the coma but had to fly home again to be with her kids. She'd seen Mia wake up, but Mia had still been confused as a newborn. That was how long Mia had been out: long enough for someone to come and leave.

Mia had waited, and the phone screen had shown her three wavering dots as Steph responded. Steph: Not sure. But you have a birthmark on the inside of your thigh. Looks like a red gummy snake. Mia had leaned in a slow lunge and looked at her thigh, a curling streak about two and a half inches long, feeble and pink. Your dumb Pisces tramp stamp tattoo that I've made fun of for years. Mia had found the symbol under the waistband of her hospital underwear. It wasn't a fish, but a symbol—two parentheses joined with a cross stroke. Mia: Does anyone hate me? Steph: I don't think so. But I'll get the first flight I can. A minute later: Booked for Saturday morning.

There was an efficiency to this unknown woman that pleased Mia and gave her a tiny bit of peace. In the photo next to her text, Stephanie was wearing a black ball cap with the word *FACTS* stitched on it.

Since leaving the hospital, everyone had prompted Mia, as if expecting her memory would soon return, easy as turning the rod on a set of horizontal blinds—the world would come into view, even if it did have pale plastic lines running through its sky. Sadly, that hadn't happened.

The first night in their home in Park Slope, she had slept next to Martin so tentatively. She'd known she was expected to sleep next to him, but although he had been nothing but kind, there was the bizarre interruption with the lawyer. Also, Martin's body was foreign. His forehead was wide and each of his features solid. His face looked like he'd lived in it a fair amount for a man of forty-six, though pleasantly so. He was in good shape and was handsome, in a way, she thought. She had called him Clive twice by accident, because he resembled the actor Clive Owen. He'd corrected her only the first time. The second time an irritated look had come to his face, but he'd said nothing.

She remembered Clive Owen in *Closer*: the way he moved through a room, how intently he looked at Julia Roberts. And then in *Gosford Park*, the shape he made where he lay on a bed. "I can't believe you forget much, Mrs. Wilson," the actor said in one scene. Mia could hear the dialogue, yet Mia didn't remember Martin at all.

Was it normal for a husband to send a lawyer to the hospital to intervene in a police interview? Because Mia was remembering only films, it seemed plausible. Then again, she could remember that films were seldom like reality.

Eventually the stiffness of their silence had seemed to become too much for Martin. Sometime after 2:00 a.m., he'd gotten up and paced their bedroom. "I was so scared, Mia. These last few weeks have been the worst. Taking care of Cameron, trying to go to work while you were lying there . . ."

If it were a performance, it would be a good one. His lips had turned pinker under his fist, and his dark eyes brimmed. She'd watched this man she'd met only a few days before melting. He'd said he would take the spare room, although he'd seemed somewhat defeated when he left their bed. She'd wondered if she should be frightened of him, or maybe the boy (it would make sense for a father to protect his son), or perhaps someone else, someone she hadn't even met yet.

That was the implication behind Officer Yang's questioning, wasn't it? That she'd been attacked, rather than had an accident.

Yet when she thought of Martin, there was something about him that seemed too pained, and also too . . . dutiful, to be a threat to her. He'd driven her to all her appointments in the week that followed; helped her in and out of the car, wrapping his arm around her or guiding her by her elbow; and when they'd arrived at the Connecticut home hoping to stir more memories, he'd walked from room to room, turning at each doorway with an expectation on his face. He'd pointed out the baby grand in the living room and told her she'd taken up piano again last year. He was waiting for her to recognize their things, associate them with some former scene.

Who were they that they had two homes? It seemed gratuitous. There was a beautiful turret that made Mia inhale deeply when they first drove up, but when she'd asked what they used it for, it turned out Martin just kept his files there. She wondered if it was what she'd loved about the house before too.

Now, Mia's gaze darted around the room; then her head tipped back, and she stared up at the high ceiling, the large raw beams, and the enclosed loft that looked down on the space. She knew which room they'd slept in together the night before, the first time she'd let him so close. But it hadn't felt familiar. She was sure her husband usually slept in the room beside. Both had windows that looked down on the living area and windows on the outer wall that peered onto a patio and pool and a sprawling wooded back acre. From here she couldn't see the distinction between the two rooms. But she knew where the wall between them would be.

The night before, she'd lied. After Martin had wrapped his arms around her from behind and softly pressed his groin against her backside, Mia broke the embrace and said she had started her period, like she was a freshman in self-defense mode. They slept in the same bed, but that was all she'd been ready for with this stranger. It was as if she'd woken up from the coma and been given the jobs of Instant Wife and Instant Best Friend. But Mia wasn't ready for how a husband and friends felt entitled to her, the ease with which they touched her. That morning, she'd disentangled from him and explored the closets and dressers. She was right: there were more of his clothes in the second room. So she was walking back into a life that was not uncomplicated. Him sleeping with her the night before, wrapping her up in his muscled arms and finding her mouth with his, had been an act on his part, at least a little. He'd been taking advantage of the situation to find what he wanted from it.

In the living room, Mia sat down at the piano and placed her hands on the keys. The first few notes of *Gymnopédies* came easy, and she had an image of herself as a young girl learning the same piece, practicing over and over again. It was a startling feeling, but her arm still hurt from her fall, and she had to stop. Mia then noticed out the window a white vehicle weaving through the trees. Thora—Agnes, she corrected herself—would be driving. She didn't know how she knew. She couldn't remember ever being beside her in the passenger seat. But it had to be her friend's car because no others had passed in the last hour, and her sister would have a rental from the airport, which meant new. This car was not new. As the Ford came closer up the road to stop outside the gate, Mia saw she was right. The woman on the passenger side got out and yanked the latch that opened the old-fashioned gate with a complaining *clank-clank*. She pushed it back over the drive, the metal foot seeming to scrape a little at the end, then waited for the driver to pull ahead before she shut the gate and got back in. Agnes Nielsen was the one in the driver's seat. The woman who'd handled the gate Mia hadn't met yet, but Martin had said her name was Zoey Wilder.

The car quickly circled to the front of the house, and the women were already out and opening the hatch by the time Mia found her shoes, pulled on a jacket, and headed outside. Her coat was a three-quarter-length sleeve, and the cool air was prickling her arm hairs. It reminded her of the mustard-yellow coat Audrey Hepburn had worn in *Charade*. *Who picks such a show-offy coat?* she asked herself. *Someone with something to prove. The same person who picked a suspicious husband,* she answered in her mind.

Who was Mia Sinclair-Kroner?

Mia descended the walk slowly. Agnes stood looking at her with a mixed expression: sadness, relief, love, worry. Just like at the hospital. The other one, Zoey, came over right away and embraced her, wrapping her long arms around her as if she would try for doubling her twice. She was the decisive one, obviously. Mia could see what her former self had done: chosen two opposites to balance her life.

"I'm so glad you're going to be okay!" Zoey exclaimed in a lilting, musical voice. She lifted her cell phone and snapped a selfie of the two of them. Mia smiled, because that's what one was supposed to do for a camera. She knew that much. But the moment left her feeling shy. She'd been good friends with these people, she told herself. This was how friends acted.

"Do you need help?" Mia gestured to the bags in the hatch that the other one, Thora—no, Agnes—was plucking at. From where she stood, she could see knapsacks and many paper grocery bags.

Before Zoey left her side, she gave Mia an extra squeeze around the shoulders. As they walked inside and set the bags on the counter, Mia felt her phone buzz in her ridiculous coat pocket. When she pulled it out, she saw Zoey had posted the photo already. The caption said #Reunion #friends #healing with a row of red hearts. Mia wondered why she hadn't waited and put the other woman in a photo too. Then she thought, *Maybe they're not great friends.* She wished her sister would hurry up and arrive already. She'd texted when she landed in New York a couple of hours before.

"Should we?" Zoey was saying, pulling out a bottle from one of the paper bags and setting it down on the marble counter. "Mimosas? I mean, it's almost noon." The adventurer. They hadn't even put their things into rooms.

Agnes dug an orange juice bottle out of one of the bags and went to work on setting up flutes. She went with a mix of orange and grapefruit juice, then draped a towel over the champagne bottle and popped the cork like an expert, smiling somewhat bashfully at the admiring glance Mia gave her.

"I think there's someone who can put this stuff away?" Zoey said, looking around as if it were her manor.

"She has a name. It's Susan," Agnes said.

Zoey looked down as her phone *chirruped* with the sound of hearts collecting on the photograph she'd posted.

"I met her last night," Mia said. "She was here earlier. I expect she'll come back any minute. When did you meet her?" Mia peered at her friend.

"At your wedding."

Mia found herself smiling at the word, even if she couldn't remember the event.

Agnes smiled back hesitantly. She had freckles, bright eyes that skimmed over you and then away, and a broad, dimpled smile when she chose to show it. Her dark curly hair spun out from her crown. Yes, Mia could see why she must have liked Agnes.

The doorbell rang, and she wondered if her sister had arrived. Zoey took off to answer it, leaving her alone with Agnes.

"Is that . . . ?" Agnes stared at the island's marble slab.

One corner of the marble was cracked, and a small chunk was gone. Mia hadn't spent a lot of time in the kitchen the night before, because the housekeeper had taken care of things. Mia watched Agnes's eyes glaze with tears. She wondered if it meant she could trust Agnes?

"You texted me that night," Agnes said, pulling with agitation on the ends of her pretty silk scarf. She looked like she would tie herself into a knot.

"What did I say?"

"Nothing. Just, you know, that you were out here."

Mia could see now that Agnes had become tentative with her answers, like Martin was—both had information they were keeping from her. She watched as Agnes abandoned the scarf and agitatedly ran a hand back through her hair.

Zoey came back to the kitchen with two armfuls of blue irises. Setting them down on the island, she said, "Does anyone have tip money?"

"In my purse." Agnes looked around for where she'd set it. "I still have extra from Martin."

"I saw it in the front hallway. I'll get it," Zoey said as she ran back to the door.

Mia reached for the vase. The card from Martin read *These were your favorite flowers. I hope you remember that and that this weekend will be good for you. Love, Martin.*

Mia sniffed the irises, but her sense of smell had not come back. The doctors said it might. Or it might not.

Why had Martin insisted on bringing her out ahead of time? Shouldn't they have waited for her sister, their friends? She replayed the night before in her mind. He seemed so edgy, like he was moving through a checklist. She decided it had been a smart and safe move to kiss him—and nothing else.

Zoey came back and picked up the card. "That's so sweet of Martin," she cooed. She turned to Agnes. "Do you think you're too hard on him?"

A look passed between the two women. There was tension there. Mia couldn't tell if Zoey was being sincere. Did both of them dislike her husband, or only one of them? She had little to go by, but already she was becoming adept at reading people's glances, the things they said that were unspoken.

"What's wrong with Martin?" Mia pressed.

The women looked at each other, then replied, "Nothing," at almost the same time.

Mia looked down at the rings on her finger. She'd had them on even in the hospital. She had a sudden image of Martin's laptop on a kitchen table. She recalled looking at it, names in red and the words *Italy Travel Budget* at the top. She had fumed. The highlight indicated her friends were being scratched from her list. Her parents were there, but not her sister. She recalled the feeling of the laptop under her fingers as she had slammed it shut, hard. The second wedding had been something she'd fought for, she realized now. Something to have when they returned, to include the people who mattered to her but not Martin.

"I don't want to say anything bad about Martin," Agnes said. "I saw him in the hospital. He was there for you."

"Agnes is a little too midwestern still," Zoey said to Mia. To Agnes, "Just say what you think."

Clearly there was a warmth that bonded them, but Mia could also see already that Zoey would never give up an opportunity to push and Agnes would never push back.

"If we tell her everything, it's not helpful. It's overload."

Mia noticed Agnes distractedly looking at the broken corner of the island before she turned back to the conversation.

"Zoey, should you be drinking if you're trying to . . . ?"

"Most people drink the night they conceive, don't they?"

Agnes looked at Mia and made a curving hand motion out from her abdomen, the way a child might instead of saying the word *pregnancy*. This Mia person had built a beautiful life of intention and color-coordinated possessions, or tried to—that was obvious—yet her friends had the maturity of twelve-year-olds. She was trying to make sense of that contrast.

"Oh, I guess, congratulations?" Mia said. "To you and . . ."

"Ethan," Zoey filled in.

"You called him Duckie," Agnes supplied.

Quit worrying. These are your besties, Mia told herself. They'd already given her more sense of her life than anyone else had. She reached out and took one of the champagne glasses.

"It's funny," Zoey said. "I don't see the Jon Cryer thing at all."

Mia tried to smile about a couple she didn't know at all having a baby. She found it surprisingly easy. She imagined the tiny kicking feet of infants. It made her feel warm inside. She could imagine the man who'd visited the hospital as a father, despite his hoodie and bright-blue Chuck Taylor sneakers that made him look like her stepson. "Should we drink to that?"

"Sure—to new beginnings!" Zoey said, and they all clinked glasses.

"And old friends," Mia added, she hoped naturally.

After they drank, Agnes walked around the kitchen island. Mia could tell she was contemplating her accident.

"It's really bad, isn't it?" Mia said.

"I'm surprised Martin hasn't fixed it yet." Zoey shifted uncomfortably.

"Every time I look at it, I hear a little echo . . . like, clanging."

"Could it be tinnitus?" Zoey suggested. "I read somewhere that it's common with injuries like neck pain."

Then Agnes probed: "Did you hear this sound in the hospital or only since you came to the house?"

Mia set her drink down and leaned against a barstool, feeling suddenly weak. "I'm not sure," she said, though in truth, she knew it was only since she'd come home.

Chapter Three

CRUDITÉS

Zoey could see the immediate relief on Mia's face when her sister arrived.

They had settled into the living room but all got up when they heard the scraping of the gate and saw a car at the bottom of the drive. Zoey went to the door as if it were her house, and Agnes and Mia followed more tentatively.

Zoey thought Mia recognized the woman who was arriving—and maybe she did, somewhere deep. Stephanie was seven years older, two inches taller, and ten or fifteen pounds heavier than Mia, with her hair swept back in a simple ponytail, yet they had the same mouths, the same serious eyebrows. The adjustable strip of her ball cap had been looped through her purse strap, and the black cap—*FACTS* stitched above the brim—dangled from the brown leather bag. Mia had told Zoey that her sister had worn that hat every day of the Trump administration.

Agnes helped Stephanie with the roller case, but the housekeeper came, took it out of Agnes's confused hand, and wheeled it down the hall to the bedrooms. Agnes was never comfortable around house staff, or even caterers at book events offering cold puff pastries. Zoey didn't understand her hesitation—she would grab this kind of life in a second.

"How are you feeling?" Stephanie asked Mia. Her forehead crinkled into at least five rows of concern.

Mia blinked as if she didn't really know the answer.

Agnes stepped in toward Stephanie. "Did you talk to the doctors? What do you think about her short-term/long-term memory situation?" Agnes, always with the crossing of t's and dotting of i's.

"The doctors said there are different kinds of memory: semantic— that's your facts—and episodic, which is the more emotional memory. Experiences and events." Stephanie ran her hand back over her ponytail while she talked. Maybe she expected it to be loosening after a long morning of traveling, but it wasn't. All the strands were neatly held in her elastic.

Zoey wanted to get back to the living room and the party. Being together, like old times, would be the best. She gestured to the kitchen island, where the housekeeper had come along and more prettily arranged the cupcakes, fruit platters, and plates of dips. "We were having a snack. And a drink. Do you want a drink?"

Mia turned, and her eyes widened with concern. "Don't give a thing to Anne Hathaway!"

The friends all stopped.

"I mean, sure. That Oscar wasn't really deserved . . . ," Zoey said, searching.

Steph smiled. "Okay. I get it."

"*Rachel Getting Married*," Mia said, looking surprised and slightly pleased with herself.

"Eight years clean, five years sober," Stephanie announced to every-one with a directness that sounded a little practiced to Zoey. Stephanie clasped Mia around the shoulders. "It's all going to come back. This was a good idea, Agnes."

"Thank you," Agnes said, as if she were getting a green ribbon.

Zoey followed Stephanie on social—even posting sad faces when Stephanie announced she had taken a buyout from the *Chicago Tribune* after twelve years there as a reporter—but Agnes was the friend who had truly embedded herself in Mia's family. Something about Agnes's midwestern agreeability made her a hit with parents, while Zoey knew that she herself was always labeled *that girl* during Mia's Sunday-night calls to her mother. "What did that girl get up to now?"

———✝———

That girl had once stood outside the Ace Hotel when she was twenty-six, waiting for Agnes and Mia to show up. She had tried to claim her reserved table at the John Dory restaurant, but she couldn't be seated until her party arrived. The night out was her treat to the girls, as Zoey had landed her first real job out of school as a producer on a reality show. Of course, *producer* in that world meant underpaid camera operator, uncredited writer, and glorified PA. But Zoey loved it because she loved working in a way that Agnes and Mia didn't. Mia was middle-class New York, but that counted as rich by any definition outside the city. And Agnes, she was still interning at an agent's office, sorting through piles of manuscripts.

"This is really shitty, Agnes!" Zoey had yelled into her phone as haute New York stared at her from the lineup. "Really, really shitty. You're not picking up, Mia's not picking up, and I'm going to be out a one-hundred-dollar cancellation fee."

But wherever they were, someone had thought ahead: not more than a minute after she'd left the message, Ethan arrived and climbed out of a cab. Zoey barely recognized him. They hadn't spoken in a year, ever since Mia cut Ethan off. He couldn't just be friends with Mia, and no one knew if they had slept with each other, though it only made sense that they had. Ethan explained there'd been some kind of emergency. Mia had called him to take their place so that Zoey wouldn't have to eat alone. Mia knew he'd be home, working on his script or torrenting obscure Japanese movies.

"It's called *Funeral Parade of Roses*, directed by Toshio Matsumoto," Ethan told her excitedly over sea urchin crudo. "It was a huge influence on Kubrick for *A Clockwork Orange*."

"Wow." Zoey nodded her head and smiled. "You don't say?" She wasn't annoyed by him. In fact, she saw his enthusiasm as evidence for his unbridled love for anything he was interested in. This boyishness irked her during school, but it now struck her as cute. Unlike before, he was actually wearing a real shirt—it looked as though it had even been ironed. In front of her eyes, Ethan was becoming fuckable.

Zoey thought about bringing up how hurt she'd been when Agnes and Mia didn't show, that she'd honestly thought they'd forgotten her and were crashing a private party with fake names. It was something they'd done before. Agnes was always doing anything that Mia said they should do. But then Zoey stopped herself. Mia had sent Ethan there, after all. And Agnes, though she irritated Zoey, had been incredibly helpful. In senior year when Zoey had mono, Agnes had attended her required stats class. She took immaculate notes, each math equation mimicking exactly the ones in the textbook, even though Agnes had no clue what standard deviation was. In tough cities like New York, friends are like a paddleball. The faster you smack them away, the more forcefully they return to you. Because you ultimately do need each other.

Ethan raised his glass and congratulated her. "What I think is so interesting about reality TV," he said, sucking an oyster, "is that it's all about character. Once you have that, you have everything."

Instead of venting her troubles, Zoey told Ethan, "Come home with me."

The next morning she woke up to Ethan making her breakfast, and it felt like a next step in her life. Later that day she found out Mia's father had gone into the hospital after a heart attack and Agnes had been with Mia and her mother all night. Zoey felt horrible for Mia and angry with Agnes. She could have phoned or texted. Zoey suspected Agnes was trying to keep Mia all to herself during a personal crisis so she could be the only hero.

People were Mia's art form. She could do it even in a moment when everything was falling apart: bring friends together. At one point, the friends fit like an elaborate puzzle, at least when Mia was there to bring the pieces together.

Now, in their thirties, they all seemed like sharp angles who didn't fit. When they did get together, it seemed to take a shorter amount of time before old competitions amplified into outright arguments.

———

Zoey got up and went into the living room to hook up her phone to the stereo. She knew the ladies were going to love her playlist. It started with "Ms. Jackson," by Outkast, and Kelly Clarkson's "Since U Been Gone," then slid into Florence and the Machine, and then, for Mia, Gnarls Barkley's "Crazy," and Belle and Sebastian's "Another Sunny Day." You could tell which drugs the gang had been doing during which musical phases. She and Mia had favored coke but hid it from Agnes. There were tracks from the White Stripes and LCD Soundsystem, and everything from Missy Elliott to Franz Ferdinand. For Agnes, there was slower-gear stuff on the list: Wilco, Neko Case, and Bright Eyes. When Zoey came back into the kitchen, they'd seated themselves around the island, reaching for napkins and nibbles.

As she went for the mimosa pitcher, Agnes gave her a concerned look—in the car earlier she'd questioned if her getting pregnant was the right thing to do. Maybe Agnes thought she and Ethan wouldn't hack parenthood. Yet she knew this was something Zoey had wanted, knew how many times Zoey dragged the baby conversation out of Ethan and weathered his unreasonable excuses, everything from 9/11 to Covid. Zoey took the pitcher anyway and poured another drink.

Zoey stood up and swayed with the music. Agnes was still standing but didn't sway. Instead she put her finger in the air and gestured, tapped in time to the music. It was good, she said; the list was a great way to stir things up for Mia. Then as Agnes finally began to loosen up and move a little, Zoey heard her phone ping with a text from Ethan.

Mia practically remembered me. I think I should come.

Zoey felt her back involuntarily stiffen. She jabbed at the phone. Girls' weekend, she texted. All welcome, except Ethan.

Ethan immediately texted, Why is this labor being gendered?

Zoey replied, Learn how to fold laundry before you go there.

How would he even get to Connecticut? she wondered. They had a car, but Ethan, a born-and-raised New Yorker, didn't drive. But before she could ask him, the phone dinged again—A cab doesn't actually cost that much to there. Like $100.

How do you even know that? she texted with a thinking-face emoji.

"Last Nite," by the Strokes, came on the stereo, and the others joined her. It felt like the party was about to begin. Zoey switched her phone to vibrate and set it down, even as more text bubbles appeared from Ethan.

The women took seats where they could. For a house that was generously sized, there was little furniture—just the couch where Zoey was, the modular chair Agnes was now in, and an old-fashioned rocking chair that Zoey knew Mia had brought there because it had been handed down during their college years, dragged out of an aunt's or grandparent's storage space. It was as if the room was designed more for Zillow than for people. Mia had told Zoey once that when Martin managed to keep the place after his divorce, he'd had it completely renovated and redecorated; it had been featured in an architectural magazine. But when Zoey tried to find it online, there had been no evidence of that, and she wondered if it was one of those casual rich-guy lies. Mia, getting duped.

Mia sat in the rocking chair while Stephanie remained standing. She had removed her Blundstones now, and her brightly striped socks were the only thing amiss in someone who was otherwise utterly serious.

"Did you know the police investigated?" Agnes said to Steph.

Steph nodded. "They came here, to the house. They questioned Mia at the hospital. Had to have questioned Martin too. But he says he was in the city."

"He mentioned that."

"Have they said anything to you?" Zoey turned the phone over so Ethan's incoming texts wouldn't keep lighting up. "I thought she was in the kitchen and slipped in some water."

"I suppose that *could* have happened. They thought a break-in was also possible," Stephanie said.

"A break-in?" Zoey asked. "What made them think that?"

"Just something isn't adding up." Steph shook her head.

"It's not. Like, if she hit the marble counter hard enough to break it like that, why isn't she dead?" Agnes asked. Zoey was taken aback: Agnes had been so direct just then. The question hung between them, and no one answered.

Zoey looked at Mia, who had her eyes closed and brows scrunched.

Stephanie pressed on. "Why did she wander out into the road instead of calling for help?"

Mia quietly asked, "Could you please stop?"

"Who told you about her slipping?" Stephanie asked Zoey as she got up to turn the music down slightly.

Zoey swallowed the rest of her drink. "Martin told us that. There was water on the floor of the kitchen. It's possible that didn't happen, but what can we do? Expose him like he's a mobbed-up alderman? You're not a journalist anymore. You're a sister-in-law staying in his vacation house. And Agnes here is just a copyeditor."

"My title is senior—"

"So you don't think she's in danger?" Stephanie cut in.

Zoey held up her hands in an I-don't-know pose but didn't comment.

"The attacker is definitely someone she knew," Agnes said. "She could have let them in."

"Help," Mia said in a small voice.

"Agnes," Zoey snapped. "What are you talking about?"

"Help me!" Mia called out. Everyone turned and saw blood dripping from Mia's nose onto her shirt. Agnes went to her and tilted her head up and back.

Zoey said she'd grab a washcloth. She darted from the room.

In the small bathroom down the hallway, she opened cupboards and drawers fruitlessly before Agnes yelled, "That's okay. It's stopped now!"

Once again, Agnes was there first for Mia.

Feeling paper between her hip and the basin, Zoey looked down and took out the wrinkled letter she had found in Agnes's purse when she'd gone for the tip money for the flower delivery: *Notice of Eviction*, it said at the top. *Rent owed: $4,400.*

She read it again and then thought, *Saint Agnes seems to have her own secrets after all.*

Chapter Four

Parlor Games

Agnes leaned forward, holding her scarf ends to keep them from falling on the veggie tray. She swiped at the dip with a carrot and then sat back. Agnes recalled any number of true-crime documentaries where the family could be a stumbling block to an investigation, pushing complex conspiracy theories. In some ways, that might help Mia, but in others, it might continue to traumatize her. Agnes swallowed the carrot, which felt too large and hard going down. It took a couple of airtight seconds to clear. She coughed, and Mia reached forward, like a friend, and handed her a glass of water.

Looking in Agnes's and Mia's direction, Stephanie asked, "When was the last time you two saw each other before the accident?"

The women had been together at Agnes's apartment only a week before Mia's injury, a Sunday tea that quickly led to wine uncorked. This time the meeting grew quickly from work talk to giggles to the stage where texts from partners asking "When are you coming home?" were ignored or answered with "Stuck on subway."

By the third glass, they were adult women sprawled in a rosé puddle—the painting version of the scene would have been called *The Last Brunch*.

Agnes wanted to get into talking through her recent breakup with her girlfriend, Charlie, but on that particular Sunday there was no cutting Zoey off when it came to her fretting about sex, or her and Ethan's lack of it.

When Agnes confessed that she worried about being single during her sexual peak, Zoey had stood up and announced she was going to the roof for a vape.

She worried that she had offended Zoey in some way, but then Mia had spoken up. "When did you know we would always be friends?"

Agnes had snapped her fingers and said, "Binky." Mia had gotten Agnes a job out of college reading for the literary agent Binky Urban. To Mia, the born New Yorker, it was a casual fact that her mother roomed with Urban at college and could send an email on her daughter's roommate's behalf. For Agnes of the Great Lakes, the gesture was magical, and it wasn't the only time Mia had helped her friends navigate the invisible maps of New York.

When Agnes had realized that all the greatest moments of their friendship somehow had to do with selfless acts of Mia-ness, Agnes raised a glass and toasted her. "To you!" she'd said.

"That's not why I asked!" Mia had protested.

But drunk Agnes didn't think to ask her why she had. "Where's Zoey?"

Too much time had passed for a vape session. Agnes jumped up from the floor with a tipsy wobble. "She got locked out on my roof!" It happened to Agnes all the time in such an old building. But as she made her way up the worn stairs to the roof egress, the metal door was swinging open. "Zoey?" she'd called out as she stepped onto the tar paper roof.

There had been no one. Just a rusting bicycle and husky remains of a roof garden. Zoey had pulled a French exit.

Now, Stephanie's question seemed to hang in the air between them. When had they all last seen each other?

Zoey looked like she wanted to say something but paused. Agnes, too, waited a minute to see if Mia would be the one to answer.

"We were always dancing, weren't we?" Mia said. She clutched a wadded Kleenex in her hand.

The last time Agnes had seen Mia had nothing to do with dancing. It had been years probably since they'd gone out dancing. Maybe Zoey's playlist had triggered something.

"We did that. Parties we were never invited to but bluffed our way into. The W, Gramercy Park." Agnes rattled off swank hotels they'd hustled their way into, though it wasn't hard to get into a private party if you were young and hip, if you looked like you belonged. With her looks, Mia belonged anywhere, much more than Agnes. Mia was good at finding a group to walk in with. She would say "We were just looking for . . ." and wait for the other person, usually a man, to supply the answer, then add an enthusiastic "Yes, we are going to the same place." What sounded awkward and cagey the first time Mia did it became as normal as spreading butter on toast. As long as they didn't drunkenly knock over a carved-ice logo, torment a human sushi board, or twerk in front of Graydon Carter, it was easy to be allowed in, to stay, to mingle. Being from New York, sometimes Mia even knew someone, which strangely only added to the ease of ruse. "You work at *HuffPo*? I didn't know that." A bonus was if they scored swag bags at the end of the night, full of free magazines and, once, a pair of Bulgari sunglasses. Midwestern Agnes had been thrilled by the opulence, the newness, that could coexist with her own aspergillus windows and flooded subway commute from Brooklyn. This was around the time of the financial crisis, and if they were going to have no career prospects, Agnes and Mia were at least going to get whatever fun there was out of the city.

"We made up lives for ourselves. Histories. Fake names," Agnes said.

"Didn't she meet Martin that way?" Stephanie asked.

Agnes didn't like the way she talked around Mia, almost as if she weren't there. Even though she *had* met Martin that way. Mia's relationship with him had started with the smallest of lies. Agnes wasn't even sure she'd originally given Martin her proper name.

"No, I wasn't thinking of that," Mia said, looking vacantly out the window, unaffected by the story of how she'd met her husband. "I remember dancing in a studio—studying for a performance, and you hated me for some reason."

"Me? Hate you? Never," Agnes said quickly.

The three women all began naming dance movies as Mia glanced from person to person, more curious than anything: *Flashdance*, *Footloose*, *Save the Last Dance*, *Dirty Dancing*—suddenly they were all laughing at how many dance movies there were.

Step Up, *Chicago*, *Suspiria*.

"*Talk to Her*," Zoey suggested.

Agnes waved her hand at Zoey like she should stop. It wasn't a good pick. *Talk to Her* was the Pedro Almodóvar film where the ballerina falls into a coma and is abused by her male nurse; no one suspects him even though he lives across the street from her old dance studio. But it didn't register for Mia, and the group moved on without discussing it when Stephanie suggested *Frances Ha*.

"Oh no, not *Black Swan*?" Agnes put her hands over her face. "It is *Black Swan*."

The film title clicked for Mia, but she still didn't seem convinced her recollection was a movie. "I don't dance ballet?"

"That must be it," Agnes offered. They'd watched *Black Swan* together at the theater. She remembered glancing over at Mia during *that scene* to see if she was feeling awkward as well.

"Oh, wow. The memory felt really real." Mia seemed to sink into herself a little, her confidence shaken. Then she said, "The doctors told me this could happen: that things that aren't true might seem very authentic."

Agnes left the room. As she was going, she heard Stephanie say not to worry, that it would get easier to distinguish between the memories—she was sure of it.

Agnes went to the kitchen and examined the broken marble corner again. She took out a pen and began tapping on things around the kitchen, listening to the tinny sound of the bread box. She moved to the baker's rack. She picked up a pan and dropped it lightly on the burner. More a *clunk* than a *clang*. She cocked her head. Perhaps that was a matter of semantics. *Clunk* and *clang* were similar enough. Somewhere in her scar tissue, Mia—and Mia alone—knew what had happened.

Agnes found her way into the room at the back of the house where her things were. The pen she'd tapped the objects with wasn't going to cut it. The room where Agnes's stuff had been placed was an office with a daybed. Earlier she'd noticed a six-inch metal ruler on the desk—she picked it up. That would do it.

Out the window she could see there was a large guesthouse across the back property, just beyond the pool and down a path. She had expected they would all want to be together in the main house, though, for the remembering party to work.

When Agnes opened the door of her room to leave, Stephanie was standing there. "Hey, Natalie Portman. Mia said you two texted. Tell me more about the texts that night."

"Mia's already upset, and that's not good for her," Agnes said. "We should probably call the doctor."

"Was it about Martin?"

Agnes sighed. "No. She said she was lonely and felt isolated."

"That's it?"

"I wish I knew more. You're her sister. Doesn't she tell you everything?" Agnes had always assumed that in the pockets of time when Mia had sometimes stopped calling, she must have turned to her sister for advice instead. The minute Stephanie had arrived, Agnes could see the trust she won from Mia, as quickly as cat hair sticks to velvet. She was trying hard not to be jealous.

"No!" Stephanie snapped. "Do you think I saw the Martin thing coming any clearer than any of you? I was finishing college when she started high school. She was a little kid. I have so much to make up with her, and COBRA does not cover new therapy."

"It's weird they'd name health coverage after something that can jump out of a wicker basket to kill you."

Steph didn't look thrilled about the joke, and Agnes could see she was busy going over other things in her mind.

Agnes realized how similar she and Stephanie were. They both worked hard at jobs with little reward and no security. When Agnes started in New York publishing, she'd felt she was competing with the same five women with the same Warby Parker frames for the same jobs. Agnes tried to make herself more a "personality" but bombed at Twitter and Instagram, and her Facebook was taken over by racist relatives in Michigan. In the end, she was somehow the last Warby Parker wearer standing, but no richer for it.

"Why *Black Swan*?" Stephanie said. "Isn't Natalie Portman obsessed with her best friend in that movie?"

"No, they're not best friends," Agnes corrected. "They're competitors."

Stephanie arched an eyebrow. "That's not all."

Agnes nodded. "Sure, there's an intimacy in the movie, but that's what I think she's tapping into. I mean, *all* the friends are in love with Mia, each in our own way."

It was what Mia thrived on. And what, Agnes had told herself many times, they had to forgive her for.

Her arms crossed, Stephanie looked more saddened than defiant, and leaned back against the door. She asked if she could please see the texts. Agnes located the phone and opened the text chain. Steph held the phone up and peered at the tiny text. She pulled a pair of reading glasses from her pocket and put them on. She read her sister's words in a flat voice: "You'll always be my friend, won't you?"

Hearing them aloud, Agnes realized they meant something different than she'd thought that night. What she had interpreted as unhappiness, maybe depression or despondency, may have been guilt and an admission that Mia could take advantage of Agnes and they both knew it.

Agnes tapped the metal ruler she had been holding in her hand against the metal doorframe. *Plink*, not *clang*.

Steph stopped the sound by putting her hand on the ruler. "Do you need to do that right now?"

"I was looking for a sound."

Steph shook her head. "What's this text mean? 'Even after what happened to Gatsby you stuck by me.'"

"Gatsby was my dog. It's . . . nothing."

"Sometimes it's the nothing that solves something." The two women locked eyes, Steph's gaze as unwavering as Mia's could sometimes be. She had a very good point. Agnes tucked the ruler into her back pocket.

"What are you trying to solve?" a voice in the hallway said.

The teenage boy, Cameron, was standing behind Stephanie, his little whiskers and his goatish smell rising from the basement into what had been a mature female atmosphere of champagne and Flowerbomb.

"I'm good at puzzles," he said as they both stared at him. The phone in his pocket dinged with a text, but he ignored it, his expression pleading to be invited in.

Agnes remembered the conversations she'd had with Mia about stepmothering. The kid was moody, but he'd been a pawn in a divorce that had played out long before Mia entered the picture. Agnes recalled Mia telling her about taking him to see the Strokes reunion concert because she wanted to go and Martin didn't—the child had been excited at first but quickly grew bored and sneaked drinks. She mentioned driving him places, shopping for him, nothing that would say they had a complex or antagonized relationship, Agnes realized. Maybe she herself distrusted him because she distrusted all teenage boys.

Cameron followed her and Stephanie into the bedroom/office with a stack of faded boxes in his hands. "You guys are having a game night, right?" Agnes went to him and examined them. She pulled a box from the stack.

Ouija, it said. It showed two people's hands meeting on a heart-shaped white plastic pointer amid the letters of the board. It was from the '70s or '80s.

Cameron said the boxes had been in the basement since the magazine did the photoshoot of the house—they'd added some vintage touches to make the place look more lived in. Then they just left them behind. Agnes realized Martin had told the truth about the magazine profile; Zoey had always doubted his stories, though Agnes had wondered if her skepticism grew out of jealousy. Cameron unpacked the box and set the board up on the large desk. Agnes pulled up a hard chair that had been against the wall.

"It won't work if you sit out," Cameron said to Stephanie, who pulled up a chair and asked what to do. "Fingertips on the planchette."

Agnes rested two fingers from each hand beside Stephanie's and Cameron's. No one said anything for a minute; then Agnes made a surprising sound. She giggled.

"Careful," Cameron said. "It's not going to work if you're not respectful."

As they sat quietly, they could all hear Zoey's music down the hall from the living room. Agnes wondered what Mia and Zoey might be talking about, and then just as she felt her mind wander, the planchette inched over, like someone had nudged it.

"Spirit, are you with us?" Cameron lowered his voice as he tried to sound like a guide. *Ding.* His cell phone gave him an alert from his pocket. The planchette swooped now, almost in a figure eight. It stopped at *YES.* "Are you a friendly spirit?"

It swooped again, and Agnes felt her hands trail along with the others, a little more reluctantly. She didn't really believe in spirits. The planchette stopped again at *YES.*

"What should we ask first?" Cameron asked.

They began moving the planchette until Stephanie asked, "Has Cameron ever had a girlfriend?"

Cameron was silent for a long second before their hands pushed the planchette toward *NO*.

"That's not true," Cameron grumbled.

"The spirit sees all," Agnes deadpanned.

"I get more than you, Millennial Cat Lady."

"Cameron!" Stephanie chastised.

"What did you call me?" Agnes challenged him to say it again.

"Nothing Mia wouldn't say. She tells me things. She says you put women on a pedestal because you're too afraid."

"Mia said that about me?" Through her hurt, Agnes saw an opening with Cameron. "What else has Mia told you?"

"That's too general a question for the spirit."

Agnes took the lead in swirling the planchette around the board. "Did anything unusual happen on March fifth, the day of Mia's accident?"

The planchette slowly moved to the alphabet at the top of the board. The pointer began stopping at letters.

F—I—G—H—T. Fight.

Agnes took a deep breath and looked at Stephanie. But Stephanie's face wasn't surprised. She wondered if Steph knew about more fights. Agnes was sure the kid was moving the pointer. He was telling them what he knew.

Cameron guided the game. "So she had a fight with someone? Was it anyone in this room?"

Agnes thought about the last time she'd seen Mia by herself, when she'd started to ask for a favor and it had turned tense. But that had been a couple of weeks before the accident.

NO.

"Who was it?"

The planchette hesitated, then moved slowly, as if it didn't want to, to the *M*. From there it went to *K*.

"Martin Kroner," Stephanie muttered.

"*Did* they have a fight?" Agnes asked, this time to Cameron, not the board.

He said nothing, but the pointer went to *YES*.

It made sense—that was why Mia had texted her that night and come all the way out here from Brooklyn.

Stephanie jumped in. "He's not the kid from *The Sixth Sense*. Just ask him about it."

"So what time was that?" Agnes asked.

"Five or six," Cameron said.

Stephanie took her hands away and pulled out a small leather notebook. She wrote down the words *Fight, 5 p.m.*, then looked at Agnes. "That's three hours before she texted you."

Beneath Cameron's and Agnes's fingers, the planchette zoomed around like an angry bumblebee. "If you don't respect the spirit, we'll suffer the consequences," Cameron implored.

Stephanie closed her book. "Sorry," she said, and the pointer slowed down. She put her fingertips back on.

"What did they fight about?" Agnes asked.

The pointer went to *M*.

"Money?" Steph interrupted.

Then the planchette swooped quickly back to *A* and *N*.

"A man," Steph said, staring.

"Was the name Ethan?" Agnes asked.

"That's all I know," Cameron replied.

"I'm not asking you. I'm asking the spirit," Agnes said now earnestly. "Spirit, was it Ethan?"

Zoey and Mia stood in the doorway, peering in at the group. Mia had changed out of her bloodstained shirt into a clean one. No one had seen them standing there. Zoey fixed an icy-hot glare on Agnes and asked, "Why would you think it would be Ethan?"

Chapter Five

The Hummus Truth

Mia headed back to the living room. She didn't want to say it bothered her that they were discussing her life over what appeared to be a board game, but it bothered her. What did it mean to any of them, Mia wondered, for her to remember? Was it just to feel as though they were proving something? What they really should have wanted was not just to see her remember someone or something that had been, but to . . . *what?* she asked herself as she grabbed a carrot and swiped at the dip on the tray. *To be safe.* They should want her to be safe.

Mia looked out the window and recalled walking down the driveway, the road, feeling a sense of urgency, as if someone might be back here in the house.

She bit down and tasted horror scented with paprika and garlic. She began to cough, then found a napkin and spit out carrot splinters and dip. "What—what is that?" she sputtered, putting a hand to her throat as the group reassembled. "I think I'm having an allergic reaction."

"Sit down. Here's some water." Stephanie guided her to the couch. But Mia jumped up again. "I'm dying!"

"Oh," Zoey said, glancing at Agnes. "She had the hummus. Agnes, I told you not to get the hummus."

"You didn't say that!" Agnes protested.

Mia ran for the toilet before the friends could sort out who was at fault. Her body heaved, but she didn't actually vomit. The door was shut, but she could hear them talking in low voices outside it. *This party was a bad idea,* she thought.

"Don't you remember? She ate hummus all night at the party, then left with that guy who worked at Tumblr. You know, *that guy.*" Zoey's voice trailed away, and Agnes's picked up.

"Yeah, the night she drank too much and picked him up. I always thought it was pretty baller."

"No, it was not good," Stephanie declared, the final word.

Mia began to quietly cry until the tears fell into the toilet. It was some kind of past hurt, but one she couldn't exactly recall. Again, all she saw was her reflection in a TV that wouldn't turn on. Why would Zoey and Agnes give her a food they both seemed to know she hated? She had a terrible thought: *This is why I left them.* It felt like a message from the other side, a ghost more real than anything the boy could conjure with a Ouija board. She'd left her friends to be with her husband because she was tired of them, tired of not being able to grow up. That must have been it. It felt true.

Mia washed her face and stared into the mirror. Her face didn't match the stories she was being told about herself. Light-brown hair hung to the chin, framing the face of a woman in the second half of her thirties. She brushed her teeth, feeling the bristles dig in. There was a light knock on the door. Mia let all three of the women into the bathroom. They stood or sat around the tub ledge, a hot ticket to trauma. Mia said, "His name was Christian."

Agnes nodded. "Of course."

Zoey said, "No, she's using an actor. Christian Slater."

"Slater was his real last name, though," Stephanie said.

Mia closed her eyes tight. "I remember looking up at his headboard, and he had stacks of pickup-artist books up there. It was so creepy. I was so fucking weirded out that I tried to get up. I just wanted to leave, and he—when I said no, he said, 'You're already here.' He kept pulling off my clothes, and I actually—I clawed his face. I grabbed my stuff and bolted."

Agnes pressed her into her arms. "I'm so sorry. Zoey didn't tell me it was that bad—I just thought it was a date with some guy. I was with you the next day. I held your hair back while you laughed about it and threw up."

"Why would I do that?" Mia said. "To show I was indestructible? Was I the kind of person who would say anything as a joke, make it an *experience*? Am I that person?"

Mia watched as Agnes cast a glance at Zoey, as if to say *Why didn't you tell me before I bought the fucking hummus?* They'd brought back the worst memory they could have—hummus, gin, and sexual trauma— and Mia was pretty sure it wasn't a film. Her memory was detailed now, and they all seemed to know something about it.

"Poor Christian Slater," Zoey said. When the women glared at her, she corrected herself. "The real one. I mean, having his name ruined in your mind like that. Remember when we watched *Untamed Heart*? We were making fun of it so hard and then bawling our eyes out at the end."

"Was that the one where he had a baboon heart transplant?" Mia asked, sniffing back tears.

"Movies are so stupid sometimes."

"Thank God," Mia said, breaking into a laugh. "They wouldn't match life enough otherwise."

———◦———

In the kitchen, the housekeeper, Susan, helped Mia with her five-o'clock meds before leaving for the night. Stephanie was chopping tomatoes for dinner, and Mia joined her, finding both the repetition of the chopping and Stephanie beside her soothing.

"Cameron said you and Martin were fighting that day?"

Mia nicked her knuckle. "Shit." She sucked the cut and walked to the farmhouse sink. "Is it important for me to remember that? Because it's looking like I'm remembering only shitty things."

"Do you trust Martin?" Steph asked.

"No. I don't trust my husband. And I don't know if I trust those women out there either."

Stephanie asked, "Were you fighting over Ethan?"

But in the moment Mia found the name meant nothing.

Stephanie corrected herself. "Duckie? Whatever."

Mia shook her head. In her mind, she could see a picture of a different man, but she couldn't find a name for him. Just a feeling. "No. I think I know his real name."

But before Mia could say it, they heard Zoey's voice erupt like a blowtorch from the living room. "The hummus wasn't an accident, was it, Agnes?"

Stephanie and Mia pushed over to the doorway and saw Agnes red faced on the couch and Zoey standing over her, waving a sheet of wrinkled paper. Zoey turned to Mia. "She was asking you for money again, wasn't she?"

Chapter Six

SET ANOTHER PLACE

Zoey saw the look of embarrassment on Mia's face, because what kind of friend would pressure you for that sum of money? Zoey felt a small flicker of vindication. Something in Mia remembered.

Agnes looked at Mia and said, "When my building got bought, they jacked the rent and tried to evict everyone. I had a lead on a new place, one that was more affordable, but I would've needed first and last."

"You didn't ask me for money," Mia said.

"I was going to a couple times, and then I put it off. That night I was just worried about you."

Zoey had been ready to usurp Stephanie's weekend role and lay out the entirety of the Agnes Theory: Jealous of Mia's life, she needs a loan, again, and Mia ignores her. She texts Mia one more time the night of the fall. Did they phone and talk about the eviction notice? Did she drive out here? It wasn't entirely logical, but Zoey could see it might be a starting point. It was certainly an unusual coincidence.

Before Zoey could explore her theories, Mia's cell phone began chirping with notifications.

Stephanie grabbed Mia's phone from the kitchen island and brought it over. "They're from Martin."

Zoey and Agnes stood looking at her, waiting for her to read the messages aloud.

"I know you're drinking." Mia paused, bracing herself and the room for the rest. "Your friends are always a bad influence. Please stop. Second text: You know we will work this out. You just have to get better."

Zoey noticed Stephanie had already scratched half the messages down in her notebook. It seemed to Zoey that Agnes and Steph had begun to compete for the weekend-detective job, Stephanie taking the forensics-and-evidence route and Agnes a looser, more intuitive, route. Almost like performance art. Zoey watched as Steph finished copying the messages verbatim. Agnes had left them and gone to the window and was peering out.

Cameron rolled his eyes. He was drinking wine from a juice glass. He slurred, "An investment guru with control issues—who could have guessed he's also an asshole to his family?"

Mia and Cameron had a conversation about whether his first mother experienced the same behavior. Cameron revealed, after a few questions from Agnes, who came back slowly, that since the divorce, Martin had nicknamed Cynthia, his first wife, Cunthia, which for a second Zoey found hilarious. She let out a snort. But disturbing too. Absolutely wrong—it was his son's mother. The group began debating how serious the fight between Mia and Martin might have been the afternoon of her fall. Zoey got up and went to the window that Agnes had been looking out of. Beyond the driveway and the gate was the forest—treetops flapping in the brisk spring wind. The sun had hit that five-o'clock low.

"How did he know you were drinking?" Agnes asked.

Zoey cut in. "It's like the movie *Sliver*. Do you have a surveillance system? Or . . . a secret one?" She glanced around nervously.

"If I knew about it, would it be secret?" Mia looked at the wine-glass still in her hand, now empty. She looked at Cameron, who shook his head.

"Martin kind of looks like a young Alec Baldwin," Agnes said.

Zoey snapped back, "It was *William* Baldwin in *Sliver*."

Instead of going back to the window, Agnes went to the door. She walked bravely out, and Mia and the gang observed her as she went to the edge of the property, out near the gate across the drive. Her curly head turned in two directions as she surveyed the woods and the road. She came back toward them, then headed around to the back of the property. When she returned, she held up one finger, then repeated her movements, making a second sweep.

"Why did your first mother leave?" Mia said.

Cameron ducked his head, like he didn't want to say.

Agnes came back in, her face flushed from moving quickly, or from fear. "There's no one out there."

Mia gazed out the window. "Who's that, then?" she asked, and everyone looked.

Zoey watched as a black car made its way slowly up the road.

⸎

She looked at her own phone and cursed. The Instagram photo of her and Mia had collected ninety likes, and she had nearly as many texts she hadn't looked at—because two hours ago she'd silenced her phone—all from Ethan, who was now stepping out of the car in front of the gate. Zoey could feel a throbbing in her temples.

Ethan had done it. He'd taken a fucking Uber from Cobble Hill to Connecticut. His dark hair lifted and rippled in the breeze. He pushed the gate open, and it complained: *clank-clank*. Mia flinched at the sound of the iron as it dragged on the paved driveway. Zoey noticed Agnes's expression as she saw Mia's reaction. The Uber didn't use the circle but backed out and pulled away, leaving him to walk the rest of the way to the house. It was not an insubstantial walk.

"Duckie?" Mia asked.

"Yes, Duckie-slash-Ethan-slash-soon-to-be-ex," Zoey said and quickly grabbed her coat and strode out to meet him—and tear a strip off him where the others wouldn't hear. She was halfway down the drive, and already he was holding up both his hands, defensive, as if she might knee him in the balls then and there. "Why?" she said, letting the word hang, a single syllable infused with all her disappointment.

He pulled a knapsack higher up on his shoulder.

Looks like he's planning to stay, she thought.

He shifted his weight from one sneakered foot to the other. "We all love Mia, and we all need to help her."

Before he could say more, Zoey yelled, "Yeah, let's talk about how much you love her!"

Ethan flinched, his head snapping back like he'd been punched by the force of her voice.

Zoey glanced at the living room window, sure they were all watching, but only Agnes's face was peeking through the curtains before it quickly withdrew. Zoey felt her mouth go dry.

"Like a *friend.* She's my *friend.* Just because I want to be here for her doesn't mean I'm not in love with you. I mean, I wouldn't not respect you."

"There were so many double negatives in that sentence, I have no idea what you're saying." Zoey stared down at her feet. "I don't think you see me anymore, Ethan. You know you can't even pay me a compliment?"

He breathed out hard. "You're an exhausting person to pay a compliment to, Zoey. Even that you argue against." Ethan fumbled with his knapsack. He pulled out a copy of a book, *Taking Charge of Your Fertility,* and pushed it into her hand. Zoey felt the weight of Ethan's love for her, that he would come here and bring it with him. What did it mean? Was it everything—or nothing? A smear of watercolor flowers on the cover, as though a woman were nothing but a garden, a place for something to grow in.

"Okay. For real, this is why I came out here," he said. "This is your window, peak fertility, this weekend." He pointed to the ground, like her menstrual cycle was written in the flagstones.

"How did you know that?" Zoey stared at him.

"You have the app on your phone that tracks your cycle. You take your temperature every morning. We only live together. You think I don't notice anything?" He flapped his arms around. Zoey wasn't sure if he was frustrated or frightened of the whole idea. His voice rose as he argued. "I thought we were trying for this."

She ducked her head, hoping the others couldn't hear. She thought about the cryotank and all she'd done to get it. "We've been so disconnected, I thought we should take a break from trying."

"People change," Ethan told her. "You have to allow for that, and you don't."

Ethan had never changed physically, and she had forgotten you could change in ways that weren't outwardly apparent. She'd gotten used to him being the boy she'd found and rescued from an anime collection and taped-up My Chemical Romance posters in a messy bedroom. Even though she saw him every day, maybe she was the one who had stopped seeing him.

Ethan headed for the house, then jerked open the door without waiting for anyone to greet him and let him in. Zoey followed quickly.

"Hi, Ethan!" Agnes was overly bright—as usual. She came across the room and gave Ethan a hug. Ethan accepted the hug and nodded to Steph, then, without a word, turned to Mia and beckoned to her.

Zoey wanted to shadow them, but let them go—she didn't want a round two. Agnes caught her eye, and Zoey shook her head slightly. Everyone was obviously aware of their disagreement outside. She watched as Stephanie followed Mia and Ethan through the house and onto the back deck. Given that, Zoey suspected Stephanie may have heard some things about Ethan.

Zoey kept an eye on him, as well, through the window looking onto the back garden. She watched Ethan's face turn serious. He must have been talking quietly to Mia, because Stephanie moved closer to them to hear.

"Are you okay?" Agnes asked her.

"You're the one I'm concerned about, falling that far behind." Zoey plucked the eviction notice she'd left lying around and handed it to Agnes, who folded it and hid it away in her pocket.

Zoey walked over to her iPod, which had played through her list a couple of times already and was blasting "Hollaback Girl" for the third time. She disconnected it from the stereo.

When she came back, Agnes had poured them each a gin and tonic. She must have decided they needed something stronger than wine.

"Should we—" Agnes started, but when Zoey turned, she stopped speaking.

"What?"

"Should we be worried about Ethan? I know he can sometimes be a little, uh . . ."

"You can say it. Impulsive." It bothered her that her friends tap-danced around the issues, even though she knew, deep down, they probably took their cues from her. *Issues* was what she always called it, though they both knew it was deeper and more medical than that. Ethan had bipolar disorder. When controlled, things were great. His intensity and creativity were as choreographed as a fireworks display. When it wasn't controlled, Zoey stepped in to be both nurse and spin doctor.

"Yeah. And it seems like the two of you are . . . having discussions?"

"We are, but he's fine . . ." Zoey felt the heat rise in her cheeks. Zoey realized she had pushed Agnes too far in questioning her about the loans from Mia. She suddenly remembered how Agnes had once waited two hours when she and Ethan were supposed to meet her after work for an art show at MoMA that required reserved tickets. Ethan had been crashed out in bed with the blanket over his head, and although he'd already been snoring for twelve hours, nothing Zoey did would rouse him. He had come through a manic phase and hadn't slept in five days. When Zoey hadn't been able to pull him out of bed, she'd eventually left him to meet Agnes on her own. Agnes had said she didn't mind, she'd had work to catch up on—staying into the evening never hurt. They could still try to get in, Agnes suggested. But it was long past their ticket time, and Zoey had admitted she was too embarrassed to try.

Instead, they had grabbed french fries and Shake Shack burgers without Zoey having to explain anything.

Agnes had said, "No doubt it's hard for Ethan, but I bet it's also tiring to do so much caretaking all the time."

"It's exhausting," Zoey had admitted.

They'd gone from dinner to a bar Agnes knew in the West Village called Marie's Crisis, where a man played show tunes and everyone sang "Tomorrow," from *Annie*, and "Seasons of Love," from *Rent*, together at the top of their lungs, not as karaoke but as one big chorus. The night had probably gone on Agnes's credit card without an argument.

"He's my friend too. I care how he's doing," Agnes said, her expression a little softer now.

"Look, Stephanie is working us up," Zoey said now in an effort to bring Agnes back on her side. "We can find who hurt Mia without cosplaying *Murder, She Wrote*."

"You're right," Agnes said. But then she pressed again. "So his moods? He's managing them?"

"He's . . . spirited," Zoey said, raising an eyebrow.

"So no danger of the thing with the knife happening again?"

Zoey sighed. "He threatened *himself*. When he was locked in the bathroom." The party seemed to be becoming about rehashing all their old hurts. "Don't stigmatize mental illness."

"Sorry, I don't mean to poke the wasp's nest."

"Well, it's like that line Bette Davis says in *All about Eve*, 'We're all busy little bees, full of stings, making honey day and night.'"

"I don't think wasps make honey," Agnes said.

Zoey straightened her back and answered without thinking: "They do. They totally make honey."

The women sipped their gin in silence. Agnes stared out the kitchen window, and her gaze settled on Mia. Then, tentatively, Agnes asked, "Cameron said they fought about a man. Do you think she could have been seeing someone else? She would have told us."

Over the years Zoey had become Ethan's protector, mostly protecting him from himself, and sometimes from his Mia thing. The night in question, Zoey and Ethan had fought. He'd been texting Mia— and Zoey hated knowing that. Zoey had also hated hiding it from her friends. He'd thought he'd been so adept, but the Messenger function on his computer had brought the texts up easily, so that even without looking for them, Zoey saw. He had been in their bedroom, but the open laptop in the living room emitted a piercing ding every time a new text arrived. On went the conversation between Ethan and Mia—and on, until about eight at night, when Zoey couldn't stand it anymore and barged into the bedroom, where Ethan lay with his phone cupped in his palm. Ethan was hardly a Don Draper at this thing.

"Come on, Agnes," Zoey deflected. "All the cougars prowl out here. Did you see that Starbucks we stopped at? It was Club Hedonism in culottes. These aspirational suburban wives have so much time. Not like us. We're career women."

"I am?"

"We've made lives for ourselves."

"I have?"

"We have it all."

Zoey tapped her phone and went through Mia's social feed, but it contained few clues of her life. Some pictures of Mona Lisa (Mia's cat), a selfie outside a bookstore in her neighborhood in Park Slope, a movie marquee with *Roman Holiday* playing. Zoey had noticed a long time ago she seldom put Martin in her photos, and Zoey wasn't sure if it was because he didn't like to be photographed or because Mia didn't care to photograph him. Zoey photographed Ethan often, even if he seldom let her post them. Zoey held out the phone to Agnes. She indicated the movie marquee. "Audrey Hepburn. Could be a date?"

Agnes shrugged. "Would have to be a hell of a date. A straight guy seeing an Audrey Hepburn movie willingly?"

Zoey felt a flicker of relief. It was true. Whenever a black-and-white film was on TCM, Ethan would fall asleep, claiming it must be his meds. His idea of film canon only went back to *Taxi Driver*. Of the group, Victor was much more the film classicist.

"Anyway, if she was going on secret afternoon dates, why take a picture?" Agnes said.

"Sometimes it's on purpose, to end things. Not all of us are good on confrontation."

Affairs, interventions, and murder-mystery weekends. Maybe all of them had begun to swipe left on their dreams long ago. Mia had been the first to shine after graduation: two short stories in small literary journals. She'd given Agnes and Zoey copies, undercutting her own pride with the statement "These aren't famous journals. No one has heard of these."

Zoey remembered she had told her it was okay. "No one has heard of the famous literary journals either."

And then Mia stopped. She said it was pointless and vain. She had been in several short films made by Zoey and Ethan and other friends, and a play—really, a workshop—but likely no one remembered them except their little gang. Mia had interned at *Vanity Fair*, but that was years ago. Zoey had been jealous, and so had Agnes, but at the end of the internship, there had been no job for Mia—probably because she'd never taken it as seriously as them.

"Ethan wants a baby," Zoey said to Agnes, surprising even herself by putting into words what had just occurred between them out there.

"Yeah. We talked about it in the car."

"No, I mean with *his* sperm," Zoey said.

"Wow, okay!" Agnes's voice brightened again, like someone who had been given a present. "There isn't a problem with his stuff? I assumed that's why, you know, you went with a donor."

"Maybe. Probably not. I didn't want to waste any more time finding out. Should I give him a chance?"

Zoey watched as Agnes pressed her lips together, considering. After a minute, Agnes said, "You should maybe talk to him more about that. Raising a child that he thinks is his own. It's kind of a big deal, you know."

"Am I just trying to get his attention with this whole . . . project?" Zoey gazed at her boyfriend outside the back window. The thought hung there. *Not using his sperm does give me an escape if things don't get better, a side door,* she realized.

"What do you think they're talking about?" Agnes asked instead of answering Zoey's question. Zoey had noticed long ago that Agnes seldom gave her direct opinion.

"I don't know, but let's go—" Zoey stopped at the sound of the gate, *clank-clank,* and then the sound of a car came from the front of the house, the thrum of the garage door rising on the side of the mansion.

Cameron, whom Zoey hadn't seen when she'd come back in, appeared now in the doorway, as if he had never been far away. She wondered how much of their private conversation he'd overheard.

"Um, it's my dad," Cameron said. His face was sweaty and pale, as if he were nervous at the arrival of his own father.

Chapter Seven

Gin and Toxics

Agnes heard the door. Martin didn't come through the front but through the side hall by the staircase, just off the garage. To Cameron, she whispered, "Don't let your father see you with that wine," and Agnes watched the teenager casually deposit the half-full glass into a potted plant beside him.

Agnes pasted on a smile and walked toward him. "Martin! You're back!"

Martin moved slowly, a look of distraction on his face. She'd seen him only that morning, but he looked years, not hours, older. The folds of his hair were messier. His eyes seemed sadder and his cheeks slacker. He pocketed his car keys, indicating he intended to stay.

"Yeah, yeah, some papers. There's stuff I need to settle," he mumbled.

"I'm so sorry about the drinking. I only let her have half a glass." For a moment Agnes felt guilt coil deep in her guts. She supposed she hadn't been an accountable friend. She *had* let Mia drink on her medication. Mia was *hers* to care for over the weekend. She'd only stirred bad memories so far.

Martin looked up, surprised she was still addressing him. He glanced around. "Oh, fine then. Whatever."

Agnes glanced at Cameron. He shrugged as Martin walked back down the hall to the spare bedroom / office, where her things were. She heard drawers being opened.

Agnes heard a sound, a light rapping on the glass doors, and turned to see Zoey beckoning the others to come inside from the deck.

Especially after the aggressive texts, she'd begun to really suspect Martin was full of anger, maybe even abusive. Now he'd walked in meekly and didn't seem to give a damn about Mia at all.

Cameron whispered to Agnes, "He's spacey when he's working."

Stephanie came in from outside. She moved down the hall to talk to Martin, unfazed by anything they'd discussed prior to his arrival. "This," she declared, standing in the hall outside the room where he was. Steph was pointing in at Martin and back at the side door. "This coming and going isn't good for my sister. We should talk."

Ethan and Mia came in from outside. Mia was holding his laptop, as if he'd had it out to show her something. She set it down on the kitchen island.

"I don't know what's going on," Agnes whispered to Ethan. "Martin's like a medicated kitten. Yarn could knock him over."

"Don't be fooled," Zoey said.

"Martin has Resting Murder Face," Ethan agreed.

Zoey shook her head. "You're making that up. That's not a thing."

Agnes said, "Ethan's right. We're all here—and it is very likely that her attacker is in the house right now."

Ethan and Zoey exchanged uneasy glances.

"I'll go listen," Ethan whispered.

But Agnes put her hand up to stop him. "I'll go," she said.

Out of a protective instinct for Mia, she crept farther down the hall. Although she couldn't see into the room, Agnes heard Martin's voice.

"What are you saying to me?" His tone was flat, as it had been when he came in.

Stephanie was blunt. "Pretty simple. You should go."

Martin stormed out of the office, followed by Stephanie.

Agnes backed up. Ethan backed away, too, toward Mia.

"This is my house. You know that, right?" Martin yelled at Stephanie; then his gaze darted around to all of them. This was more what Agnes had expected.

Agnes hadn't considered it until that moment, but Stephanie, despite her rounded shoulders and athletic attire, was perhaps five-six. Not large. And Ethan, with his tall but wiry frame, was not much protection either. Zoey was perhaps the fittest of them, but even she was slim and feminine.

"You don't need to check up on her. She's my sister. I'll take care of her," Steph insisted.

"Jesus. I invited you here. I offered the space for this—thing, this whatever party. I came back for some contracts . . ." Martin stopped in midthought, as if he realized he had been arguing from the defensive position. He pivoted to offense. "I know you already think I did something, and you know what? I'm tired of it. The way you all look at me." He lifted his chin at Agnes, acknowledging her. "It doesn't surprise me, though. You think you're all open minded and creative, but you're the most judgmental little turds ever. You think I stole her away from you?"

Martin looked at his wife, hiding on the other side of the room. "Mia *ran*. I know I'm not cool, but I love her. That's what she ran to."

"I'm sure," Stephanie said. "But why didn't you phone us right away? Is it because you fought?"

"Jesus. Couples fight," Martin said. "Ask your ex-husband."

Agnes watched as Zoey nudged Ethan with her elbow, as if to say *Oh shit, he went there.*

"He didn't crack my skull on a marble island," Stephanie spat back.

"What if she *was* pushed?" The room went silent after Martin improvised this murder scenario out loud. After an excruciating moment, he laughed in an attempted recovery. "Now it's in the open—you think I tried to kill her." Martin scoffed as he looked at all of them. "I was fifty miles away. But that doesn't matter, does it? You watch your crime shows and podcasts, and you read your little novels"—he pointed to Agnes on that one—"and you're suspicious of success and happiness, 'cause you don't got any."

He strode past them, and Agnes flattened herself against the living room wall to let him by. He smelled like Ralph Lauren's Polo and pompous indignation as he said over his shoulder, "Crime rates are dropping, you idiots."

Then Martin lurched to the corner chair, where Cameron had been skulking. "What did I walk into here, Cam?"

"Whatever, Martin." Cameron was more like a defiant coworker than a son. "I did what you said. I texted you updates."

There was a spy in the house of Martin and Mia. Cameron was why Martin had known she was drinking. Agnes had almost felt a kinship for the sullen teenager earlier that day, but now it appeared everyone was on their own side.

Martin turned to Mia. His voice seemed more hollow than angry now. "Tell me honestly." He held out one hand for her to take. "Do you love me?"

Mia didn't seem to pick up on the cue, and Martin's offered hand fell in a fist.

"I loved you," he said, and the past tense wasn't lost on anyone who was there.

How can anyone flip to past tense so quickly? Agnes wondered. *As if love is a light switch you turn off at the end of the night.*

"I'm sorry," Mia said, though if the apology meant anything, only she and Martin were aware.

Martin crossed the room to Cameron, who hunched before his father could touch him. Martin looked into his son's face, waiting for something, some sign. Cameron swallowed. "Go to your mother's," Martin said, and leaned down and kissed the boy on the hairline. Then he dodged out the front door.

—⊢—

Agnes noticed Zoey had her phone camera up, filming Martin through the picture window as he walked into the garage to go to his car.

"Good move. Thank you," Stephanie said.

Zoey flipped the phone around so she was in her own shot, then slated it with her name and the date, time, and address. Then she clicked the circle on the screen to stop filming. Agnes couldn't imagine what the title on YouTube would be. *Murder Dad Freaks Out? Brunching with the Enemy?*

"Do you think he saw you filming?" Stephanie asked. "Did you get the whole thing?" She took her notebook out and started jotting some thoughts down, documenting what had been said. Zoey shook her head no, to one or possibly both questions.

"Part." Then Zoey said, "I think we should turn this over to the authorities. That was fucked up. 'What if she *was* pushed?' I mean, that's almost going the full *If I Did It.*"

"Zoey, you're not going to go viral over this," Agnes said.

No one said anything for a minute; then Mia got up and hugged Cameron, who looked like he might cry. Like all teenagers, his face looked like it strained to hold in his emotions at the best of times, skin waxy with seldom-shaved hairs. Now, he'd turned downright blotchy. It made Agnes wonder how her friend knew to do that, but then, Mia had never been afraid to touch people. She'd made friends easily. She could touch a stranger on the arm and learn their whole life story in a bar, then leave without saying goodbye, never to see them again. Of course she would comfort the child who was her stepson, even when she barely remembered their lives. That was Mia. She cared deeply and made you aware of it; even if it didn't last, it meant everything for a moment.

Agnes sank down onto the ottoman, exhausted. The remembering party had to continue, she thought. In a way it was becoming bigger than all of them. She remembered last December, in that week between Christmas and New Year's. Mia had said she had a gift for her and had come by to Agnes's third-floor walk-up on DeKalb. Mia's brownstone wasn't far, and when Mia walked over, the two usually met on the stoop to go out, as if they both knew Mia's designer clothes would clash sitting on the mismatched vintages of furniture Agnes had, and that Mia could no longer help herself from brushing a thumb over the chips on the teacups before sipping. It didn't help that Agnes wasn't a great house-keeper. She cringed, thinking of the unscrubbed baseboards and stacks of recycling in her crowded kitchen.

Mia had confided that Martin was going out for New Year's, enter-taining clients, and she would be spending the night alone. Agnes had quickly volunteered to do something, but Mia said it was fine. "Are things all right with Martin?" Agnes had voiced, and Mia had said something about space being a healthy part of any relationship.

In a pretty gold gift bag, Mia had given her a stainless steel water bottle and a leather bracelet, things that seemed impersonal or, maybe now that Agnes considered it, masculine. Things she might have chosen for someone else—Martin, or another friend. But what had Agnes given in return? A candle. A pair of silly socks, pale green with spotted basset hounds on them. The kinds of gifts that were safe. Sitting there in Mia and Martin's *Town & Country*-perfect house, Agnes felt ashamed now that she hadn't pressed her friend for more details about her life. The friendship had begun to have gaps in it.

Agnes remembered how close they'd been a decade ago. The Christmas break during sophomore year when Mia's folks were having a trial separation, Mia had come home with her to avoid taking sides. The girls had flown to Detroit and then driven out among the small farming towns to Agnes's tiny home village outside Ann Arbor: a land of wool-blend shirt jackets, denim and Sherpa collars, Campbell's Soup–based casseroles, and hot dogs sliced into mac 'n' cheese; a place where all the women had Hillary Clinton–campaign hair. They wore their Christmas sweaters right into spring because YOLO.

Agnes had seen the sociological wonder in Mia's eyes when she met the Nielsens. Agnes had prepped her about the Nielsens' middle-class ways: a split-level house, a mother who was a retired grammar school principal, and a dad who was a bookkeeper. Every present cost twenty dollars or less, and at night Agnes's dad offered to drive them around to look at Christmas lights, as if they were twelve. Her mom made up the double bed in Agnes's old bedroom with two sets of blankets folded as if they were sleeping bags so the girls wouldn't touch at all while they slept—it was clear even then that her mom had fears about her daughter's sexuality she could articulate only through linen.

It had occurred to Agnes many times that marrying Martin was the biggest rebellion Mia could stage—to leave her Film Forum–supporting, Upper West Side world permanently behind for a finance guy who thought watching the Godfather trilogy marathon on AMC in fleece pants was culture. It was part of why Agnes, unlike Zoey, couldn't stay angry at her—because Mia had to rebel. And maybe she'd glimpsed a different life in Agnes's hometown. Something simple and secure. That day after Christmas, Mia hadn't been able to believe the Nielsens all went and exchanged their gifts for items they liked better without shame.

———

The group had moved back into the kitchen when Agnes joined them. "Stephanie, can you come with me for a minute?"

When Zoey looked concerned and asked why, Agnes said it was to check and see if Martin wasn't still hanging around, which Zoey thought was a good idea.

What Agnes didn't say in front of Zoey was that she could guess who the bracelet was originally for, and that it was time to talk with him.

Chapter Eight

Dinner and Cocktails

Mia was beginning to suspect she was a terrible person, despite everyone telling her about her wonderful qualities. Or maybe it was that the people around her were like a warped mirror, emphasizing all her flaws.

There were dozens of movies like this: a person wakes up one day and has to discover who they really were. There were the Bourne movies, but where would Mia have seen those? Martin seemed the type to watch them, home theater sound system cranked and the walls shaking with every explosion. Mia realized that unlike the protagonist in those movies, there was no do-or-die reason for her to remember who she was. It was her friends who needed her to remember, as if they didn't exist without her.

Then there was the '90s indie movie *Amateur*, where Isabelle Huppert plays an addicted-to-porn ex-nun and befriends an amnesiac who, it turns out, doesn't remember any of his life of crime. It was the kind of farcical scenario with a bleak ending she could relate to now. She remembered meeting the director, Hal Hartley. He was rumpled and talking about *funding* this and *money* that. But how did she know him? Agnes had explained that she and Mia were roommates and English majors at NYU. They had taken an elective class, Adaptation Studies, and that's where they'd met Zoey, Ethan, and Victor—all film majors. Maybe Hal Hartley had visited the class?

Getting changed for dinner was Zoey's idea. She said a bit of glam would make the night special. Apparently she and Agnes had packed for it. Stephanie came in at the end of Mia's nap to check on her and see if she needed help getting dressed.

"Is that more blood?" Stephanie asked, pointing to Mia's collar. The blouse she'd put on earlier already had a small rusty smear on it. Mia got up and stood in front of the closet, staring at things she kept there. Stephanie walked over and pulled out a crisp navy blouse, saying she'd seen Mia wear it before and it looked great on her. But Mia shook her head. "It doesn't feel like me."

"Can I borrow this?" Steph asked, picking up a long necklace from the top of the dresser.

Mia nodded. Her hand reached farther into the closet to flip through garments. She stopped at a shapeless gray sweaterdress.

"I think Mom bought you that," Stephanie said as she fastened Mia's necklace around her own neck. "Do you remember?"

Mia removed the dress from the hanger and laid it on the bed. She stared at it and remembered her mother crying. Mia remembered she was the one who made her cry by saying "It's a bit matronly for me."

"Was I a bitch to people?" Mia asked Stephanie.

"You grew up. Eventually."

"Is that what happened between me and them? I grew up?"

"They're your friends."

"I don't know them anymore."

Stephanie sighed like an HR rep forced to tell the truth. "Agnes. She tries to do the right thing, but she's too nice for New York. Zoey is too perfect for New York. She's the person who gets a job and tells the boss what to do in her first week. Ethan . . ."

"Is in love with me?" Mia's fingers went to her blouse buttons, and she undid them without any hesitation.

"I guess even you can see that, huh?"

Mia handed her sister the old blouse, assuming she would take it and find a way to lift the stain. She was naked in front of her like someone can only be when they've undressed many times in front of a person before. The fact that she had no memory of it didn't change her demeanor.

Mia turned and looked at the sweaterdress on the bed.

"This bruise," Stephanie said from behind her.

Mia glanced down her body. "Where?"

Steph walked up and softly took Mia by the arm. She held her arm up and peered at Mia's elbow. There it was: a yellow-brown bruise across the back of her forearm, still fading, even though it had been weeks now since her fall. The shape of it was on an angle, as if she'd been struck by a police officer's baton. Stephanie said it didn't look at all like something you could get in a kitchen.

"I guess I didn't think about it," Mia said.

"Could you have hit the counter here, instead of with your head?" Steph asked. "But to hit your head, you'd need to fall a second time . . . it doesn't make any sense." Her eyes narrowed, and then she pulled out her notebook and scribbled some things in it.

Mia went over to the long dresser and picked up a round jar of blush and dashed it onto her cheeks with a nearby brush. The reflected face in the mirror looked tired. But why was she judging a person she barely knew?

"I wish I could start over. Like, really start over," Mia said to her sister.

"Don't be that way. It'll come."

"But maybe I don't want it to. I don't want to remember. What happened. Who this person who lives here was. I'd rather walk into a new life somewhere else."

Mia looked down at the sideboard where her makeup lay. A man's valet tray was beside it. The only things on it were a pair of enamel

Montblanc cuff links and a crumpled pack of American Spirit cigarettes. Mia closed her eyes, and a scene played before her again, one she had been working on. She hadn't told anyone else yet, but something different was happening. She suspected she was starting to make her own original movies in her head. Bits of her own memory, but now overproduced—streets wetted down to catch the glint of lights, dialogue flying a little too fast and sharp. The scene running through her mind should have starred Scarlett Johansson and Clive Owen in a meet-cute scene, but instead had Mia and Martin.

———

In the scene Mia exited the hotel, defeated. She turned around to say something to the security guard but then stopped herself. Agnes had gotten in because she legitimately knew someone—Mia hadn't. Agnes hadn't wanted to leave her, but Mia had told her to go in while she could. They were too old for such games, and she felt silly now.

Down the street a few yards, a man leaned against a building, smoking. He saw Mia and seemed to clock her as she walked down the street toward him. He was well dressed, and she didn't mind his glance. She felt herself wanting to feel worthy.

As she passed, he called out to her. "I know who you are!"

She stopped and sighed. She had to snub a man—even a good-looking one—for using such a tired old pickup line. She used the opportunity to dig in her purse for her MetroCard.

"Your name is . . . Ashley Tisdale. You're an editor at *Vogue*. We met at Soho House. Last month."

Mia's annoyance changed to a guardedness. "You're thinking of someone else."

Martin, with his pressed shirt and rumpled hair, came closer. "No. I remember. You told me Anna Wintour has no fingernails. Like a salamander."

Mia winced. "I did say that!" Mia snapped her purse shut. "I made it up. The name. The job. Anna Wintour has normal hands. As far as I know."

He regarded her coolly. "I know that game. Messing with the Wall Street bro?"

She shrugged, surprised he'd called her out so easily. "No. It's because I'm bored. With myself. I'm not an editor at *Vogue*. I'm a copywriter at a nonprofit. Actually, I'm not even that. My contract ran out."

She gestured for a cigarette. Martin paused for a beat before handing his over.

"At least you're not an investor in this app. I mean, come on, 'daily short stories'? What's the rate of return on . . . jack shit?"

Mia laughed, took a drag. She hadn't had a cigarette in a long time. She assessed him: a few years older, a few more stress lines around the eyes, a full head of hair, a nice smile.

He continued, knowing he had an audience with her now. "Or ten percent of . . . absolutely nothing."

Mia took another pull on the cigarette. She and Agnes had already tipped back a couple of glasses of wine, and she felt light headed. "You're not investing?"

Martin smirked. "I have to. Everyone else is."

"So that's how this capitalism thing works."

"Pretty much. But the smart ones know when to stop pretending."

She registered the subtle advice sent her way. She passed the cigarette back to him. "Want to get a drink?"

"That depends." He took the last drag off the cigarette, then flicked it to the curb.

"On what?"

"Who am I getting a drink with?" He pointed at her, questioning, then let his finger trail down her arm.

"Mia Sinclair."

"Tell me about Mia Sinclair," he said.

Now, Mia and Steph went down to join the others, the scene in Mia's head temporarily paused. Remembering her life through film scenes left her feeling isolated, a lone viewer at a matinee show. But this new kind of memory gave her a sense of power. She wanted to tell the others but wasn't sure how true the details were or who she could trust yet.

As they walked downstairs, they passed an empty black frame on the wall where a photo had once been on display. Now there was just a blank rectangle. Mia tapped the white wall just below it and looked at her sister questioningly.

"Was there a picture of me here?"

"I don't know. But something is definitely gone."

Mia looked at the empty frame, slightly askew, feeling her face crease with concentration. "It went missing during a party. We thought it was a friend of Martin's. From England."

"And he stole a photo of you?" Stephanie straightened the frame and felt for dust on her fingers. "How long ago was this?"

"I don't know."

Steph marched back to the bedroom and grabbed her notebook, scribbling in it. Then she said, "Let's keep thinking about that," and continued down the stairs.

Mia followed, stumbling a bit on the steps. Steph turned back to look at her, but for a second Mia instead saw the British man—white hair and intense eyes—asking, "Are you okay?"

Downstairs, the group assembled around the long dining table. Cameron had retreated to the basement, Ethan had shaved, and the women were wearing jewelry and had dabbed on perfume. Agnes had tamed her curls and replaced her scarf with a gold necklace that clung to her clavicle. Adult decorum had taken control, until Ethan poked at avocado halves on a plate. "Do you think these are ripe enough?"

A tipsy Zoey admonished him. "Babe, stop finger fucking the avocado."

They drank more wine and passed a plate of charcuterie around while Agnes ladled the linguini into bowls—grilled zucchini, shaved parmesan cheese, tomatoes, and fresh basil. Zoey had made crostini to go with it.

"Women used to get drunk so we could have sex. Now we get drunk so we can eat in front of each other," Zoey said, laughing, twirling the linguini strands with her fork.

"Yeah, I've decided to actually eat bread tonight," Steph said.

"Are straight women okay? Should someone check up on you?" Agnes asked, pushing a forkful of pasta into her mouth.

Mia nodded her head. That was the note of otherness this woman carried with her. She hadn't recognized it in Agnes until now.

"It's so weird, Mia," Ethan said. "I can't stop thinking of you like Uma Thurman in *Kill Bill*. Rising from a coma, looking for revenge."

Agnes jumped in. "That's not what this weekend is about."

"Besides," Zoey said, "I don't think that movie holds up too well now."

As they gorged themselves and poured more wine, a game of Never Did I Ever began, informally at first, then picking up steam, for all of them except Steph, who drank soda water. It began with Zoey asking, "What's a story about yourself you've never told anyone?"

The friends were eager to share their memories, even embarrassing ones, and Mia realized the group had been around each other long enough to have no fear of judgment. Ethan told a lengthy story about the time she and Zoey had found him in somebody's back bedroom tattooing *Kid A* onto his thigh—that the number of people there had overwhelmed him, that he'd felt anxious and paranoid and had hidden in the room to get away from the party. What to a stranger would sound like trauma was, among friends, a great story.

"I remember that," Zoey said. "I thought, 'Oh my God, he's so intense. If he doesn't die of hepatitis, he's going to be a great artist.' I was probably really drunk."

Mia watched as Ethan ducked his head a little, maybe embarrassed after all.

To Stephanie, Ethan said he had some old school movies on his laptop that he and Mia had starred in when they were twenty-one. They could watch them later, on Martin's projection system.

"What happened with the tattoo?" Mia asked, pointing down. She tried to remember if she knew what Ethan looked like pantless.

Ethan shrugged. "Zoey thought I should have it removed. So . . ."

Stephanie raised a glass of soda water. "Unlike tattoos, marriages are not a permanent bad decision."

The group raised their glasses too; then Zoey, already clearly tipsy, smacked the table like a lectern. "You and Agnes have the same tattoo, don't you?"

Mia looked at Agnes, whom, out of all the friends gathered, she felt the most for. She had noticed that Agnes sometimes looked away if Mia caught her glance, as if Mia was causing her some kind of embarrassment.

"It's the same as yours," Agnes admitted. "A Pisces symbol on my lower back."

"Why do we have the same tattoo?"

"It's how you became friends," Zoey said. "You have the same birthday. I'm two weeks later. Aries. Of course. You Pisceans are such classic sexual explorers. Though you wouldn't know much about that lately, Agnes."

A hurt look passed over Agnes's freckled face. "What do you know? We barely hang out anymore."

"Everyone knows—you're afraid of intimacy. Look at your Instagram. Every shot is leaves, rocks, or close-ups of ponds. You're sending out the wrong intentions to the world, unless you want a tree to fuck you."

Ethan cut in with a quiet "Stop it," but Zoey finished her thought in defiance.

"Or Mia." Her glass sloshed a little as she gestured with it.

Agnes looked mortified at Zoey's words. Mia felt the heat of panic and confusion as she looked around the table.

"You two hooked up, way back." Zoey waved her fork in the air, like a magic wand, between them.

"We did?" Mia felt her brow creasing.

"I mean, Agnes was more serious than you."

"It was one time," Agnes corrected. "We're friends. That's what we decided." She glared at Ethan despite his attempt to help. "You know how that goes, right?"

"So we've all had our thing. It's not really a big—" he started, a defense that confirmed everything Zoey had said.

"It's always more of a 'Mia' decision than a 'we' decision," Zoey said, half into her wineglass.

Mia put her fork down. She stared at Agnes and tried to draw up feelings or a sense of intimacy, but it was blocked by something.

Zoey interrupted with a witticism. "Did I just out you to yourself? I mean, that's pretty unique, but this is a unique situation."

"Shut up, you bitch!" Agnes burst out.

The room went silent.

Mia didn't know if Zoey was being cruel or factual. Maybe she used to be like Zoey, witty to the point of glib, but whichever Mia they were talking about was not the Mia of now. Mia in her twenties was the one they knew, the one they were reconstructing like a Coachella hologram, stilted and flickering. *That* Mia was someone who flitted without focus, who didn't know yet that friendships don't die from hurt—they die from neglect. Mia saw that Agnes was trembling with anger.

Mia had a sudden flash of an apartment—had she shared it with Agnes? She remembered a set of hooks, and their jackets hung side by side. She recalled a green leash hanging there.

"John Wick," Mia said, putting down the crostini she'd been nibbling on.

Stephanie picked up on what Mia was trying to articulate. "Who's John Wick here?"

"Agnes is."

"That makes sense," Zoey said excitedly. "Keanu Reeves is a lesbian icon."

Stephanie took control again. "He's an assassin in that movie. You're not saying . . . are you saying?" She stared at Agnes in near shock.

"No!" Agnes yelled. "Mia just remembered that she killed my dog!"

Mia felt her head tighten as everyone looked at her. "His name was Gatsby." It was out before Mia could think about it, almost as if the old Mia had spoken through her. "I was taking him for a walk when it happened, and you never forgave me, did you?"

Suddenly Mia felt goose bumps on her arms. From across the table, Steph said her name loudly, though she wasn't sure if it was the tone of a chastising sister or if Steph was shocked that Mia had remembered something.

Mia closed her eyes and saw the small black box behind the garbage cans. It was a rat hotel. Gatsby had eaten the poison while Mia had stood chatting with someone, loosely holding his leash. The poison had fallen out of the box, and the dog had gotten hold of a wheat-colored cube and snarfed it down as if it were a Milk-Bone. When Mia opened her eyes and looked at Agnes, her face was drained.

"You were never the same with me after. It was the first time I totally and utterly failed you." Mia wasn't sure where the words came from but felt like something struck inside her as she said them, like there was a ringing in her chest. And that sensation seemed true.

Ethan broke the silence. "I don't know, but that sounds like motivation."

"Motivation for what?" Agnes replied. "Gatsby was years ago."

"Deep-seated resentment. Anger, jealousy, revenge?" Zoey said.

"Have we all talked about that night? Where was everyone?" Ethan asked.

Stephanie leaned over the table toward Ethan. "That's a good question. I was at my house in Bucktown, Chicago. Where were you?"

Zoey answered for them. "We were at home, watching Lars von Trier's *Nymphomaniac* on Netflix."

"*Volume I* or *Volume II*?" Stephanie pressed.

"Both. We got horribly depressed, then fell asleep."

Mia watched as Agnes got up and left the table. She exited through the sliding doors in the kitchen, which led to the back deck, the pool, and, across the yard, the guesthouse. Mia rose and followed. She watched as Agnes stood there and held herself as though cold, her hands on her elbows. The shirt Agnes had changed into for dinner was thin—sheer black sleeves. She wore a black buttoned vest over it, her look both masculine and feminine. She turned when Mia came up to her on the deck.

"I don't think that," Agnes reassured her. "I would never believe that. I know Gatsby wasn't your fault. We were roommates for another six months after that."

"But John Wick never forgives," Mia said as an image of Keanu Reeves, sad and in the rain, filled her mind.

"I do now." Agnes reached for her and hugged her around the shoulders. Mia listened as her friend tried not to cry. "I mean me, Agnes. I forgive you."

Then Mia pulled away. She felt light headed, as though standing next to Agnes were somehow intoxicating. She couldn't remember if she'd had more than a full glass of wine with her meal. "It's not a movie, is it?" She pursed her lips, trying to decide. It wasn't, Agnes told her. It was real life.

They stood there another moment, Mia's hand resting lightly on Agnes's arm, and then Mia suggested they go back in. She felt somehow protective of Agnes, and wondered if they had always felt that way about each other? Maybe it was why whatever had been between them was only a moment. Or was that what she was telling herself so she didn't have to confront the fact that she seemed to be someone who used others for a thrill, then abandoned them?

Martin may not have been the best choice for Mia, but she had to guess she had matured with the role she'd stepped into.

They found Stephanie and Zoey still in the dining room, though the dirty plates had been cleared. They seemed to have come to a truce. Stephanie was explaining the Bathtub Theory. Mia noticed how her sister's steady voice stilled Zoey enough that she hadn't even tried her "*Godfather* cocktail." An amber row of glasses full of scotch and amaretto sat lined up on the table, waiting to be claimed and sipped. Stephanie clutched a mug of coffee, a square of tiramisu sitting in front of her on a scalloped ivory plate.

For a second Mia vaguely remembered she'd been like Stephanie in the group, back when she was herself, extolling the virtues of some theory or other, the person who made them all sit still and listen for a minute. Already, Agnes and Zoey seemed transfixed. But Mia could barely tune in. She didn't know if the medication she was on was making her suddenly sleepy or if it was the food and drink and the overwarm room. Someone had put on the fireplace in the adjacent living room—through the doorway she had noticed, before, that it was a gas one, not real. So why was there a real fireset beside it, a brass shovel and brush? It must have appealed to Martin's rustic side, or to the decorator, or possibly even to Mia, though she couldn't relate to it now.

Mia listened to Stephanie talk about how friendships fall along a bathtub graph. Steph drew it in the air with her finger. "On one edge are the friends you have at twenty. You've seen each other naked. Drunk. Everything. You can say anything to each other, and they're the ones you know you can call anytime, even if you haven't spoken in forever. On the other edge are your friends you know now, parents you carpool with. Coworkers and associates. And you can laugh with them, but you cannot say anything too honest to them. Name, rank, and one-pan recipes."

"What's in the middle, oh forty-five-year-old Gandalf?" Zoey asked, raising her glass and squinting at the light through her cocktail.

Stephanie didn't blink at Zoey's sarcasm. She answered: "Mistakes. When you're thirty, there are a lot of people you think are important who don't mean anything. They fade out—and you're back to your old friends again, the people you don't have to try to impress."

"I don't think that drifting away is wrong," Agnes put in. "It's more like we take a break and we discover another side of ourselves."

"I wish you'd discovered you wanted your own model of phone, instead of picking the color I got." Zoey snickered.

"Let me see," Steph said, and Agnes held up her phone. "You have good taste. Take it as a compliment, Zoey."

There was a shout from the living room, followed by Ethan cursing.

"What is it?" Zoey asked, and everyone quickly moved through the double doors to see what the commotion was about.

"My films—they're gone." Ethan peered at the screen of his Mac laptop. He reached out and moved the cursor around, opening different windows. "I was going to show *Ghost of You*, the short film we made from that time when Mia was blonde—but my stuff! It's just—fuck, where is it?!"

"Calm down." Zoey leaned over and squinted at the laptop. "We have backups of everything at home."

"We can see them another time," Steph said, as though she'd not been looking forward to watching student films from two decades before.

"But they should be here," Ethan said, slapping the ottoman hard enough that the laptop sitting on it jumped. "I just don't understand. It's like someone erased them on purpose. Because everything else is where it should be."

———✦———

Night in the country came on fast, with its velvet darkness and boredom. The heels the women had put on to be chic in Mia's own home were kicked off. Zoey slid down enough on the couch that her wrap dress was slouching off one shoulder and now appeared more *Flashdance* than Diane von Furstenberg. Intentionally or not, Agnes's blouse had an extra button undone. Even Stephanie had become a little disheveled, playing with the borrowed strand of pearls and staring at the ceiling before announcing she could barely keep her eyes open.

Mia went out to the kitchen to get some water, then stood plucking peach candies out of a dish with an addict's speed. They seemed like an incongruous treat for the party, but her tongue enjoyed the pop of sour-sweet they brought. Ethan followed her and poured his own glass of water. He had cleaned up but hadn't dressed for dinner like the others and was wearing a boyish striped T-shirt, his hoodie discarded somewhere.

"What is it, Duckie?" she asked, instinctively feeling he had something to tell her. She was important to this person, and with that realization came a vague discomfort that felt familiar.

"I just wanted to explain myself about what I said in our texts that night."

"Our texts? But I don't remember, so there's nothing to explain?"

"I just—I wanted you to meet me, instead of coming out here."

"But why, Ethan? We're just friends, right?"

He avoided answering for a moment, and she watched his face, his dark eyebrows, one of which seemed to dance a little over the top of his horn-rims. She put another candy in her mouth and sucked on it.

"I remember holding your hand," she said suddenly. "While watching bears?"

He glanced at the candy dish on the counter and then looked back at her and rolled his eyes. "IFC Center, 2005, *Grizzly Man*. Halfway through the movie I put my hand out for you to take, thinking it was a date. You had this candy bag, and you put it in my hand instead."

"Oh," Mia responded. This seemed like something she would have done.

"We never did hold hands. I laughed my head off to save face, but . . . one of the more humiliating moments of my life. And now I'm telling it to you. Go figure. You'd think we would all take advantage of your state right now, cover up those bad moments."

"I don't think you'd do that," Mia said.

"I guess I'm glad you remember something about me."

They were standing close now, hip to hip against the island. Her water glass was empty, and as he poured another for her, she changed the subject.

"You're very kind, and it's so big of you, what you're doing. I mean, that you're okay with Zoey going to a sperm bank. This afternoon when she told me, it seemed so important to her."

Ethan stiffened. "What?"

"Okay. Maybe I don't remember right . . ." Mia put her fingers against her temple, which had begun to ache.

"Well, we're trying to have a baby, but—*what* did she say, exactly, about a sperm bank?"

"She said you were okay with it. You told her, 'Babe, if a farmer can afford A-list seed stock, he goes for the A-list.'"

Ethan's forehead creased, and he stuttered, "She—she said I put down my own sperm? And a farm metaphor? My feet haven't touched grass in years."

"Maybe if you talk to her—"

"It's like she's cheating on me."

"It's more like shopping, if you think about it."

He looked like he might crumble. Mia knew the signs of a man about to cry, and she knew she should think of something to say, quick. But she was drunk and couldn't find any words that would help, so she hugged him, completely unsuspecting of the scotch-scented dive he would take at her mouth.

Ethan's lips pressed against hers, and he attempted to open her mouth with his tongue before she knew what to do. She'd felt this kiss before, she realized. She knew the shape of his chin, the faint pinpoints of stubble on his neck, the circuitous route his affections would take, from mouth to earlobe—and probably back. But she firmly pushed him away with one hand. He stopped. During the kiss, Mia had felt nothing, despite all the feelings others said they had for each other. It was like what she had felt whenever Martin touched her since the accident: nothing. She wondered if love didn't need memories to work. That it was something you felt or didn't.

"I'm sorry. I know you're in no state to consent right now. Please forgive me."

"It's okay," she said as she left the room. "I know what a kiss is." Why was it always a woman's job to reassure a man after he'd done something stupid and gross, she wondered as she went down the hall and climbed the stairs to her bedroom. She heard the sliding patio doors, as if he was going out to catch some air. She was relieved he didn't follow. Leaving was the surest way to end the conversation.

Chapter Nine

FASHIONABLY LATE

Zoey remembered the long rows of chairs and one-arm desks. It had been a lecture hall class, not a workshop, but the professor had called on them more and more as the semester went on. On Mondays they watched a film, and on Wednesdays Dr. Lemper would lecture and discuss "the text-film dialectic." It was still the first month when Jonathan Halichuk tore Mia down in front of everyone. Jonathan was a sophomore film major who was in two of Zoey's other classes. He was tall and spindly and had tousled brown hair beneath a fedora she seldom saw him without. He wore Fluevogs and had those round glasses that could be a tribute to either John Lennon or the melting Nazi from *Raiders of the Lost Ark*.

They had watched Mike Nichols's *Catch-22*, which Mia called cold and austere. "It's as though the director didn't know which direction to choose in adapting the book, and so he didn't choose any," Mia had critiqued during the class.

Mia had not yet seen *The Graduate*, so she held no affection for Nichols. But she wasn't wrong, in Zoey's opinion. The long shots of bombers flying overhead were striking, but the comedy was off, never committing totally to funny or serious.

Rather than put his hand up, Jonathan stood, as though to tower over Mia, when he said, "In my opinion, often the failure is not on the part of the director but of the audience. That's what *I* always look at. Is it him or is it me? Nine times out of ten, I later realize: it's me."

It had been condescending enough, but when Mia quietly replied that she felt she was entitled to her opinion, Jonathan refused to let it go.

"It's because your taste is lachrymose," he fired at her. "A film shouldn't be determined as good or bad depending which week of the month it is."

Zoey had seen Mia struggling with his put-down. *Lachrymose.* Who wants to be sent to the dictionary to understand what someone has accused them of?

Agnes, the curly-haired girl Mia always came to class with, had said nothing but glared and began loudly flipping through her second-hand copy of the novel for some ammunition she clearly couldn't find. Although Zoey hadn't known Mia well at that point, she'd raised her hand. The prof had been quick to call on her.

"One: I'm capable of bleeding and judging a movie at the same time, and I assume she is too." Other students had chuckled. Mia had raised her gaze to Zoey, the shame falling away. "And two: the director himself would agree with Mia's point," Zoey had said. "If you had listened to the DVD commentary track with Nichols and Steven Soderbergh, you'd know that. Nichols said his own movie kind of lies there."

"Fine," Jonathan had snarled. "I guess he also made *Regarding Henry*, so what does he know."

The following class Mia and Agnes had changed seats and sat just a couple of spots away in Zoey's row, as though they were aligned against the Jonathan Halichuks of the world. It hadn't been long before Mia and Agnes asked Zoey to come with them to the bar after class. The guys in the class were *arrogant dicks*, they'd agreed. Except maybe Ethan, whom they thought was the cutest, and Victor, the nicest. They would form a strategic alliance with them and start a study group.

Zoey, transplant from California, had quickly realized the benefits to being friends with Mia, born New Yorker. Mia knew not just every *it* place in the city but how long it had been an *it* place and when the *it* status would be revoked. From birth, she'd been given an education in culture: restaurants, books, bands, theater, films. If you could set aside the fact that every guy would look at Mia first, she was worth knowing. It wasn't that she was prettier than Zoey, but people were always saying there was something about her. Agnes always said she had a way of looking at you that reinforced you. Fifteen years of the Mia Mystery, men and women falling under her spell, yet Zoey could tell you exactly what the mystery was: she had big tits. It was just a bra size, 32DDD.

As a freshman, Zoey had found friends but hadn't really discovered her crew yet. She had a tendency to befriend other students, then quickly alienate them with her outspokenness. She was a woman who told the truth about others. Living in residence her freshman year, she'd been constantly told, sometimes by huddles of girls, that she was too loud, too brash. And while the "We're all goddesses" crowd loved Zoey's theories and ability to talk for hours, they couldn't get past her manicured hands, her side bangs à la Scarlett Johansson in *Lost in Translation*, and her California fixation with exercise.

In contrast, Mia and Agnes were a perfect pairing. Mia stood out, and Agnes lived to be slightly invisible, leaving room for a wild card like Zoey. The only problem was that sometimes Mia was just too perfect; things came to her too easily. Jonathan Halichuk had shown the one flaw of Mia: she had never learned to fight back.

—⸙—

Zoey was waiting for someone to wake up and entertain her. Tossing on the bed in the guest room but unable to sleep, she stared out the window as the morning brightened. She'd changed out of the dress the night before and into sweats, but the comfort clothes did nothing to relax her. Instead, she'd watched a low dawn fog dissipate through the woods. Now, at almost eight, it was bright. A day that promised to unfold into a beauty.

When she saw the housekeeper's car arrive and slalom up the drive, she flopped back into bed. Now at least she wouldn't have to make the coffee herself. But she felt guilty at the thought of treating Mia's home like a hotel. She also felt guilt over the fight with Ethan last night and how she'd acted after he'd stormed out to sleep in the guesthouse by the pool.

Zoey cradled her phone and started typing a search: adult woman kissing 17-year-old legal? She panicked about even having the search on her phone and was about to erase it when a scream reverberated through the wall, the kind of wavering shriek that left no doubt about its meaning. Zoey, her nerves still raw from being up all night, bolted up and dashed out of the room to the garage, which ran along the east side of the house. Opening the door into it, she saw the housekeeper, Susan, a grimace on her face. Her own car was parked on the far side of Mia's and Martin's silver Tesla. The Tesla was small for a big man like Martin, and he was slumped over the steering wheel, his head practically against the windshield.

"Oh my God," Zoey said, her voice climbing in register.

Susan had left the door to her own car open. She was standing between the two vehicles, looking like she might collapse. She was a slight woman with gray hair. Zoey lifted her phone for an embarrassing second, but she resisted the urge to immediately photograph Martin in the Tesla. Documenting everything had become second nature. Instead, she dropped the cell phone on the workbench by the door and rushed over to Susan. She shut the door of Susan's car to make more room.

Susan was in shock, and Zoey knew she should just help the woman inside. The housekeeper held Zoey's elbow as they walked toward the door. Agnes was there because, like Zoey, she'd had a room on the ground floor and heard the scream.

"What is it?" she asked.

"Help her," Zoey said, transferring Susan into Agnes's arms.

"I'm fine, just . . . I need a sit," Susan said. She leaned into Agnes for a moment, accepting a stranger's hug, then pulled away and straightened her back.

Agnes craned her neck to see into the garage and yelped, a high, thin sound that didn't fit with her personality. Even from a distance, Zoey and Agnes could tell that his color was all wrong. His skin was splotchy and unnaturally violet.

"Did he kill himself?" Agnes asked, speaking low, like she thought the neighbors might hear from two miles away. "You know, carbon monoxide."

"In a Tesla?" Zoey asked.

"Electrocution?" Agnes asked, in all seriousness. Zoey's glare sent her back toward the house. "I'll tell the others."

Before Zoey could answer that they shouldn't let Mia see this, Agnes had gone back in, shutting the door and leaving Zoey with the body.

She edged toward the vehicle to check on Martin and see if he was still breathing. She noticed he was still in the same clothes from the evening before—cable-knit sweater and new jeans—as if he'd said his rant to the room, come out to his car, and never left. She recalled she'd stopped filming after he walked to the garage. There were no injuries she could see, and that made her worry less about Ethan and where he was. Zoey thought about everything that happened during the night while Martin must have been sitting here, dead. Her body involuntarily shook as she reached in the car's open window. She felt no breath coming out of his mouth. She quickly touched his neck. He was as cold as the concrete under her bare feet.

She snatched her hand out of the vehicle and began looking for something to clean it with. Finding a pile of rags on a workbench, she wiped between her fingers. Through the open door of the garage, she saw that a car was pulling in from the road. Was it the police already? This was, after all, the richest zip code in Connecticut.

Zoey noticed it was a BMW as it steered up the curve of the drive-way and stopped outside. A man in Ray-Bans and tailored Helmut Lang pants eased out of the car and stepped into the garage. *Are those Savile Row bespoke shoes?* Zoey wondered. He took off his glasses, and Zoey could see him adjusting to the dimness.

"Zoey?" he asked.

"Victor?"

Why was Victor Thomas there at eight in the morning? Had Stephanie invited him? And when? Probably while they were all downing cocktails the night before. Zoey recognized Victor, but not. In college, their gang had been a cross section of New York: Victor, Black and from Queens; Ethan, pale and Jewish, from Long Island; and WASPy Mia of the Upper West Side (who had many arguments about the UWS not being as horrible as the UES). Victor had broken away first, looking for his own life on the West Coast. Sometime in the last fifteen years, his shoulders had become two broad gym-hardened points above his paleo-diet-trim waist. He'd always had a goatee on his chin, though now it suited him more. He'd grown into it. And the sad eyes she remembered were now smiling, at least until he took another couple of steps toward her and glanced inside the Tesla.

"How's your friend there? He's not looking so good."

"It's Mia's husband. He's dead."

"Whoa." Victor's response was as physical as it was verbal as he stepped back. He looked ill but recovered quickly. "How long has he been like that?"

Zoey shook her head.

Stephanie appeared in the doorway. She was wearing pajamas and blinking, her hair down, like a blanket on her shoulders. "You're Victor?" she asked.

Of course, Zoey thought. *Sisters—always up to some kind of intervention.*

"Martin's not breathing," Zoey said, and it was the first time Stephanie noticed the body in the car.

Stephanie turned two shades paler. "Was it a heart attack, you think?"

"I only checked for a pulse."

"We should call an ambulance, to be sure."

"Then Mia will know!" Zoey yelled before quieting her voice. "She almost died a month ago. Last night was stressful enough. This will kill her."

"What are you proposing? Shut the doors and leave his body here until you figure something out?" Stephanie asked.

"Yes, that's exactly what I mean."

"Why not go the full *Weekend at Martin's*, then? Put sunglasses on him and a beer in his hand."

"One: I don't find that funny. Two: Ted Kotcheff's good. He's a really underrated director," Zoey retorted.

Victor expertly cut into the argument and nudged them away from the scene. "Whatever you decide, we should leave the garage and not touch anything out here. That's the best thing we can do right now."

She felt slightly annoyed at how well Victor took charge of something she had thought she was in control of. Ethan always showed up and did the same thing, but worse, pretending to know more or make the decisions as if she hadn't already made them. She felt vindicated by her thoughts, then guilty a second later. Why was she already getting irritated by Victor, a friend she hadn't seen in over a decade?

Inside they could smell coffee. The housekeeper had snapped into gear and returned to her routine as if it were a regular Sunday. When they walked in, she was cleaning with vigor, putting all her distress into wiping down the patio doors.

"Wait, what are you doing?" Zoey asked with renewed authority.

"They were covered in soot," Susan said in a heavy New England accent.

"What do you mean, *sut*?" Zoey went over to look at the sliding glass panel.

"Soot. You know. Ash, from a fire. There were smudges and handprints all over the doors."

When they'd all gone to bed the night before, the house had still been in order, save for a few empty glasses on end tables. The sliding doors had been spotless.

Zoey knew Victor's eyes were rolling before she even looked back for his reaction. "Maybe you should go home for the day," Zoey told Susan, who seemed relieved. "If the police need to talk to you, we'll call you." With Susan gone, Zoey had a better chance at protecting Mia from the impending nightmare of ambulances and police interviews. This left Cameron. She knew he wouldn't be up yet, as she'd left him passed out on the couch in the basement just before sunrise.

After Ethan had excused himself to the guesthouse, Cameron had knocked on her door. The little shit heard everything in the house, apparently, even discussions of farmers and A-list seed, and here he was with a small baggie of white powder in his hand. "Some distraction?" he'd asked, as if he actually had game to go along with his suburban coke.

In the basement she and Cameron did lines, and she opened up to him about everything: loving Ethan but not understanding him, worries about her fertility and beauty and having her career so tied to Ethan's. Cameron's advice was for her to let him feel her up. She'd laughed and said, "Okay. One breast," thinking it could be like a French movie. But she felt ashamed now that she had come down. No matter what Zoey and the group decided, she would have to get Cameron to clean out his stash before they called in the authorities.

Zoey, Victor, and Agnes settled around the broken kitchen island to discuss what to do. Agnes set her phone on the island and went to find a sugar bowl in one of the cupboards. She was the only one who took her coffee with sugar. Mia was still sleeping upstairs, Stephanie said, taking a long sip from her cup. Should they wake her? And what about Martin's son; they had to tell him, but how?

"I'll talk with Cameron," Zoey said. She cringed at herself and tried to cover her shame by coughing into her hand.

"I can't believe Martin didn't go last night. Did you hear the garage door, or that old gate?" Steph asked Zoey.

"I noticed it was open," Agnes said. "I figured he didn't bother to shut it behind him."

Steph said, "Let's update our evidence before we call anyone. I left my notebook here last night."

Zoey watched as Stephanie got up and began moving things around on the surrounding counters. She moved a stack of clean linen napkins, the paper towel dispenser, and a bowl of fruit. She pushed Agnes's phone off to the far side of the island. She moved the caddy with the salt and pepper and other spices. The notebook was nowhere.

"The housekeeper must have moved it," Zoey suggested.

"Well, we should also look in the backyard and see where that ash came from. Agnes, can you do that?" Stephanie asked.

Victor cut in. "I came here to help Mia, but I have no idea what I've walked into."

"It's a remembering party," Agnes reminded him. She was seemingly exhausted at her own concept but still playing the hostess.

"I get that. I read the email attachment on the red-eye. But there's something else going on here. Who else is here this weekend?"

"Just us, you know, the *gang*," Zoey said.

"Where *is* Ethan?" Stephanie said, snapping out of her fog.

Zoey gestured out the back window to the guesthouse. "He slept out there. I'm a terrible sleeper after drinking. He can never stand my tossing."

"Ethan's here?" Victor asked. After a pause he added, "That's great," but Zoey was unsure whether he truly thought it was great.

When Zoey had broken the news to Ethan a few years before that Victor had landed an executive job at Watchr, a streamer that was now approaching forty million users, her boyfriend had started going through old terrible scripts to pitch. (*Rock Ness*: A Scottish indie band experiences supernatural goings-on at Loch Ness while recording. *Empire* meets *Stranger Things*.") She'd explained that Victor was in VR and user experience, not content development, but still Ethan pushed: "He'll see it's great and pass it to the right person."

She'd never mailed the scripts. He was capable of writing good stuff, but these were dashed off and manic, and she'd wanted to save him from future embarrassment. This had led Ethan to believe he'd been ghosted by an old school friend. Ethan had stalked Victor online for weeks, liking all his posts and commenting overenthusiastically until he realized Victor wasn't going to get back to him. Then he'd stopped interacting with him. He'd pace around their apartment, privately trash-talking Victor. Several years on, he was still picking at things. "Did you see he got married? He didn't invite anyone. He thinks he's above us."

There had been no photos. Only a change in relationship status. Even Zoey had thought it odd. The wife, Casey Somebody, had seemed to disappear before the year was out. In her profile pic, she was wearing a striped T-shirt and a jean jacket, squinting into the sunlight and smiling. She looked a little older than they were, and Zoey had always meant to ask Mia what she knew about it, but in the crush of days and deadlines, she'd forgotten. And now Mia wouldn't know either.

"That's not a little crack there," Victor was saying as he moved around the broken island corner. He bent to examine it. The expression on his face changed to apprehension. He lifted an eyebrow. "No wonder Mia doesn't remember anything."

Zoey could see Victor getting lost in his thoughts—putting the facts together and not liking them. She was about to say that they'd already discussed the possibility of an attack by Martin when Mia appeared in the doorway to the kitchen. She stood there, wrapped in a lilac kimono.

"Victor?" Mia said from the doorway, and everyone's head turned. She had shuffled down the stairs so quietly they hadn't heard her coming. Now she closed the space quickly and threw her arms around his neck, nearly toppling him from the kitchen stool. "You came back!" she said into his neck.

Zoey exchanged glances with the other women. They all recognized the same thing: Mia had just remembered someone, easily, effortlessly. She hadn't remembered her sister, or Agnes, or Zoey. Yet she remembered Victor.

Chapter Ten

In the Mood for Victor

Mia stared at Victor and could see the look of someone who has waited too long. He'd been waiting for her longer than the time she'd spent in the hospital. He'd been waiting since the first time she'd known him—or had she been waiting for him? She took his hand. "Let me get dressed quickly. We can go outside," she said.

Victor glanced at Stephanie for permission, which wasn't the first time Mia noticed people doing that—as if she were a ward of her sister's. Stephanie looked more nervous than usual and muttered to Victor, "That thing we talked about."

He nodded. "Right. The . . . uh . . ."

"Possum in the garage. Someone is coming out today for it."

"We won't go near it."

"I didn't hear anything last night," Mia said. "They're not going to hurt it, are they?"

"He's already . . ." Stephanie stopped herself. "No one will hurt him."

Victor walked Mia out the front, down the circle drive, and through the gate without speaking. She had thrown on the first clothes she'd touched in the drawer and smoothed her short hair back with a hair band. She'd pushed on her shoes, and they were ready to go. He looked troubled for a moment as he glanced back at the house and the garage.

"I remember we walked so far once. I was wearing a light-blue dress with red flowers," Mia said. "I had heels on."

"No," he said. "It was a blue shirt, but there weren't flowers."

Victor had an easy way about him—everything about him felt familiar. Mia asked if they had met in Hong Kong once, but he said no, they hadn't.

He reminded her that he lived there for a year, when he'd been overseeing the launch of Watchr in Asia. Maybe that was the connection in her memory.

"I was carrying a container, some kind of thermos, full of noodle soup . . . I climbed a dark staircase in an alley. I went up as you were coming down. You said hello as we passed."

Victor shook his head. "Is this a film you're remembering? The only stairs we climbed together were in New York. The High Line."

"We walked the High Line?"

They had now walked almost as far as the neighbors' stone wall, the one where Martin had said she'd found help. She looked at their gate and the shrubs that lined the properties but didn't recall anything from that night. Instead she remembered the hot city, how ecstatic and lonely she felt every time she and Victor glanced at each other.

He told her the first time they'd seen each other was in the fall— warm, not hot. They'd had a perfect day, and since then, they'd video chat. They'd seen each other a few times, any time he could fly in for business. When they'd seen each other last, it had been early March, the day of her accident.

"Wait," Mia said. She stopped and drew circles in the gravel road with her toe.

Victor put a hand in his jacket pocket and played with a car key or something that was there. He breathed out through his nose. "What is it?"

"I remember being covered in blood the last time I was walking this road. But I don't like to think about it. I'd rather remember that day with you."

"If that day is a day you actually remember," he said, "then we're going to have to be honest with each other."

She reached out and snagged the corner of his suit coat for a second, a coquettish gesture—she wasn't sure where it had come from. Was she playacting?

There was another time, in a booth. She recalled him smoking. It had risen up all around him in feathery twists and curls. They'd drunk tea from jade-colored cups and talked about their partners. Another time, still in the back of a cab, when he'd almost held her hand, just his fingers touching hers lightly for a moment.

"I've never smoked," Victor said. "But there was tea, and we took cabs several times, no doubt."

"You were staying in a hotel. And you invited me back there."

"Yes."

"With red curtains all down one hallway," she said, certain.

"No. It was Cachet in Hell's Kitchen." His lips picked up at the corners.

So she was wrong about things that felt more vivid than anything she'd remembered so far.

He said that they *had* eaten dim sum at Momofuku once, last fall, and now that he thought about it, that was how it began.

"What do you mean, it began with food? Just like in the movie?"

"So it is a movie you're thinking of."

Mia hesitated. "It's a movie, and it's also *us*. Because we were never supposed to do this."

He squeezed her arm just for a second, then let it go. They kept walking as they talked.

"That's why. Because they can't either—the characters. They're a husband and wife, but they aren't married to each other. Their partners are having an affair. Oh, and there's a soundtrack that makes you ache." Mia looked up at the trees and the azure sky and felt as if she could sink into it. She felt perfectly content for the first time since she'd come home, even if all she could remember were half truths.

When she glanced at Victor, she saw the hint of a smile on his face. "I know which film it is. But tell me more on our way back." He turned around on the road.

She took his arm and leaned against him. She asked why they hadn't eaten that morning. Susan was supposed to make breakfast, and he said he didn't know but that no one had seemed hungry. He was cagey, and she wondered why. Things felt calm with him, so there was no reason not to trust him, right? Maybe he was just nervous.

"Tell me about our date," he pressed. "The real one."

"We met for lunch," she said.

"You're telling me what I just told you. Tell it to me your way."

Mia leaned into him more. She did feel shaky, and part of it was hunger and not being sure of whether she'd taken her pain medication, but part of it was anticipation. She liked how he smelled. She didn't want to get all the way back to the house yet, where the others were waiting to taunt her and each other or take turns trying to unknot her from herself. The man beside her seemed to understand her. She wondered what he'd been like when he was young—could he have been as immature as her and the others? That seemed impossible. But he wasn't asking her to remember back that far. Only as far as last fall. Mia licked her lips.

"I didn't know married life would be so . . . dangerous," she said. "I thought it would feel safer."

She remembered leaving early to get there, taking two subway trains and arriving ahead of him because she knew he was busy—*in town for a day and would love to catch up*—and she hadn't wanted to keep him waiting. But after putting her name in, she'd stood outside in the October sunshine. It wasn't cold yet, and when he'd come, she'd spotted him from a block away. He walked the same as he had. From far away it was as though nothing had changed. He could have been walking back to her from a place lost from time. He'd had on a brown blazer, something he would never have worn in his twenties but which she instantly felt suited him. She had a feeling if she saw him at one hundred years old, she would know him, even if he didn't turn his head to acknowledge her. Then, at that moment, he looked up and locked eyes with her.

Why was it so simple to remember now, like walking out a doorway and into sunshine?

She went for the hug; he gave her a kiss, not quite on the cheek. He hit the spot between jawbone and earlobe. She sucked in a breath. "Victor!" she said, her delight obvious.

She was surprised that he could take as much time as they had. She'd expected him to need to leave for meetings or constantly check his phone like Martin did, but he ignored several texts and listened to her instead.

Now, Mia squinted. "You told me a funny story about when you first moved to LA. You drove up the coast to a Hitchcock location and got so excited when you saw it you jumped out of the car and locked your keys in without thinking."

"Busted. Still a nerd," Victor confirmed.

They walked slowly.

"This was ten years ago. I was living in this apartment in East Hollywood, four roommates, all white guys named Josh." He laughed. "I had been passed over for story editor on the reboot of *Police Academy*. I'm so angry. Then I realize I don't want to be angry over something that meaningless ever again. So I'm done. Moving back to New York. But a friend calls from San Jose and says he has a job for me at a streamer. I don't really believe it, never heard of them, but on my drive up I plan to visit as many Hitchcock locations as I can. Then, if it doesn't really happen, I can say goodbye, California, hello to living with my mom in Queens and teaching screenwriting at City College."

He continued, "I start with *Psycho*, and I make my way up to *Vertigo*. I'm at the mission at San Juan Bautista. Middle-of-nowhere Northern California. Me, trees, and the Zodiac. I see the stables where Jimmy Stewart brings Kim Novak so she can remember her past life."

As they walked, Mia listened to Victor's voice, full and mellow. *Sonorous*. She liked that word. But what did it mean? Was it possible to trust a person based only on their voice?

"And that's when you lock your keys in?" Mia asked, and Victor nodded.

"Oh yeah. I find this park station with one ranger there. She's helpful and small. A Tig Notaro type—if I were writing this as a script. She calls a tow truck, but it's going to be at least three hours. She looks at me, claps her hands. 'Let's use this time constructively and learn about the El Camino Real and mission culture in the area.' And I learned."

"She taught you things?"

Victor smiled. "So many things. Now, I'm missing the interview, and I don't care. But that night I find out: I still got the job. My biggest win to date, and I wasn't even there." Then Victor's face sobered. "But that's ten years ago. What do you remember about us?"

But Mia wasn't ready. She stared at her feet. She had a sudden realization that she hadn't been wearing heels, like the woman in the movie. She'd worn a pair of Camper ballet flats. She grasped that she'd put on several different outfits before meeting him, spent time on the intricate details—which shoes (more casual), which earrings (small pearl droplets). She had wanted to seem insouciant and at the same time catch his eye, even if she didn't know why. She remembered his hands, looking at them, his mouth, his ears. She recalled sipping green tea and peering over the rim at his shirt buttons, the gap where his throat emerged above his collar, the contrast of his skin and the crisp white shirt, his soft dark beard. They had spoken in glances, as people who have affection for one another do.

Mia watched their feet walking along the shoulder of the road. "I didn't know I was sad until that day . . . no, I did know," she amended. "I just didn't know I was still capable of feeling joy."

For a second he looked so serious that she wondered if she'd said too much. Maybe the relationship hadn't progressed beyond passing each other too closely and eating dumplings. She remembered the hotel with the red curtains—but no, she told herself, *That was the movie. Don't get all out of order. Keep the chronology simple.*

"In this dream, we take a cab to the . . . High Line," she said uncertainly.

"Oh, it's a dream now?" Victor cocked his head. His tone was mocking, but in his expression she saw his concern for her brain. "At Watchr we have stats that show thirty percent of people turn off a movie during a dream sequence. I don't disagree. I always thought dream sequences in movies were redundant because you're already kind of in a dream."

On the High Line, the city buildings were all around them, but they had a path through—it almost felt like they had it to themselves, even though it was such a nice day. Early October, Victor said. It was a weekday at one o'clock; that was why it felt private even though they were exploring the whole city from that elevated vantage, the old rail tracks running beside everything, planted with shrubs that were turning golden, the flowers of summer gone. There was a staghorn sumac that had turned bright red. He had taken off his jacket and rolled up his sleeves. They'd bumped and nudged each other as they walked, always a little too close. "We sat on wooden lounge chairs, and you said . . ." Mia peered into the distance. "You said you never had time for love when you were younger, that you didn't even think about it, not like the rest of us."

He had said more, she recalled. That he'd thought there would be time for it once he'd established himself in his career, but now that he was older and had money to do anything, he didn't have time for any of the things he loved. He said all he did was drive and talk on the phone. Mia could hear his voice beside her that day: "I buy all these things that I dreamed of buying, that I would kill for when I was twenty, but fifteen minutes after buying them, I forget why I did." He bought thousands of dollars in camera gear, and it stayed in its case. He was too afraid to talk to anyone about filming a short he had an idea for.

"I'll act for you," Mia had offered out of the blue. "I do nothing during the day. Literally nothing."

They had eaten gelato. They'd spent two hours in the sun, walking from Thirty-Fourth Street down to Fourteenth, and while Mia had known she should go home, she couldn't think of a reason. Both of them were reluctant to leave the day where it was. There was one place on the High Line where they'd stood over the traffic and watched it shoot away from them through Plexiglas, all the yellow cabs and Ubers and delivery vans. Victor had said he wished he'd brought his camera, but it was back in LA, in a case on the shelf. He took some photos on his cell phone, then stood beside her, peering down. She'd said to him, "I always liked you. Is that wrong?" He'd said, "No, why?" For a moment she'd debated lifting onto her toes to kiss him, but she changed her mind. He'd looked at her intently. She had turned and climbed back up the wooden block seating in that area, which acted also as stairs. She'd suggested they go inside Chelsea Market to get out of the sun. They'd wandered past craft and clothing tables, then from restaurant to restaurant, unable to decide. She hadn't been hungry. A drink maybe.

They'd gone into a bar, already thick with tourists and Chelsea men with their massive thighs and biceps. Mia and Victor had made fun of the drink names, pretending to be above it all. Afternoon Delight,

Booty Collins, Hush Money, and Thank U Next. The kind of place they would have loved in their twenties, or maybe still. She'd ordered an It Was All a Dream, a gin drink with vermouth and bergamot that wrapped her tongue like a silvery ribbon, immediately going to her head. He'd gotten an ale of some sort—she couldn't remember. They'd sat on high stools at a ledge, and the wall they'd been looking at had an antique mirror on it so they could catch each other's glances in the glass.

As Mia recalled, she gazed up into Victor's face. She could see he was eager for her to remember everything—not just that day last fall, but the other times, too, including the date he'd spoken about in March.

"We didn't pretend that you were my husband and I was confronting you about your mistress, who was actually your wife?" Mia asked.

He shook his head. "Do you know the movie yet?"

"Yes." She remembered she'd been the one to touch him that time in the bar. She had reached out simply and put a hand alongside his face, cradling his cheek. It was all that had needed to be done. They'd kissed to the soundtrack of chattering strangers, a soft touch of their lips. "It was Wong Kar-Wai's *In the Mood for Love*."

Victor smiled and leaned back against the gate at the edge of the Sinclair-Kroner property.

She had gone to his hotel room. More than once. There just hadn't been red curtains. She recalled a private outdoor terrace, almost as big as his room. It had been outfitted with modern furniture, a café table, and a lounger that was nearly a bed. With the five-o'clock magic light, he'd wanted to photograph her. He'd held up his phone camera—"Pretend it's a Hasselblad and you're in *Blow-Up*," he'd instructed, and she'd laughed and stretched and posed. She remembered this time the cool March air on her skin, making her shiver. She was in a different memory, though the tone of the movie seemed the same.

"Was that all that happened?" she asked.

"Maybe a little more," he admitted. "We were friends, and . . ."

"Friends and . . . ?" She recalled the taste of beer, how wet and open his kisses had been. She recalled unbuttoning her blouse.

"You were trying to decide if you should tell him about us."

"Us?" she asked, and he nodded. "What was your feeling about that?" But she could see worry in his face, and seeing it here and now told her that he hadn't thought she should. She had a vague feeling that she'd thought it was the right thing to do—and Victor had argued with her. But she couldn't say if it was real or not. She felt the words in her throat like stones. "Did I tell him?"

Victor shook his head. "That's just it. I don't know. You didn't text me back."

Mia took out her phone and opened it. His number was there, but there were no recent texts from him. The last one said Landed . . . and here in Midtown. Her response: See you there!

He held her wrist with the phone in it and stared. "Someone erased them."

He yanked out his phone now and showed her the texts he'd sent. Did you talk to him? You all right? was the first, the little bubble marked just before 8:00 a.m. the morning after the accident. The other was twenty-four hours later. Back in LA now. Call whenever you can. They were unanswered because she'd already wound up in a hospital bed.

"It must have been Martin," he suggested. "No one else could access your phone."

"It's too creepy to think about it, Victor," she said. She ran her hands up and down her arms to stop them from being goose bumpy.

"Maybe something nicer to think about?" Victor accessed his iCloud drive. Mia stared at her own face. Her hair was a little shorter than now; she'd just had it cut. She was in profile, her back to the viewer. She was staring at the potted palm beside her. It was the terrace at the hotel she'd been able to visualize. The blouse draped off her shoulders because she had undone it, but nothing showed except her shoulder blades. He was right—it was blue and did not have a flower print on it.

"Was that the only time you took my photo?" Mia asked Victor, searching his face.

Victor looked at the ground, then back up again. "No. There was the time on the High Line too."

"And you've never been out here before? A party?"

"First time," he answered. "It's like you're putting something together right now?"

"It's all I've been doing. It's like a scrambled-up Soderbergh movie."

Mia knew the photo he'd shown her was the last time she'd seen him—in March before her fall, how it had felt the same as that other day on the High Line, only now with more urgency. Every touch had begun to have more consequences. The relationship had become real, not just a passing idea.

She remembered leaving the hotel that last time and turning her phone back on. It had begun ringing right away. A man had been upset on the other end, and she'd thought at first he must have known already about her and Victor. The voice had told her to come straight home and not talk to anyone along the way.

"I want you here now!"

She ran the voice through her head again. Who else could it have been but Martin?

Chapter Eleven

Selections from the Grill

Agnes paced the pool area, eating pistachios from a bag she'd found in her coat pocket and uncertain what she was meant to do there. She was grateful that it was brightening into a warm morning, an arching blue sky above the woods that the property gave way to at the back. The whole lot could be gone over, she supposed, but Steph had specifically said to look for the source of the ash. Steph stayed back to make sure Mia didn't go to the garage, and Agnes hoped her half-assed evidence search wasn't being watched. It was Zoey's job to come out here to the guesthouse and tell Ethan what had happened, but somehow she remained in the house still.

As Agnes wandered around the pool and outdoor furniture, she marveled again that her friend could have such a perfect house, the kind of dollhouse made life-size that anyone would imagine for themselves as a child. Agnes had thought about her future and where she might live, but she'd never fantasized about getting married, like other little girls. She remembered making up those details as easily as reading a story when asked in the seventh grade by a friend what she imagined her future would be. "My husband, David Hyde Pierce, will take me out to dinner, and I'll have three different kinds of potato, and I'll make the funniest jokes about Susan Sontag." The trick to blending in with the other girls had been storytelling; she'd never considered it lying, not then. It was imagining—it wasn't meant to be real. No matter, her constructed fantasies were off kilter enough that the girls just knew and gave her the nickname "Fagnes."

The swimming pool was empty, and Agnes flicked several pistachio shells into the mulch of leaves at the bottom.

It wasn't right for Zoey to tell Mia her past so insensitively. As Agnes stood there, more early nicknames came back to her. She'd learned to camouflage her heart better in high school by reading a lot and saying much less. In tenth grade she'd realized track was the perfect sport for her because she could take buses with other girls in short shorts to faraway events, but there had been no pressure to strike up any friendships, no need to participate in team rituals or talk about boyfriends and makeouts. The kids who ran track had been largely introverted, but being on a sports team had kept them from getting beat up or singled out. Zoey had been poking at all that hurt by bringing up the near relationship between her and Mia, but Agnes knew that Zoey hadn't any clue of the things she'd been through to arrive at herself. Zoey was so desperate to be cool, but her understanding had all the depth of a rainbow filter on a Facebook profile.

Over the years, Agnes had learned what clothes suited her frame, and she knew how to cook well and pack a lunch, things that had eluded her in her twenties. She had briefly joined a soccer league, then switched to queer soup night—and although neither had been quite right for her, she'd learned you could make a social life for yourself as easily as showing up. Most people were friendly if you let them be. But she was stuck in the same job and had many of the same goals longer than she'd wanted to. The two-month relationship she'd had with Charlie was one of her longer ones. She'd assumed, like Mia and the rest, she'd have had a partner by now, that she would be thinking about things like in vitro or home ownership or . . . dog ownership, at least.

She had become independent, though, and mostly self-sufficient. Even if it felt like there might still be a missing piece.

————⸙————

Mia had once said to Agnes, "You can either have expensive sheets or good sex. You can't have both." Looking around the estate, she wondered which one Mia had gotten from Martin. Everything was stone out in the backyard. When he'd had the property redone, Martin had constructed a kind of rustic haven, erasing any feminine touches. There was a gray rock half wall beginning by the pool, then ending in an outdoor kitchen complete with stone countertops, a sleek stone fireplace, and a grill station. Once, Mia had asked her to house-sit the Connecticut place, and Agnes had driven out alone to check up on things. Martin had been away for work for an extended period, and Mia had been in Chicago with her sister. Agnes had lounged by the pool for a week. At night she'd lain in their bed and written poems for the first time in years. Mia's pillow had smelled like her: lilac and Earl Grey tea. Mia had known she'd needed a vacation and couldn't afford one. God, she'd really tried to continue being a good friend through the Martin years.

Agnes was just about to head for the back of the patio where the grill and firepit were when Ethan came out of the guesthouse on the other side, still pulling a T-shirt over his head, catching it on his glasses. He saw her, then lifted a hand in greeting before he wandered over.

"What were you doing out here?" Agnes asked, though she had her theories.

"You know Zoey when she's up late—tossing and turning. So out to the guesthouse for me."

"Upgrade from the doghouse, right?"

Ethan laughed and straightened his glasses. He glanced at the pistachios in her hand and asked if he'd missed breakfast. Agnes had heard the fight in the room across from hers the night before and knew he was saving face. She also knew she needed to tell him about Martin, and knew from all the thrillers she had copyedited at work that this was the moment someone could be tripped up. They had no idea what killed Martin, and Ethan had been in the guesthouse alone, only ten paces away. It made her nervous, and she blurted out, "There's no breakfast and Martin's dead."

For a long moment he said nothing, but Agnes saw him thinking, stalling for time and mouthing silent words. *What*, or *But* . . . she couldn't tell which.

Then he said, "You guys get a call from the city or something?"

She told him they'd found him in his car in the garage. Ethan went on to ask all the things discussed around the island, including whether anyone had properly checked the body to determine the cause of death.

"With all our medical training we learned in film and creative-writing classes?" Agnes shot back.

"Yeah, I guess not."

"Victor said we shouldn't touch anything."

"Victor's here? Whose idea was that?" Ethan was still blinking the sleep from his eyes.

"Mine," she said. "Steph and I asked him to Zoom and say hello, but he said he'd fly in on a red-eye." She didn't tell Ethan about the nondescript holiday gift Mia had given her, or how she suspected it might have been intended for Victor.

"I don't think he likes me. He never got back to me when I sent him scripts." Ethan peered toward the house as if he were looking for Victor.

They walked slowly around the entire back area, prying pistachios open, then dropping the shells in the woods as they ate and talked. They spotted both a hawk and a cardinal as Ethan attempted to reconstruct the events from the night before. He was obviously more hungover than Agnes was, or maybe it helped that she'd at least had a glass of water and some coffee. He said that Martin could still have been the one to hurt Mia, even if he was dead. It didn't change anything.

"Why were you yelling at Zoey last night?" Agnes asked.

"She's cheating on me."

Agnes dropped the nut she'd just pried open. Zoey, the one who usually couldn't stop talking about herself, had managed to hide something? "Wow. She didn't say anything on the car ride up."

"Cheating with someone else's sperm. And I can just picture him in the come catalog. Six-two, Harvard. Works as a French translator. I want to punch his *visage*."

"You want to punch this bilingual person you made up?" Just as in high school, Agnes found it better sometimes to shake her head than to talk to men. The sperm was still in the cryotank in the hatch of her car. "Don't worry—he's probably ugly. Most men are."

"Yeah, we're ugly but noble—like farm animals."

Agnes laughed, but Ethan's expression changed.

"I did do something I shouldn't have."

She felt wary again, not ready to hear what he'd done. She tipped her head back, avoiding. "Look, there's that hawk again."

"I think it's a falcon actually," Ethan said, peering up. He looked back at her. "You and I love Mia the most."

Agnes stopped at the wall and leaned against it, her shoes sinking in spring mud. "I love her enough to let her have what she loves," Agnes said decisively, staring at the outdoor-kitchen area. "If you love someone, you let them have the person they want and don't try to make them want you."

"No one loves a martyr, Agnes." Ethan scraped his shoe with a stick to get the mud off the bottom of his sneaker.

"What did you do?" Agnes finally asked. She heard her own voice grow rough with trepidation. Normally she had a low, steady tone, but when she was nervous, her voice could crack like an adolescent boy's.

"I kissed her." Ethan looked at the muddy stick in his hand with resentment; then he cast it away. "Last night in the kitchen."

She wondered how Mia had reacted, but Ethan didn't give any more. Agnes considered it. Making a play for someone who couldn't remember how they felt about you. It was desperate. She'd thought Ethan was above it. That like her, he would always put Mia's needs first. But maybe she needed to reconsider what they were all capable of.

She herself had done some things she wasn't proud of, like writing a whole manuscript of poems about Mia while house-sitting for her and sleeping in her bed. The titles were a little bit Sylvia Plath and a little bit stalker-ish: "Permission," "The Last Time I Saw You," and "The White Lace of Her Breath." A thing she really should have stopped herself from, especially so long after they'd decided they were just friends. She'd learned to repress a part of herself, a tiny little closet in her pocket, every time she saw Mia, yet she couldn't bear to break away from her completely. What if what Zoey had said was true, that she feared intimacy?

Ethan had never managed to keep his boundaries, now that she thought about it. There'd been a time she recalled Mia telling her about when she'd come home from a date with Martin—back when they were dating, before she'd moved in with him—and found Ethan in her apartment. She said she couldn't remember if she'd left the door open or not. It was an old New York lock, she'd said, waving a hand as if it didn't matter. "You know how I lock myself out half the time." Mia and Ethan had talked until 2:00 a.m. or so because Ethan had been going through one of his moods, and she'd instructed Agnes not to tell Zoey because nothing had happened so it was no big deal. As always, Agnes had obliged.

Agnes examined her friend's features. He was pale and lanky, and his tortoiseshell glasses made him seem nerdy. That didn't mean he was harmless. Had the door really been open that night, like Mia said, or had he found a way to let himself in?

"You know, usually the wrong people get hurt. But sometimes the right people die," Ethan said, gazing back at the garage. "I mean, there's no point in pretending we liked him."

The idea that someone had intentionally hurt Martin had occurred to her, but she was trying not to think about it, even though Stephanie had sent her outside to investigate the source of the ashy fingerprints on the door. It was a futile task, since Agnes knew where they came from.

She supposed she'd been assuming that Martin was old enough to have a heart attack, although maybe it had been suicide. He had told his son, "Go to your mother's," with a kind of intensity that might have been a last wish. But what if it had been a violent act? Wasn't that why she'd been questioning Ethan for the past half hour? She blinked and tried to recall the glimpse she'd had of Martin through the car window—she didn't think there were wounds. If she thought about where everyone was in the night—Mia upstairs, Stephanie sleeping upstairs in the adjoining room, Agnes downstairs in the guest room. Ethan out here in the guesthouse . . .

She didn't want to tell Ethan that she'd heard Zoey and Cameron partying in the night. At one point she'd sneaked downstairs to search for those poems, which she never should have given to Mia and now didn't want her to ever remember. Mia would have them stashed in a box with her files, the things relegated to the country house because there wasn't room in the city, or maybe stashed there because she didn't want Martin to go through them. When Agnes had given them to her two years ago, she'd said it was a manuscript and maybe Mia could tell her if she thought it was worth submitting to a publisher. She had no idea if Mia had read them. For several months afterward, whenever they'd met, she tried to will herself to ask, then found herself tongue tied. After a while she'd decided too much time had passed to discuss it. Maybe her friend hadn't even recognized herself in the work, she told herself. Agnes had quietly sifted through the file folders in the box, then found the manila envelope with the sheaf of poetry inside. *Agnes's Poems* was written in pen in Mia's dainty handwriting on the outside.

As she'd clutched the envelope against herself, Agnes had heard Zoey and the teenager at the far end of the basement in the rec room, laughing. Agnes had flattened herself behind the little room that held the furnace and listened.

"That is not how you handle a tit," Zoey admonished him. "It isn't a softball!" Then she'd laughed hysterically.

———

Ethan handed the pistachio bag back to Agnes with only a few nuts left in the bottom and said he needed a drink of water. He started toward the sink in the outdoor kitchen. "Look," he said, pointing. "Someone's been using the firepit."

"I don't think that's important right now, Ethan." Agnes hurried toward the house.

Behind her, she could hear him scraping at the fireplace, the papery sound of remains being lifted off the grate. "Aggie—it's documents!" he said, catching up to her, the burnt layers of papers cradled in his hands. "Do you think this is, like, business . . . documents? You know, for whatever Martin did for a living?"

"No, definitely not," Agnes said, because she had once been hired by Mia to copyedit Martin's book proposal, *Gain without Pain: Going Beast Mode on Portfolio Diversification.*

Also, she had done the burning.

It had been damp at 4:00 a.m., and still half-drunk, she'd barely been able to get the pages to ignite. Once they had caught, they'd begun rising from the heat, floating off the log grate. There had been a pair of barbecue tongs lying beside the firepit. She'd picked them up and chased after half a dozen ember-edged pages. Her words might have been leaden before the fire, but somehow the pages were now weightless: a black tatter of adjectives dancing in the air.

Chapter Twelve

Breakfast Club

"Mrs. Dalloway said she'd buy the sperm herself," Zoey said ironically as she slipped on her shoes to run outside. She had forgotten the sperm in the trunk overnight, as if Mia's memory condition were contagious. Zoey had been so focused on everything that was happening, she hadn't thought to transport the tank into her room.

She crossed to the parking pad just outside the garage, thankful they'd put the door down so she didn't have to see the body a second time. She had a philosophical moment in which she thought about the short space between life and death. It was about twenty feet, she figured, given the location of what was in the trunk and what was in the garage.

She grasped Agnes's key fob, but the car made no sound and didn't click open no matter how many times she pressed the button. *Figures,* she thought. Agnes hadn't replaced the batteries. Zoey stuck the key into the driver's side and opened the door manually.

Inside, Zoey pressed the unlock button to open up the whole car so she could get in the hatch for her junk. She heard a chime and felt a little buzz in her pocket, but the ding wasn't her usual one for messages. She took out the phone and stared at it. The phone had the look of hers but was obviously Agnes's. They'd switched them again. Maybe when they had been sitting around the kitchen island? Floating on her home screen was an email notification, over the top of a selfie of Agnes and her cat: Pay your E-ZPass fine for 03/05/2023.

To her surprise, when Zoey pressed the notification, it opened automatically to Agnes's email. *Is she really so trusting as to have no pass code?* Zoey wondered. She scrolled, snooping. The bill was for the Connecticut Turnpike toll. She sucked in a breath as she stared at the date.

Agnes had lied to her. The one friend she could count on to not lie. Ever. A girl with no pass code on her phone certainly didn't have the skills for it.

In fact, now that Zoey thought about it, the one time she'd seen Agnes lie had been to protect Ethan's pride. The night he'd planned to screen *Ghost of You* to a handful of other students and friends at a bar, he hid in the bathroom for twenty minutes past when it had become uncomfortable that nothing was on screen. Agnes had taken the mic, thanking everyone for coming. The moment she'd grasped a microphone, Shy Agnes had displayed surprising stage presence.

She'd apologized and said Ethan had been pulled away by an important phone call, hinting it could be an agent, then cued the projection for Ethan. He'd crept out slowly, just in time for the second scene, and stood at the dark in the back.

But Agnes's ability to spin a tall tale didn't extend beyond the stage or the page, did it? Zoey had confronted her in their last year at NYU about why things had gotten weird between Mia and her, and Agnes had gone wide eyed and stammered until it was clear that the two of them were boning.

So what was she up to, hiding the fact that she'd been headed to Connecticut that night?

Around the back of the Ford, Zoey lifted the hatch and picked up the cryotank. It was square and plastic and looked no different from a cooler. She had to hold it on her hip in order to shut the hatch. She didn't want Ethan to see her walk in with it after the battle they'd had the night before. She had no idea whether tonight would be the night, but she had cashed in a 401(k) to pay for the fertility treatments, and—because being upsold always gave her body tingles—she'd splurged extra on the portable tank. She wasn't about to give Ethan the satisfaction of giving up.

Inside, she wedged the cooler in a corner of the guest room. She heard her name being called. It was Stephanie. She trotted out of her room before anyone came to find her.

When she walked into the kitchen, Ethan was looking over burnt papers, and Stephanie was googling legal terms on her phone. Without looking up, Steph asked Zoey, "Did you tell Cameron yet?"

"No . . . I had to get something from the car."

"Did you know Martin had been indicted?"

Zoey nearly dropped Agnes's phone. "What? No."

"I went into Martin's office, and I found that—it was in one of the folders he pulled out yesterday and left lying around. And Ethan found this other stuff in the firepit."

Stephanie slid the manila folder and a clean piece of paper toward her. Zoey picked it up and examined it. It was a subpoena with Mia's name on it.

"Who puts an indictment in a file folder like it's a normal part of their business?" Zoey asked. "Is this why he came back?"

Ethan held a torched piece of paper up to an Edison bulb that hung above the marble island. "This looks like a journal entry. What if Martin was getting rid of evidence last night and then—"

"What if someone decided to get rid of Martin?" Stephanie finished for him.

"Tell her about the notebook." Ethan nudged Stephanie.

Dear God, Zoey thought. *The obsessives at the party are bonding.* But Zoey already knew that it was missing—Stephanie had been looking for it earlier. It was how she must have grabbed Agnes's phone, because Steph had moved everything around.

Stephanie pointed to the stamped and official-looking document in front of Zoey. "Look at the date."

The subpoena Stephanie had found was issued to Mia in the case of *The Southern District of New York v. Martin Kroner.* The issuing officer's name was at the bottom, and the date had been written in by hand: *March 5,* the day of Mia's accident. After a few seconds of letting Zoey scan the subpoena, Stephanie took it back and asked if Mia had ever told her about Martin's business. As far as Stephanie could discern, Martin was being accused of running a Ponzi scheme.

Zoey just shook her head. "I cannot see Martin confiding in Mia enough that she could testify at a deposition. He didn't even let her pick the color of the kitchen."

Agnes walked into the kitchen and stood there awkwardly.

Stephanie, now obviously keeping tabs, asked, "Where'd you go?"

"I was looking for my car keys."

Zoey quickly offered the key fob from her pocket. "Sorry. I forgot something in the car."

Stephanie scanned the paperwork again. "Jesus. It's accusing Martin of stealing twelve million dollars from Mike Jeffries of Abercrombie and Fitch and six million dollars from *Hellboy* star Ron Perlman."

"Seriously? I love Ron Perlman," Zoey said.

Agnes jumped in. "That seems way more important than anything else. Really, let me throw these out. In every investigation, there's a distraction." She reached for the sheaf of burnt pages, but Steph was in her way.

Stephanie took a burnt page from Ethan and squinted. "She's right. Whatever these are, they're just nonsense. 'The world turned velvet.' What the hell does that even mean?"

"Could be code for 'the shit has hit the fan,'" Ethan said. He continued to argue with Stephanie. "'Your jewelry, your perfume, your house, your pool.' It's like a list of purchases he's hiding from the IRS."

"But that word *your*—that's the second-person voice. That's not business," Stephanie debated.

Zoey tried not to stare at Agnes. *Did she actually come here that night?* she wondered. *But then, wouldn't she have known the route better on the drive up? Of course, people lied, but the E-ZPass cameras did not lie.*

Ethan was now leaning against the counter, a box of Post Honeycomb cereal in his hand that he was eating dry from the box by the handful.

"Why are you eating children's cereal?" Zoey snapped.

"No one made any breakfast," Ethan said with his mouth full. As if someone was supposed to cook for him. Usually Zoey did; being able to make a perfect omelet was one of the few things she'd learned while growing up that was still of use to her. But today, Ethan's assumption that he would be waited upon rankled her.

He started to speak again but paused with a finger up to bear with him as he dry swallowed. "I'm no criminal profiler, but there's something about using the second person that says 'You are a sociopath.'"

"I know what these pages are," Stephanie announced. "They're poems."

"Martin's?" Ethan asked.

"They're mine," Agnes whispered almost inaudibly. "Mine." Agnes sighed, her breath picking up ashes from her burnt poetry. "I'll tell the truth. I took them out there last night because I felt stupid. I want her to remember, but not these. Maybe it's better if she doesn't know—"

"Doesn't know what, Agnes?" Stephanie gave her an assessing stare.

"I was processing some feelings. From a long time ago. And I stupidly sent them to her, asking what she thought."

"You asked her to read your poetry?"

"I know. And at dinner last night, I realized maybe it's time to leave some things behind."

Dinner, Zoey thought. *She* had *been drinking too quickly.*

Ethan brushed the cereal crumbs from his fingers on his pants, then touched the pages as if he couldn't believe it, his disappointment obvious. He'd hoped to have caught Martin at something. "These are yours, Agnes?"

"Don't read the fragments—you're not getting the whole poem. They were much better than you think," Agnes protested. "Zoey, you keep telling Mia about all our emotions, mine and Ethan's, like they're nothing. You can't just read out the past to her like it's . . ."

"Voice-over in a bad script?" Ethan suggested. "*Eastern Promises, Blade Runner, Interview with the Vampire*. Pick one." He dug a paw into the Honeycomb box again. "I agree with Agnes on that. Mia has to remember on her own."

"This is yours, too, isn't it, Aggie?" Zoey took the phone and set it on the island where the burnt pages sat.

Agnes leaned forward and looked at the phone. The email with her E-ZPass details was on the screen. She blinked. Zoey could see she knew exactly what it was.

"Looks like you've got an unpaid bill." Zoey spun the phone toward Stephanie so she could see. "And may I have *my* phone back?" Zoey put her hand out, palm up toward Agnes.

"You must have set it down somewhere. I don't have it," Agnes said.

Stephanie picked up the phone. "The back rent you wanted to borrow. The texts that night. The E-ZPass bill. Did *you* hurt my sister?" Stephanie asked, her voice calm but cold as she stared at Agnes.

"No. I would never do anything to hurt her. I—I love Mia," Agnes stuttered.

Zoey watched Steph assessing Agnes. For a second Zoey almost felt sorry for Agnes. She recalled the glances between Agnes and Mia for all those years. The same kind Mia and Ethan shared. There was a power that came with having intimacy with someone and then not reciprocating. It kept them hopeful, acquiescent, yours. That was what Mia had done.

"Maybe something in you just broke—gave out. Maybe you couldn't keep your composure anymore," Zoey said.

Zoey found herself moving her body slightly so she was standing closer to Stephanie than Agnes. It felt better to be on that side of the counter.

Agnes ran a hand over her eyes. "My car broke down on the turnpike, just past the old tolls. I had to get towed back."

"Why were you coming?" Ethan asked.

"I thought she needed me. Her voice—it wasn't Mia. She was shaky. Now I know why. There were obviously things she was going through that she wasn't ready to share with me—with any of us." Agnes picked up the folder containing Martin's indictment.

To Zoey's ear, Agnes sounded worried, but also guarded.

"Wait—I thought you only texted?" Stephanie said.

"Maybe we talked on the phone for a minute?"

"Why didn't you tell me this before?" Steph's face turned pink, and her voice sounded pinched. It was clear she'd trusted Agnes and now she didn't. Zoey watched the veneer come off as the two women stared at each other.

"Jesus Christ, you guys! This party was *my* idea." Agnes woke up her phone screen and scrolled through her history. She showed the call list to Stephanie.

Ethan interjected, "You were the one who said, 'It's likely that her attacker is in the house right now.'" Ethan leaned in. "What's this other number?"

"It's for North Bronx Towing. And if you want the paperwork, it's probably in my glove compartment."

"A five-minute call isn't *a minute*—there was lots of time for Mia to have told her about the subpoena!" Zoey shrieked.

Agnes shook her head but looked like she might crumble. "You're all questioning me, but how do you think I feel? If I'd actually made it out here, I could have stopped something! Or someone. I failed her and—"

"I believe Agnes," Stephanie said. "This isn't her."

"You *failed her* because you don't make regular oil changes? Which does sound on brand for you." Zoey felt tears in her eyes; the side effects of the fertility meds could do that. She heard herself raising her voice. "Or did you actually come here? What, does Mia have an app on her phone where she presses an icon, Dial-a-Sidekick, and you arrive within fifteen minutes?"

Agnes reached out suddenly and grabbed at her burnt poems. They trailed sooty pieces behind on the marble island as she swept what was left of them up against her. "Do you know how shitty you're all acting? This is my life. Not a Joe Eszterhas movie! The homicidal lesbian didn't do it."

"You are holding an entire sheaf of burnt love poems." Ethan gestured at Agnes with a honeycomb between his thumb and forefinger.

"Do you recognize yourself, Ethan?" Agnes asked. "I guess that's a mark of good writing. Connect with your reader. Even if he's a stalker in Chuck Taylors."

She left them and took the pages with her down the hall. Ethan peered at his shoes. "I don't know what she's talking about."

Zoey knew what Agnes was referring to, even though the word *stalker* was a little harsh. Ethan had tried to hide it. It had been just after Mia had begun seeing Martin three years before. Ethan never came in at 2:00 a.m. after having just "been out to a movie with friends." To do that, one had to have friends. The only places Ethan went were Film Forum or the Metrograph, but usually alone at three in the afternoon. Zoey and Ethan had been through a fairly rocky stretch at that point, but their web series had finally started doing well, so she had overlooked the fact that he'd obviously been at Mia's.

Zoey recalled she'd actually stooped to phoning her mother for advice. Her Orange County parents watched only faith-based movies starring Dennis Quaid. They thought Zoey never should have moved in with Ethan without a wedding. "Ignore it, or you'll make it worse," her mom said. But when Zoey thought back over her entire life, her mother had always instructed her to be quiet, say less, and take up less space in the universe. Zoey had spent her whole life attempting to do the opposite of that, yet for some reason, that time, she'd listened. She'd let Ethan have his excuse. But she wasn't going to let Agnes have it.

"I don't trust her," Zoey said, gazing down the hallway after her.

"Means, motive, opportunity," Ethan said, holding three fingers aloft. "She's only got one of the three. Opportunity. But she definitely has that."

"You need to have a life to have motive!" Zoey shot.

"Yeah, but people always have their little reasons, don't they?" Ethan said.

Zoey nodded. "Good point. Even if they're emotional ones."

It felt like when they worked on one of their *Movie Fails*, combing through a film together and documenting the errors. Zoey took his hand in hers, folding down his fingers gently.

Chapter Thirteen

The Unbearable Lightness of Mia

Agnes glanced back at the main house to see if any of them were watching from the window; then, assured they weren't, she turned the handle to the guesthouse. She hadn't organized the party for the purpose of trading put-downs and comebacks with Zoey and Ethan. Maybe this was why the distance had been growing between them all—gradually they'd come to a point where they knew so much about each other that they didn't respect each other anymore. What a horrible shame. No, she'd put this weekend together to help Mia, and that's exactly what Agnes intended to do.

At the hospital, the first thing Mia had said to her was "We were friends, weren't we?" Following that subconscious desire for reassurance of a relationship, Agnes considered that perhaps Mia herself, on some level, considered those she knew untrustworthy. The friends, therefore, weren't wrong to question Agnes. But that meant *they* couldn't be disregarded as suspects either. Especially now, with a body languishing in the garage.

The guesthouse rooms were dim and smelled tangy, either from lack of use or from Ethan sweating out the alcohol through the night. They'd all had too much—mixing and matching—and it had impaired their thinking. They all loved the thrill of a good story, and they'd told plenty the night before—letting drama matter more than truth. Now they were turning on each other.

Agnes could see from the doorway that Ethan had slept in the bed—it was unmade. The couch cushions were also disheveled, as though he might not have been comfortable or had switched from one to the other before completely crashing out. The windows had blinds that hadn't been opened or rolled up. Walking around in the guesthouse in the slant of half light, Agnes felt suddenly like Richard Gere's character in *American Gigolo*, trying to prove he's been framed.

Agnes desperately tossed back all the covers and the pillows on the bed, not sure what she was looking for—smears of Martin's blood, maybe. Something that would show Ethan had been in the garage and done Martin some kind of harm before crashing out here. She knew he had gone through the garage after his fight with Zoey—she was certain of it. She'd heard them arguing, then the thump of the door into the garage slamming. So he had to have seen or encountered Martin. Maybe Martin had stuck around to spy on the group—he'd already had Cameron doing that for him earlier. When Agnes had sneaked out to burn the poems, she'd gone through the kitchen and hadn't heard anyone in the hall again all night.

Agnes pulled back a sheet, and a single tube sock flew out of the bed like a jump-scare cat. *What is it with men and socks?* she thought. She had two brothers and always wondered: Was it the soft weave of the fabric that was irresistible? The virginal whiteness that asked to be sullied? Still, DNA was DNA, and, holding it by the tip of her fingers, she put it into a Ziploc baggie she had taken from the pantry. Maybe there were actually more female murderers out there, Agnes realized. They were just harder to catch because they didn't leave evidence everywhere.

Agnes had always had complicated feelings about Ethan—he was sensitive and intuitive to the moods of people around him, but that also made him intense. And he was good at putting his emotional distress to work for him. It was always perfectly timed to draw Zoey or Mia back into his life. No matter how much he proclaimed himself a feminist or reached for the proper politically correct terms, he could make a whole room of women concerned for him, treading carefully around his male ego. He always had.

In the bathroom Agnes found Ethan's travel kit, containing his medication, a toothbrush, a travel-size tube of Crest, a razor, and a bottle of Kiehl's aftershave. There was nothing anywhere to say that her friend had decided to do something he shouldn't have. Yet she couldn't help thinking he had the most motive of any of them. If he hadn't suspected Mia and Victor of being involved—and until this morning it seemed likely none of them had—then Martin had been the only man standing in Ethan's path to Mia. He had, by his own admission, kissed her the night before. Agnes wondered again how Mia had reacted.

She wondered about the meaning—the value—of the kiss Mia and Ethan had shared. *A kiss is a data point,* she thought. *But each person interprets it in their own way.*

There had been several kisses between Agnes and Mia, but it was hard to say whether they meant anything on Mia's side. Girls like Mia had a habit of rounding down their number of sexual partners based on arcane rules. "That docent from MoMA?" she'd say. "He didn't count. I only did that because he looked like Mr. Bean."

Still, there was one particular night Agnes could never think about without the fragrance of Dolce & Gabbana's Light Blue suddenly floating through her mind. They had been coming home from the Delancey on the Lower East Side and walked the Williamsburg Bridge back from the city. As they'd stood in the middle of the bridge, looking down at the water and the lights, the subway rattling below them almost violently, it had been Mia who had said, "Kiss me."

It had seemed more serious. Agnes had felt it but would never have proposed it. But immediately she'd known the answer was yes; and as Mia had searched her mouth, it was yes; and in an instant her whole body was yes. Mia had tasted like lemon Absolut and stolen cigarettes.

Back at their shared apartment, there had been more; it had felt like a lifting of something that had been lying over their friendship for a long time. The next day Agnes had woken up hoping it might happen again, feeling like it was a thing that was always meant to happen, that she had been led to that moment. But Mia had buried everything with seven words shoveled on top of Agnes's heart: "That got a bit out of control."

Mia didn't mean to hurt anyone. She was just a person who shouldn't be possessed by anybody. She spent her twenties searching for orgasms like she was writing the great American novel. For someone afraid of attachments, Agnes supposed, it would be the ultimate nightmare if Mia had fallen for her roommate. That was the difference between her and Ethan. Agnes accepted that Mia was a feeling: you took a moment with her for its beauty. You couldn't hold it forever. That was why she'd burned the poems—she'd overstepped and tried to fix that feeling with ink on paper.

Agnes breathed hard through her nostrils. *You have to understand that about Mia,* she thought. Ethan was greedy and couldn't think far enough outside himself.

Or maybe she simply felt superior to him because her midwestern skill at repression was next level compared to his.

Agnes bit her lip and swept back the shower curtain. She wasn't sure what she was looking for. The retro wall tiles interlocked, white and black. Clean and empty throughout the oversize shower area. In the medicine cabinet, Agnes found only an organic rose deodorant stick and a bottle of Mia's perfume. She uncapped it and inhaled.

Then, as she was putting back the bottle of perfume, she paused. Why had Mia never given her the same consideration? Agnes had respected Mia's feelings. Mia should have known and seen how Agnes had felt about her.

There was a large walk-in closet just off the bathroom, about six feet by six feet, with white-painted shelves, and there Agnes saw the usual cleaners, toilet paper rolls, and stacked towels of any guest bathroom.

On the other side of the closet was a bar where some of Mia's swimsuits and cover-ups hung, like tropical ghosts swaying in the murky light that came from a single small window. She reached in and ruffled through the towels for no reason except that she was furious. If knocking over a stack of toilet paper rolls was her only revenge, then fine. *That's how we throw down in Ann Arbor.* Then, her finger snagged on raw wood. She drew her fingertip back and put it in her mouth, sucked. Inside the closet, the old guesthouse remained. Before Martin's reno, the place had once had '80s wood paneling that no one had torn out inside the little room. A panel here was loose, and that was what she'd torn her finger on.

She reached out and traced the edge of the wood paneling. Why was it bent out like that? Why didn't it lie flat? Agnes yanked the fake wood forward, and there it was. Her hand closed on it, an object wedged in between the wall and the panel. It was long, cold, metal. Agnes swallowed. She pulled it out into the light and saw the glint of the brass fireplace poker. Immediately Agnes knew it went with the set in the living room that stood beside the hearth.

She backed into the bathroom light, where she could see it better. It rang on the stone floor as she dropped it. *Clang.* Like in the kitchen, the flooring here was stone and heated, if you turned the dial next to the light switch.

Agnes peered at the oblong brass object.

She didn't want to pick up the poker again, afraid of putting her own fingerprints on it, covering what evidence might be there. There was no blood on the curved end of the poker. It was still shiny and new. But without a doubt, it had been concealed in a strange place. She remembered Zoey had said in the car on the drive up that she and Ethan had been invited more. How often had he stayed in the guesthouse? There was no doubt—she had found evidence. Agnes leaned back against the bathroom doorway, breathing hard.

Agnes wanted to run into the house at full tilt and declare she'd found the weapon, but she knew that approach could provoke the others. She had to be careful about this.

In the dining room, Stephanie and Victor were eating. A plate of pineapple and the last of the grocery store cupcakes sat on a tray in the middle of the table. Victor—very LA and health conscious—had scraped off the frosting. Zoey was at the farthest end of the table. Looking like she was nursing a hangover, she held on to her cup of coffee with two hands like it was a teddy bear. She glanced up just long enough to give Agnes an icy stare. Agnes could only assume the teenager was still passed out in the basement. Ethan was in the living room on his laptop. Was it possible the missing student films had been a ruse, something to distract them the night before? He'd spent a good thirty minutes, confounded, raving angrily about it. And now here Ethan was, acting as if everything were completely normal—even when there was a body in the garage and their friend had been nearly killed a few weeks ago in the kitchen.

"Where's Mia?" Agnes asked, hearing the hoarseness in her voice that only happened when she was stressed. But none of them heard how concerned she was.

"Resting. She needed to lie down after our walk," Victor said.

Agnes remained standing in between rooms, where she could keep an eye on everyone.

Stephanie continued with whatever she'd been discussing with Victor. "And you were with her that whole day?"

Another interrogation, the kind of drilling Stephanie could pull off as if she were asking for driving directions to Costco. It must've been from her years as a journalist. Agnes could see Victor tensing up as Stephanie made notes, now on her phone instead of in her notebook.

Agnes had planned to walk in and tug Steph away and tell her about the poker, which she'd left lying on the floor of the guesthouse bathroom. But now she inserted herself into the conversation. "You must be tired?" she asked Victor.

"I'm feeling the red-eye now, for sure."

"Stephanie, we can do this later. He should rest." Agnes touched his arm and felt him relax.

Stephanie's eyes narrowed at Agnes, but Victor said it was okay. He wanted to help. He turned to Stephanie. "I didn't fly back to LA that night."

"The night of March fifth?" Stephanie clarified.

"Mia called me after she left the hotel and said she was worried about Martin. That he was really worked up, in legal trouble. She was on her way home at that point."

Zoey interrupted. "I don't understand. If Martin was indicted for fraud, why wasn't he arrested?"

Victor grinned. "Do I have to tell you that the rich are even arrested differently? It's as civil as getting a letterpressed invitation that says, 'Join us as we celebrate your deposition . . .'"

"So you stayed an extra night?" Stephanie asked Victor.

"I stayed in case she needed me," he said, steepling his fingers. "But she never phoned again that day or the next."

Zoey's eyes widened as if she had put something together. "Why were you expecting the call?"

"We were seeing each other. At first just as friends," Victor said. "I reached out after some personal things happened. Then it got serious. I think I should be clear and everyone here should know that." There was nothing nervous in his demeanor, but he glanced toward the door to the garage. "It's kind of a weird situation, but honesty is called for."

———⊢———

Agnes had always liked how up-front Victor could be. Years ago he'd asked Agnes, "Is Mia your girlfriend?" when they'd all hung out at a bar after Adaptation Studies class together.

She remembered laughing so nervously. "Oh no, not at all," she had answered.

As well as the Adaptation course, she and Victor had taken one creative-writing class together where his criticisms were incisive—and fair. But aside from that elective, he'd been singularly focused on the visual: photography, film, technology. Like Ethan, he hung around dissecting pop culture, but he was also more his own person—never seeming to search for anyone else's approval, even Mia's. He was "Agree to disagree" personified. If Agnes thought about whether she'd ever seen any energy pass between Mia and him, she couldn't recall. Maybe once.

They'd all gone to a midnight showing of *The Princess Bride* at the IFC, but Agnes had messed up and read the calendar wrong. They'd been screening *The Wicker Man* that night instead. After the group had decided to stay, Victor and Mia had lingered together at the popcorn stand longer than necessary. But there wasn't that desperate energy that Ethan always had around Mia. She recalled Mia sitting in between Victor and Ethan that night, laughing out loud at the nude hippie dance scenes but sobbing by the end as Edward Woodward is burned alive in the pagan ritual.

Too much had changed since then, yet also not enough. Glancing at Zoey, Agnes realized she hadn't even changed her style since those years. The same was true of Ethan. In some ways, Victor and Mia were the only two of the group who'd transformed their lives and become older, changed who they were, developed new priorities.

The remembering party was making her reassess not just the past, but her present self. Zoey and Ethan were a tight knot—that was the only difference since college: they'd become more and more tangled and ensnared. They supported each other even while they tore each other down, like trim, vegan versions of George and Martha from *Who's Afraid of Virginia Woolf?* Of course Zoey would protect Ethan at every turn.

Victor picked up his overnight bag. But before he could go claim a guest room, Ethan shouted at him, "You met Mia through me!"

Victor set his bag down. "Seventeen years ago."

"Weren't you already married or something?"

Victor looked at Ethan with genuine hurt before replying, "Yeah, well, things happen." Hoisting his bag again, Victor made his way upstairs.

"Stephanie, I really need to talk to you," Agnes said, and this time everyone looked at her. Her face and tone had betrayed her worry.

Stephanie rose, and Zoey stood and, uninvited, followed them through the kitchen and out onto the back deck. *Fine, so be it,* Agnes thought. It was likely Zoey would try to cover for him, deny and protect him. She always did. But Stephanie needed to know about the possible weapon. They needed to examine Martin's body more thoroughly.

After stopping just outside on the deck, Agnes turned to Zoey. "I don't know if you should leave her alone in there."

"Who, Mia? With Ethan? Victor?" Zoey's disbelief came out in fluttery hand gestures. There it was, the denial Agnes had suspected would come, and she hadn't even shown them what she intended to yet.

Agnes had been about to say "Ethan" but didn't think it was a good idea. She'd wait and tell Stephanie alone. "Let's be smart."

Stephanie nodded. "She's right. Go back."

Zoey turned and made her way back through the sliding door. She gave them a pissy look. "All right, I'll babysit."

———

As soon as she was gone, Stephanie asked, "You realize that Victor admitted he was on this coast the night of?"

Agnes shook her head. "Yeah, but I don't think there's anything to worry about there. Mia recognized him. She wouldn't run to hug Victor if he had tried to hurt her. She wouldn't go off with him. Some part of her would know." Agnes led the way to the guesthouse. "Also, Victor's never been here—he sent a gift from Taipei when she had the wedding. I think only someone who has stayed here before would think to hide this here."

"Hide what?"

They entered the guesthouse and walked through the main room, Steph glancing around, wrinkling her nose at the stale male odor.

They came to the door of the bathroom, and Agnes pointed, though it wasn't warranted. The object lay amid the scattered paper rolls and knocked-over towels. "It was there, with everything in the walk-in closet. Tucked in behind a loose board."

Steph stopped abruptly, her whole body rigid. She stared at the fireplace poker on the floor. "That could kill someone. No one would carry it out here except to hide it, or to use it again."

"My thoughts exactly. Ethan is the one who stayed out here all night after his fight with Zoey. And then there's this." Agnes held up the white sock in the Ziploc. "He admitted to me he kissed Mia last night. And then he obviously jerked off."

"Unless he did that . . ."—Stephanie looked ill before finishing—"after killing Martin." She sank to a squat, still staring at the brass poker.

"Too far," Agnes said, holding her hands up. "You've watched way too many Netflix documentaries."

Stephanie tossed her ponytail back from her shoulder. "Sometimes *it is* the one you don't suspect. Ethan was just telling the sweetest story about a book club he's part of. It's all men, and they only read books by women."

Agnes scoffed. "Okay. He is definitely hiding something."

"We have to call 911. Not an expert, but the longer you keep a body sitting around, the more explaining you'll probably have to do."

"Let's be sure first. Let's go look at Martin closer," Agnes said.

Agnes led the way to the garage, indicating the trail Ethan would have walked when he came out of the garage the night before to go to the guesthouse.

They opened the back door of the garage and went inside. It was dim, even now; the only windows were two high-up glass arches in the garage door letting in a meager amount of pale-gray daylight. They heard the sounds before Agnes saw anything.

"What's that noise?" Stephanie said as they walked into the cold space. It sounded like digging, a wet fumbling.

Agnes found the light switch, and the fluorescents came on.

Hanging on to the Tesla door with its back legs was a raccoon. Its front was inside the vehicle, and Agnes could see another black-and-white-striped figure inside.

"Oh my God, they're eating him!" she said.

Stephanie screamed.

"Shush!" Agnes grabbed Stephanie to silence her. "Everyone will hear."

"Shit! Do something," Stephanie begged.

Agnes took stock, glanced around for resources. Without hesitating, she grabbed a club from a leather golf bag that was propped on a stand along the wall. The raccoons weren't small. They were twice as big as her cat, Major Tom. She grabbed a nine iron of Martin's and ran at the car with the club raised in front of her. "Don't you do that!" Agnes hissed. "Go! Get away from him!"

The raccoon with its back legs on the sill turned and paused, calmly blinking at her. She held the club up as if she meant it, and after a moment the animal jumped down and waddled for a far corner.

"The other one." Steph pointed into the car.

"Let's open the door to let it out," Agnes whispered as if the raccoons would hear.

Stephanie regained her composure and said, "On it."

Steph circled around the Tesla. She opened the car door and jumped back as the raccoon scooted from its perch on the passenger side. This raccoon was more skittish than the other one and emitted a high-pitched shriek that was almost as loud as Stephanie's had been. As Agnes stepped after it, swinging the club lightly, it chased the other raccoon through a gap where the rolling door was bent and didn't quite meet the frame.

Both women could see the small pocked patches the curious animals had left in Martin's face and arms with their nails. They'd arrived just in time.

Agnes's adrenaline had run out, and she bent over, panting hard. "Suburbia is sick," she said between gasps.

"How on earth did you know how to get rid of them?" Steph asked.

"You should see where I live in Brooklyn. Rats are part of daily life, or at least part of the building's garbage bins. In my hands, Martin's two-thousand-dollar club's nothing but a rat stick."

Stephanie stared at her with admiration. Then she reached inside and turned the car on so that she could roll up the window.

"How bad do you think he looks?" Agnes straightened up.

"Oh, he's bad. Very bad," Stephanie answered. She held the door open and pointed at the passenger seat, where four empty plastic baggies lay. "That's what he was doing out here."

Chapter Fourteen

Manic Pixie Coma Girl

Am I dying?

Mia didn't know if she said it out loud or just thought it. She knew she was in the hospital even though she could see only backlit shapes. She felt those nurse and doctor hands everywhere: clicking IV tubes, feeling her skull with trained fingertips, shining a penlight back and forth in her eyes.

Then, as Mia lay there, she heard someone yell, "Last looks!"

Spray bottles of glycerin and water spritzed her hair down; then makeup came in. Someone dabbed purple greasepaint on her bruised arm with a *voilà*. Wardrobe lifted her gown and rearranged it on her shoulders, replacing it over her collarbone in a way that must have been more pleasing. She heard stands being moved around the bed—both IV stands and lighting adjusted. Oh, it was the hospital scene, she realized. How many times had they shot it? Days, weeks. Was David Fincher directing? Was it a remake of *All That Jazz*? Mia decided yes, she was starring in a gender-swapped remake of *All That Jazz* directed by David Fincher.

Mia was vaguely aware the fussing was becoming overly long. She could feel the impatience of Fincher, who was there—beyond the edge of what she could see, beyond the cables and the grips. She felt the mood on the set start to curdle.

Mia heard a voice. "We're waking her tomorrow. If the damage is extensive, we'll have to look at long-term care facilities."

She heard another voice, farther away, asking how she felt.

"I'm ready to shoot," Mia tried to reply, but her throat was blocked by something, and she had no voice. Inside she felt the words, *I'm not a diva. I'm happy with my life.* When she tried to sit up, everything was pain.

Fincher had come and taken the seat at the end of the bed. "I'm sorry," Fincher said, squeezing Mia's hand. "This is all my fault."

The apology seemed insincere. Or at least uncharacteristic for the director. He really didn't seem like the right person for this project. Maybe it wasn't David Fincher. No matter; they had to begin filming. Her lips parted just slightly to let in a breath before they began. So much preparation. She knew any inconsistency could undo the believability. *I'm dying in this scene,* she told herself. She lay as still as she could. She didn't want to ruin the shot.

Then a piercing scream startled her. Mia jumped, her hands gripping the sheets around her. But it wasn't a hospital bed—or a film set. She was in her room.

It must be hers: it had a bold wallpaper with a pattern of wildflowers and birds. There was the dresser, and there, the mirror. She sat up slowly, still worried about disappointing the director, but she was alone. She couldn't remember now who the director was—backlit, only a shadow. Mia had been dreaming. She swung her feet out of the bed, realizing she was still fully dressed. It had only been a nap. Since getting out of the hospital, she took a lot of naps. Forgetting was such exhausting work.

She was at that house—the big country estate—kept by the man named Martin. It was her house, too, she remembered now. She had walked with Victor that morning; her feet seemed to know every step of the grounds. Then there was another shriek. She recognized her sister's voice.

—

Mia edged down the stairs, carefully touching her hair, as though it somehow still mattered what she looked like. She heard another set of footsteps. Someone was coming up from the basement, and the two staircases met in the hall. She saw her stepson emerging, looking as dazed and confused as she was.

"Was that you?" Cameron asked.

She shook her head.

At the far end of the hall, Zoey and Victor came from the kitchen. "No, Mia," Victor said. "Come this way."

"I'll get you some coffee." Zoey coaxed her toward the kitchen.

Ethan came out of the living room. He looked at Mia, and a strange expression came to his face. She couldn't tell if it was guilt or sadness. Probably he was ashamed of his lunge at her the night before—although it wasn't really a lunge. *The move was more pitiful, like watching a too-confident child fall off a skateboard,* she thought. She still felt foggy headed, especially after the dream.

"Where's Stephanie?" Mia asked.

"No, that was . . ." Zoey trailed off, obviously unable to come up with a lie.

"Something's wrong," Mia said to Cameron. She could see it in their faces. They were keeping something from her. The teenager stared back at her. Then he took a few steps down the hall toward the door of the garage, where they could hear movement.

"No, no!" Victor's hand shot out, even though he wasn't close enough to really stop either of them.

"Cameron. Get over here!" Zoey demanded.

"What is it? What's going on?" Mia asked as the teenager halted for Zoey's mother-like command.

"We have some things to talk about," Victor said grimly.

The admission was enough to draw Mia and Cameron away from the garage door. Mia walked back to Victor as she'd done that morning, trusting him. She entered the kitchen and found the coffee carafe they'd promised. She passed the first cup to Cameron, then handed him the sugar bowl, knowing on some level that he took it sweet. It must have been something she'd done a hundred mornings before at that counter, or the one in the city. He stirred the coffee, then got a box of cereal from the cupboard. He sat back down with a bowl, poured the cereal in, and then ate the large pieces with his fingers, as if it were snack mix.

"Don't do that," Zoey pleaded. She seemed to be perturbed by everything Cameron did.

Victor took Mia's hand, and Mia saw Ethan visibly flinch. "How are you feeling?" Victor asked her quietly.

"I had the weirdest dream."

Mia watched as Ethan went to the cupboard and took down the pillbox the housekeeper had set up for Mia the day before. Without being asked, he brought it over to her. She flipped up the Sunday tab and stared in. She took the pills and swallowed them with her coffee, then smiled weakly at him, and he carried the box back to the cupboard. It was like he was trying to prove himself. He and Victor were having a care-off.

"What did you dream?" Victor asked.

"It was like *All That Jazz*—you know, where the hospital becomes a stage set?"

"I've actually never seen it."

"Gotta be a theater kid," Zoey said, casting an eye at Mia.

Victor took out some pieces of paper and held them up for Mia to see, steering the conversation back to seriousness. "Do you remember getting this? It's a subpoena for an investigation into Martin's company."

Mia stared at the paper Victor held out to her. She recognized her name and the date. It was the same as her accident. Mia glanced at Cameron.

"He was indicted?" Cameron sighed. "Maybe that explains the AirTag on Mia's car."

"Wait, what AirTag?" Victor asked.

"The week before everything happened. My dad and I talked about it, and he said it was probably nothing." Cameron set down his mug.

"A lot has happened since then," Ethan said.

"She said she kept getting notifications on her phone that there was a device near her. It seemed to follow her all the way home. I went out and checked her car. Found it in the passenger wheel well. No idea how long it was there."

"I don't think the government is using AirTags to follow people. They can afford real stuff," Victor stated. "So someone was following her. Who here is cheap and controlling?"

Mia felt a chill run up the back of her arms.

Cameron tossed a couple of chunks of cereal into his mouth. He chewed loudly.

"Can you please stop that?" Zoey said, her voice suddenly sharp.

"I'll make you some toast." Mia jumped up and went to the back counter to avoid the question. She pictured some bald man in a raincoat handing her the subpoena with a curt "You've been served," but it felt like a fiction to her, a timeworn scene without realness. She was making it up. But without thinking, she remembered how to make toast. She had opened a bread box, located the butter and a table knife.

"Maybe Martin tracked her—to see where she was going during the day when he was at work. They were fighting," Zoey said, looking at Cameron. "Remember what the Ouija board said?"

Victor looked confused. "Did we switch genres?"

"It was a game they were playing last night," Zoey said.

"Cameron, what else happened?"

Cameron ran a hand through his hair. "We were all at the house in Brooklyn. I heard him yell at Mia to get out, and after she left, he got drunk on the couch." Cameron's voice faltered. Mia could tell he didn't want to meet her gaze.

Ethan said, "It's kind of weird you're only bringing up this AirTag thing now."

"You don't know what's normal for my family. My dad once had a PI track my mother to Jared Leto's yurt. So, whatever."

"Listen," Victor put in. "I don't mean to rush you, but something's happened, and we have to learn as much as we can."

"He got a call from a woman that night. It woke him up."

"How do you know that?" Zoey asked.

"Oh, I could hear her, but I didn't recognize the voice. He called her a crazy bitch after he got off the phone. I mean, she was angry." Cameron glanced at Mia, then away again, as if the shame were somehow his and not his father's.

"Is he seeing someone else?" Victor asked almost hopefully. Maybe he hoped to justify the affair he was having with her. Mia wondered if their relationship had included guilt. She hadn't remembered any when they'd talked about it that morning—but it would have to, she realized.

"So it was someone he must've known?" Ethan said.

Mia glanced at Ethan. She saw Zoey open her mouth to say something, then shut it again. Mia looked at Victor. She could see what was happening around the circle. Everyone had caught it but Cameron. Ethan had used the past tense. *Must've known*, not *knows*. She felt her eyes burn and felt instantly helpless as she realized why they were all acting cagey.

The door to the garage opened suddenly, and each of them turned to peer down the hall. Stephanie ran in, with Agnes following. "We figured it out! Martin died of an overdose!" Stephanie said, sounding strangely triumphant.

Agnes caught Steph's arm. "Oh shit," she muttered when she saw the whole group sitting there.

Cameron lurched from the stool hard enough that it fell backward and clattered on the stone floor. He had realized what Mia figured out only a minute before. Ethan had known, and so had the rest of them.

Zoey jumped up too. She looked guilty and said she was sorry, but Cameron just stared at her like she was a dog that might bite. His face contorted. "He's *dead*?"

Mia took a deep breath. It was easier for her to process. She'd had no solid feelings for Martin, and it was soon after she got out of the hospital that she'd figured out why. Mia had calculated the months she'd known these people. It was a way to take friendship out of abstraction.

Stephanie: 444 months
Agnes: 204 months
Zoey, Ethan, and Victor: 192 months
Martin: 38 months

Her friends represented elephants of time. In comparison, Martin was a poodle. Her friends were more responsible for who she was than Martin, or Martin's house, or her closets full of clothes bought by Martin. He had generously provided for her, but what she could call to mind from those thirty-eight months was a disconnected montage more than a relationship. She remembered how his shirts looked from behind when he'd just put them on and they were fresh. But she remembered his pacing and angry muttering too.

Cameron had lost his father, though. She went to the teenager and tried to wrap him in a hug, but he stepped back. He walked toward the garage.

"He's out there?"

Victor was the one to block him. "We have to call 911 first."

"He overdosed, you said? Fuck!" Cameron shouted. Everyone looked at him. He stood back up. "He had to have raided my stash again!"

"It was yours?" Zoey asked.

"Don't look innocent," Cameron shot back at her.

Agnes stepped in, uneasy. "Maybe Zoey, you should, uh, tell us a bit about last night?"

She ignored the question and turned to the group. "We can't call 911. They'll have Cameron arrested."

"And you seem like you'd be really upset by that," Agnes needled.

"Cameron!" Stephanie snapped, her angry-mother voice turned up. "You're on probation. I wrote your letter to the judge asking for you to be allowed into Scared Straight."

"I never went. It was Mia who wanted me to go."

With the room starting to get out of control, Victor did his best to rein everything in. He asked Cameron, "What do you think your dad took?"

Cameron wiped a hand across his eyes. "Probably the heroin."

"Jesus." The unflappable Victor was finally flappable. "Heroin?"

"The markup out here is insane," Cameron replied.

"Cam, what your dad did is what he did. It's not your fault," Victor said. "But everything you have has to be gone, now. Flush it. And then we'll call it in. Look, everyone, I know this sucks, but it happens every day. What's out there is sadly normal, but no one's touched anything. It's not going to look suspicious."

Agnes grimaced and said, "That's not entirely true anymore."

Stephanie touched Mia's arm and whispered, "I'm so sorry."

As her sister squeezed her hand, Mia felt a rush of déjà vu back to her dream. *Who is directing this film now?* she thought as she looked around the kitchen. She watched as Cameron slunk back downstairs to dispose of his supply. Zoey and Ethan moved off to the living room and were huddle fighting. Victor and Agnes were talking, on the verge of arguing themselves.

"Nibbled on him?" Victor said to Agnes repeatedly. "Nibbled? Like George Romero–level nibbled? Shit, we should have phoned two hours ago."

"Time out, people," Agnes yelled while making a T sign in the air. "Let's talk about policing, civil rights, and public safety. Let's question why we want to call. I protested the police. So did Zoey. What if they show up guns first?"

Cameron reemerged from the basement and interrupted. "In this zip code? The closest neighbor is the attorney general."

He was red faced and sniffling, as if he'd snuffed a line while disposing of the rest. Mia noticed Zoey watching him. She started back over, Ethan coming too.

"I don't know," Ethan dithered. "I would feel more comfortable if there was an app instead."

"Guys," Victor interrupted. "It's not my job to make you feel better about it, but in this case, I think there's no problem calling."

"I'll do it," Zoey said.

Mia watched their faces as they discussed the situation, details Zoey would relay and in which order. They all seemed so familiar, and it was agonizing not to know who to trust or agree with. Were friends who would keep a death from her really her friends? But Stephanie was her sister and had done it too. Mia swallowed and broke in on their conversation.

Mia announced, "I could use some tea. Anyone else want some?"

She reached up to a shelf for the silver kettle and saw it was dented. She felt distinctly that it shouldn't be. A dented kettle didn't fit with the other things in her life. Or maybe it did.

"Can I see that again?" Agnes asked.

"The kettle? I wondered what happened to it."

"No, your arm. Just now, when you reached up, your sleeve fell down."

Mia slid her sleeve up and showed her bruise. "Yeah, it's ugly."

"Feel like getting some air?"

Mia could hear Zoey and Ethan now fully arguing with each other in the kitchen doorway.

Mia turned off the water. "Fuck the tea. Let's go."

———⸙———

In the backyard Agnes walked close to Mia the same way that Victor had. She felt protected in her friend's presence. "I can't believe Martin is gone," Mia said. "I also can't believe he was here in the first place."

Agnes raised an eyebrow. "I think that's probably everyone's opinion of Martin."

"Why'd I marry him?"

As they reached the guesthouse, Agnes answered, "You never told me why. But if I had to guess, you wanted change. I mean, love, too, obviously. But . . . it gave you direction."

It felt to Mia like a perfectly Agnes thing to say, acknowledging the flaws and the strengths of a situation. She was sure they'd had many conversations like this before.

"I was one of those women with a list, wasn't I?"

Agnes shook her head. "We're all like that. We all want something amazing."

"Was I horrible to Martin?"

"I'd say, relatively, you were a saint." Agnes moved toward the door of the guesthouse. "I need to show you something before the police get here."

Mia stopped her by touching her shoulder. "Can I ask you something?"

Agnes nodded. "Of course."

"Do we know anyone British? Older man, white hair?"

"You mean like David Attenborough? I don't think so. I'm not that fancy," Agnes answered.

"No, he was more knife-crime British. Cockney. I'm sure he was at a party here, and he stole—"

Agnes cut her off. "Given the shady stuff Martin was into, that's not surprising. But I think it was one of *our* friends who hurt you," she said with a look of intensity Mia hadn't seen before.

Mia followed Agnes into the guesthouse, and inside she saw it was a mess, like a hotel the morning of a checkout. Someone had stayed the night before, and Mia wondered who. On the table was what looked like a sock in a plastic bag, making her truly curious as to what was going on. Agnes told her to ignore it. She went into another room and came back with a brass fire poker. "Hold up your arm like I'm attacking you."

Mia was slow to process.

"Humor me. It's an experiment." Agnes took her by the wrist and straightened her arm, positioning it up. She held the poker against the bruise. Its width was a match. There was a small right-angle cut jutting out from the end of the bruise. It matched the barb on the poker. Even the wrought twisting on the poker had left dark hash marks.

"Please get that away from me," Mia said. Then, when Agnes didn't take it away immediately, Mia yelled, "Why did you come here?!"

Agnes snatched the poker back, alarmed at Mia's outburst. "It's all right."

Mia pitched herself onto the bed, hands over her head. For a second she'd felt the unyielding impact of the strike inside her arm, how it seemed almost as though it had reverberated across the bone.

She struggled to breathe. She felt tears running over her face, fear coming up her throat hard and making her gasp. She felt the kitchen floor beneath her head, the snap of her neck as she fell backward that night. She felt it as certain as the moon is the moon. It wasn't the kitchen island she'd hit. She heard the *clang*. Then another *clang*.

"Help me," she said, still gasping.

"Okay, okay," Agnes said, taking her hand and cradling her in her arms. "I've got you, Mia."

Chapter Fifteen

BAKE OFF

Zoey was starving, and her insides felt like they were vibrating. She opened the fridge and scooped out leftovers from the previous day. She went to grab the teakettle, but her hand stopped when she saw it was dented. *That probably doesn't work anymore,* she thought. She picked it up and shoved it on the top shelf of the baker's rack. She cut bread and cheese and put together hasty sandwiches on a board that she carried into the main space, where everyone was starting to regroup.

Mia sat at the piano bench, though she wasn't playing. She was trembling and holding on to the edges of the fallboard.

"What is it, Mia?" Zoey asked.

"I had a flashback. I have chills."

Zoey startled. She sat down beside Mia, the bench just large enough to accommodate the two of them. "What kind of flashback?"

Mia explained that she didn't hit the counter—she remembered being struck and falling to the floor instead.

All the friends stared.

Just behind them, Agnes was leaning in the doorway between the kitchen and the living room. Ethan and Victor were seated on either end of the couch, and Cameron sat on the floor, looking smaller than he was, with his knees up against his mouth and his arms hooked around his legs.

"Is this our fault?" Zoey asked. "Are we making Mia's memories now because we're treating it like a game?"

"What part of that didn't sound real?" Agnes said, walking closer to them, eyeing if there was enough room on the bench for her.

"It sounds like any movie. Woman alone in kitchen. Someone creeps up from behind . . ."

Victor and Ethan exchanged glances. Victor bobbed his head. "It's not your fault," Victor said to Mia. "But you're approaching things from a different place. We should keep an open mind."

"Exactly. We could be imprinting false memories on her." Zoey turned her gaze toward Stephanie, who was standing by the fireplace. "Stephanie. You're old enough to know about *Michelle Remembers*, the satanic panic."

Zoey's parents had clung to an intense evangelical fear and wild theories throughout her childhood. "Devil worshippers don't live in our neighborhood," her father said, "but everywhere else you go, watch out for them. Evil can live in anyone." It could be the soccer coach, her teacher, or even a Tickle Me Elmo doll.

Victor held his hand up to interject. "At Watchr, we've actually done some research on induced memory. Outside of a power differential—like you get with a parent or doctor or a cop—it's hard to cause fake memories."

Ethan looked concerned. "Why exactly is Watchr doing that?"

"Come on. We don't make our yearly gross on Adam Sandler comedies."

"So you're experimenting on us with Adam Sandler movies?"

Zoey wished Ethan would shut up. She put her arm around Mia. "I want to make sure we're not careless," she said. "The fact of the matter is she dropped the kettle, slipped, and hit her head. That's what the police said. I don't want to work her up anymore. She's our responsibility."

"She is," Steph said. With her eyes she seemed to signal Agnes across the room. Zoey watched as Agnes pivoted left. "And like you I want to make sure that we're all doing our best to protect her. Some of us may have different motives."

Victor asked what she meant, but Agnes had already reappeared. She walked into the room carrying the brass fireplace poker.

"What is that?" Zoey asked, her gaze fastened on the unexpected object that was clearly being displayed to all of them like an artifact.

Agnes went and stood next to Stephanie like the two of them were presenting evidence in front of a jury. "We found this in the guesthouse. Where Ethan slept last night."

"What?" Ethan looked up suddenly, as though he hadn't been paying attention. "I have no idea what you're talking about."

Agnes laid it out: It perfectly matched a bruise on Mia's arm, a defensive wound. She'd been struck from the front, an intense attack that had made her fall backward, where she'd hit her head on the floor. "If the counter got cracked, in fact, that was from a second strike," Agnes argued. "A kill strike that was interrupted."

Most importantly, Agnes reasoned, to be attacked from the front meant it was someone she knew well: she'd let him into the home.

"That's her left arm. She's a lefty." Steph gestured to Mia, who, beside Zoey, still looked like she wanted to sink into herself. "So the person who struck her is right handed. Who here is right handed?"

Slowly, all around the circle, everyone raised their right hands.

"All of you? I would think with a group of writers and artists, there'd be at least one lefty who could get ruled out." Stephanie frowned. "Shit."

"Well, none of us are *successful* writers or artists," Agnes admitted.

Stephanie charged on. "It doesn't matter. I still think you're right that someone arrived here yesterday. Saw this weapon still here. Panicked. And hid it in an out-of-the-way place only someone familiar with the guesthouse would know about."

Agnes crossed her arms. "And I quote, 'We've been invited up here a few more times. Because we're a couple.' Ethan has stayed at that guesthouse before."

Ethan had his hands embedded under his chin, and he was starting to rock back and forth. "This is stupid. Like Victor said earlier, the police will be here soon. Let them handle this."

"Martin killed himself," Zoey declared. She left the piano bench to stand by her boyfriend. "I'm sorry to put it like that, but that's what his overdose was. A cry for help because of overwhelming guilt. If someone hurt Mia, it was probably him."

"Or . . . Ethan could have hidden the poker last night," Agnes said. She whipped a Ziploc out from behind her back. Inside was what looked like a crumpled white gym sock. She held it aloft for the group to see. "He was out there, busy, doing *this*!"

Zoey averted her eyes. She knew what those crusty white socks always contained; she'd gathered up dozens of them over the years without ever complaining, chucking them into the laundry basket, sometimes after she'd tried to initiate with Ethan and he'd rejected her. Her gaze settled on her squirming boyfriend. His expression was a tangle of barely contained anger and confusion. His lips had pushed out, and he was glaring hard at Agnes.

"In their guesthouse?" Zoey asked, looking at Ethan with partner reproach.

Agnes continued. "He practically bragged to me that he cornered Mia and kissed her. Then he did this!" Agnes said.

Mia spoke up. "I wouldn't say he *cornered* me—that's so aggressive, Agnes." But her gaze flitted around the room, as if she were avoiding looking at the sock in the baggie.

Zoey almost involuntarily stepped away from her boyfriend.

"Maybe I did that, but what does it prove?" Ethan asked.

"That you can't stop yourself around Mia," Stephanie said, rapping her hand against the mantel.

Ethan began to stammer. "The last thing we had was jerking off, and now we can't even do that?"

"Oh God," Agnes spat back. "It's about the evidence."

Victor started to protest. "Things are getting out of hand."

Ethan glared at him.

"Oh, sorry. I didn't mean it *that way*," Victor said. "But I think we should just wait for the authorities now. They pick up Martin's body, they take it from here, and we all go home."

"This is bigger than Martin now!" Agnes burst out. "Someone hurt our friend, and I'm going to fucking find out who!"

A transformation was occurring in front of Zoey's eyes. Agnes was saying exactly what she really thought and wanted. It was the blooming of a frightening flower.

Agnes folded her arms across her chest and crossed the room to stand in front of Ethan. "*You* stayed in the guesthouse with the poker—hoping to make sure no one else stayed out there and found it." Her tone was firmer than they'd heard before, and the air felt like it had gone out of the room.

"Zoey and I fought. *That's* why I went out to the guesthouse."

"What happened?" Agnes asked.

"I'd rather not say," Ethan replied. "It's personal."

He looked at Zoey for backup or to issue a warning. As if to say *This isn't looking good for me. Back me up like a publicist spinning a story in a better direction.*

But Zoey knew they weren't wrong. Ethan's feelings for Mia were not close to being gone, and he barely kept them in check. All the other friends had accepted Mia's excuses about her wedding at face value. Three years before, during a phone confrontation, Mia had gone through them all again for Zoey's benefit: *Martin wanted to get married in Italy; it's so expensive, and I couldn't ask everyone to spend so much; Agnes works in publishing and can barely afford Meow Mix for Major Tom.*

But Zoey had iced her with one line. "It was because of Ethan. That's why you couldn't have us there. You still don't trust him, do you?" That movie moment, "Speak now or forever hold your peace . . ." Zoey knew deep down Ethan would be the one to stand and speak.

Mia's silence after the question answered everything. Like all friends, Zoey and Mia had forgiven each other the small transgressions—shoes never returned, book clubs bailed on, the rounding down of a dinner-bill share. But Zoey suspected her relationship with Ethan was a constant reminder that she took a risk on love and Mia never would. Martin was proof of that. Mia had chosen security—not love.

And Ethan, as much as he loved Zoey, couldn't be trusted. That was true too.

The truth was Zoey was tired of defending him. His all-around inconsistency about intimacy and the future was the reason Zoey had to *pay* for product, and now that she knew about him kissing Mia the night before, it was time to look out for herself. She walked back to sit beside Mia on the piano bench.

"There's something else," Zoey said. Ethan's eyes pleaded with her, but she turned her gaze away, connecting instead with Mia, who looked like a lost little girl.

"What is it, Zoey?" Mia whispered.

She spoke directly to Mia: "We weren't home together that night. He was messaging with you. He kept texting that you should meet up and talk about whatever was bothering you. We fought, and then he went out. He didn't come home till after two a.m."

Mia's hand fell onto the piano keys, accidentally making the saddest chord burst through the room.

"I thought you were watching a movie!" Stephanie said. "It's in my notebook, which is still missing."

"I said *Nymphomaniac*. God, everyone should have known. No woman who doesn't hate herself watches a Lars von Trier film," Zoey said.

Agnes cut in. "I liked *Melancholia*."

"Exactly! You've proven my point," Zoey shouted. When she gazed back at Ethan, she saw he was hunched over. He looked broken.

Cameron spoke up. "He placed the AirTag too. Then he followed her."

Victor let out a low whistle, and Zoey watched as suddenly his face turned serious—as if it were a real investigation and not just a group of friends pontificating.

"I don't drive," Ethan said under his breath, his head still down as if he couldn't bear to look at any of them. Zoey felt a small stab of guilt for taking away his alibi.

"And if we looked at your Uber account for that night?" Agnes asked. "Would it show you following Mia out here?"

"You're accusing me of trying to kill Mia!"

At the other end of the couch, Victor stood and moved away from the accused before realizing there was nowhere else to sit and taking a leaning position on the couch arm.

"You know, anyone could have placed that AirTag," Ethan said. "Agnes could have. And Martin and Cameron both saw her every day. Clearly they're having some problems as a family. And let's talk about Victor."

"I don't want to argue with you, Ethan," Mia broke in. "But I have no feelings about Victor being dishonest."

"Let's talk about his wife, who mysteriously died."

All the faces in the room turned toward Victor. Everyone saw the look of discomfort on his face.

"I googled her," Ethan said, as if he were the tech nerd on a network forensics show. "Casey McMurray. Lots about her accomplishments. UCB improv instructor. Writer on *Key & Peele*. Not much about cause of death in her hometown obit."

Victor stared.

Ethan charged on, swiping a hand through his hair distractedly. "Wife Number One dies, and your next girlfriend almost dies?"

Victor's eyes went wide; then his lips formed a grim line, like he was trying to control himself.

"I did *kind of* wonder about the wedding thing?" Zoey said cautiously, letting her voice uptick so it would feel softer, more of a question than the accusation Ethan had hurled. If there were a more likely suspect in the room than her partner, she would gladly entertain the thought and follow that argument.

"Casey's a friend." Victor leaned forward, one hand balled tight and pressed into the other. He gazed around at their faces and stopped at Ethan's. Victor's voice was steady as he corrected himself: "We were friends. Casey and me. She was a writer I knew in LA. She'd lost her health coverage when she was diagnosed with ovarian cancer. I offered to marry her so my plan could cover her treatment as fast as possible. We were never a couple. But when she died, it hit me harder than I thought. That's when I reached out to Mia. I needed to talk to someone."

Zoey blinked back tears. The embarrassment stung, and she wished she'd let Ethan pursue the line of questioning on his own.

"That's the sweetest thing I've ever heard," Stephanie said, setting down the phone she'd been making notes on.

"I think I was bi again there for a minute," Agnes said under her breath.

Ethan held up his hands, palms out. "Victor is perfect. I'm an asshole. But I didn't follow Mia."

"Ethan's right to question everyone," Steph said. "I wish I could check the timelines."

"I have the notebook," Cameron said.

"You took my notebook?" Stephanie peered at him, surprised by his admission.

"You were gathering evidence against my dad! I mean, he was an asshole, but he didn't do this. I was with him."

"Cameron, can you bring my notebook back?" Stephanie asked with politeness that belied motherly anger. He launched out of the room. They heard his footsteps running down to the basement.

After he left, Ethan sat up and struck a finger through the air. "Wait! Wait! Let's look at Little American Psycho here. It was his drugs in the car. And if anyone is to benefit from both Martin and Mia dying, it would be him."

No one said anything. Ethan had managed to still the room, with all looking at him, impressed.

"But . . . ," Victor slowly interjected. "I get the sense there's not a lot of real money left in Martin's bank account. Indictment and all."

"The house?" Ethan said hopefully.

Cameron came back to the room. "It belongs to my mom's family. Her grandfather bought it to have a place for his affair with Lee Radziwill."

Zoey looked around at the house in a new light. *Wow,* she thought. *Jackie O's sister getting her strange here.*

"So we're back to accusing *me,*" Ethan said, looking at the floor.

Zoey knew that look from Ethan. He looked again like he might cry. There was a red spidery blood vessel inside one of his nostrils that always seemed to show more vividly when he was upset. She wasn't sure if it was because his skin went pale or if his nostrils flared in those moments. But she stared at it now, even a few paces away, and thought of all the other times she'd stared at it. She'd never pointed it out to him; this oddly intimate detail was hers only.

"All I did was come clean about where you were that night," she said, still staring at the blood vessel. Why did she love all the little weird things about him? The quirks. He was cute once, but now seemed like an actor who was too old for the role he was cast in. "We shouldn't lie about something so important. Like you said when you got here, we all love Mia. And we have to do what's best for her."

"Okay, fine—let's be democratic, then." Ethan grabbed a tissue and wiped his eyes up under his glasses. He launched himself to his feet to pace the room.

Zoey watched as Agnes set the Ziploc sock down on the mantel and tightened her grip on the poker.

"This is the only way to get everyone's feelings out in the open." Ethan snapped his fingers. "Paper, pens. Ballots all around. We're going to vote: Who do we think is guilty?"

It was the first good idea Ethan had come up with in months. Zoey always suspected that they weren't individuals. They were The Group and always had been, no matter where they went in the world, making one decision for all: *Where will we eat tonight? Who will we allow into our circle? Who tried to kill Mia?*

Ethan had realized that only consensus could save him or damn him.

"I'll find paper," Zoey offered.

"Know this: I've never been to Connecticut without Zoey. I don't know what an AirTag looks like. I don't even know how my iCloud works. It keeps filling up. Zoey, tell them!"

Zoey said nothing.

—⸜—

As they were all people with more technology than they needed, the group set up a makeshift election center. Agnes typed names onto a laptop that was connected to the giant flat screen on the wall above the fireplace. Zoey played the part of John King and shuffled the note sheets around inside the FACTS cap.

"Are we sure about paper ballots?" Stephanie asked. "Election integrity and all."

Zoey ignored her and began pulling them out and reading them aloud to the group before placing them on the piano top.

"One for Ethan."

Ethan bolted up. "Stephanie's right. Let's restart."

Zoey watched his name appear on the screen, then dipped her hand into the hat again. She unfolded the ballot. "One for Martin."

"We're still looking at him?" Agnes expressed dubiousness.

"It's democracy," Stephanie said. "Every vote matters. Everyone has a reason for what they wrote."

Zoey looked around but couldn't read the expressions enough to guess whose vote was whose. Agnes typed it onto the screen. Zoey dipped her hand in again.

"I don't think we should debate the votes as they come up," Victor said. "We should let the votes speak for themselves."

"Victor," Zoey read.

"Okay. Who the fuck did that?" Victor asked, his tone now changing.

Zoey turned the page so he could see it. Victor looked surprised. She knew who had written this ballot, and she set the note down on the piano and pulled at her lip. Agnes's typing was flawless and fast. Zoey drew another ballot. "Oh, interesting. 'Not Martin.'"

"Does that count?" Ethan asked. "In a real election that would be a spoiled ballot. Like I couldn't say *Not Trump* or *Not Biden* and expect for it to be valid."

"Pro tip. This isn't an election you want to win," Zoey whispered. "Don't argue with ballots that don't have your name on them."

"Can we just—?" Steph sighed and rolled her hand in a forward motion.

Zoey pulled another folded piece of notepaper. "Ethan," she said.

Agnes marked it down. "That's two for Ethan."

There were only two ballots left. Zoey had no idea how the vote would lean. Who would Mia herself write? She hadn't noticed any that had her delicate lettering on them and hadn't been able to tell from her expressions as the names were called what she was thinking. Choosing the paper that was on the right side of the hat, Zoey opened it and stared.

"Wilson," she said, and handed it to Agnes for verification.

"Who's Wilson?" Agnes asked.

Around the circle: blank faces, heads shaking slightly.

Stephanie looked at Mia. "Does this have to do with the stolen photo?"

"Yes," Mia proclaimed. "A British man named Wilson stole my photo from the stairway. He was stalking me. It was during a party."

Around the room their expressions were all searching. Then Victor sprang up and went to the laptop. On a tab he opened IMDB and under Search typed *Wilson*.

"Wilson from *Home Improvement*?" Ethan asked.

Victor shook his head in annoyance. "I don't think Mia is wrong. But we do have to translate her."

When nothing came up, Victor added *Soderbergh*, which brought up Terence Stamp's page. "*The Limey*. 1999. Knew it. He steals a photo of his daughter from the home of a murderous record producer. You also probably know him as . . ."

"General Zod!" Zoey shouted like it was charades.

"It could still mean something," Victor said.

Cameron walked to the edge of the room and looked up the stairs toward the empty frame. "That picture? That's where we had a photo of me and Mom in the birthing tub. My dad took it down anytime he got a letter from her lawyer."

Mia's expression wavered, her eyebrows twitching upward like two exclamation points. "Maybe I didn't want it to be anyone here."

Zoey wasn't surprised. Mia was a peacemaker, a comforter, and although she sometimes demanded to be the star and a storyteller, a strong current could pull her. "Let's finish the vote," she said. "Should we have music?"

Mia didn't play a song, just a musical flourish, running her fingers over the keys and ending on a trembling bass hand.

Zoey drew the last ballot. Before opening it, she glanced around at the group. Then she opened it and let it fall onto the baby grand with the others. Mia, Agnes, and Stephanie were all close enough they could see what it said.

"Ethan," Agnes read aloud, and typed it in. "Three for Ethan, one for Victor, one for Martin, one for Not Martin. Do those two cancel each other out?"

"This is election fraud," Ethan said. "This is an embarrassment to democracy."

"You suggested we vote," Agnes said.

"Let's talk Martin," Steph said. "He would know where to hide something in his own house."

Agnes added, "It wouldn't be hard for him to walk right in, and he had motive if he was angry about what Mia might say to the investigators. He could also be angry about her having—" She glanced at Victor.

"You're not wrong," Victor said. "Him dying doesn't rule him out."

"But I was with him that night. I saw him get drunk on the couch fifty miles away in Brooklyn," Cameron said.

He was clearly the Not Martin ballot.

"No one's after you on this, Cameron. Anyone would cover for a parent," Victor said. "I mean, I might. Would you?"

Victor nodded at Agnes, who then surprised him by saying, "Catch me on the right day, and I'd turn my mother in for a Snickers bar."

Cameron protested and said he wasn't lying.

"Don't you see? Victor is the obvious choice," Ethan said. "It's always the husband or the boyfriend. He stayed an extra night. That's opportunity."

"But not motive," Agnes said.

Thank you, Victor mouthed across the room.

Stephanie added, "You also had opportunity, Ethan. You were missing for hours that night. Zoey said that."

"I was at Brooklyn Bridge Park, thinking about my relationship."

"Your relationship *with who*?" Zoey yelled as she stood, as if the words propelled her up.

"Wait a minute. I voted for Victor. He voted for Martin. Mia and Cameron basically didn't vote. Stephanie and Agnes, well, that's obvious. But you—*you* voted for me, Zoey?"

Agnes picked up one of the three ballots with Ethan's name on it. "It's her handwriting. She voted for you."

Zoey had always loathed when Agnes snapped into hall monitor mode.

"I can't believe this." Ethan was beside himself.

Zoey cocked her head. "I saw you walking near Agnes's the last time Mia, Agnes, and I all had tea there. After I left, I remember thinking, *What is he doing in this neighborhood?* Maybe you could have placed the tracking device then."

Cameron leaped up. "It *was* after that I found it!"

Ethan stared at Zoey, his eyes pleading for support. Zoey said nothing. They both knew it was the end of the Ethan Sharp presidency.

———◦———

Zoey couldn't face any of them. Victor huddled with Cameron, Agnes, and Mia over in the dining room, deciding what to do. Sitting at the piano, Zoey could think of nothing to say to Ethan, so she played a verse of the hymn "Abide with Me," which was the only song she could recall from childhood lessons.

"This isn't a funeral," Ethan growled from the couch, and she stopped, and they sat in a horrid silence.

Then she overheard Victor say "How are the raccoons your fault?!" to Agnes.

After what seemed like forever, Agnes made the announcement.

"Until the police are here, we would be more comfortable if Ethan was safe somewhere."

"What do you mean 'safe'?" Ethan snapped.

"We decided as a community that it's up to us to keep everyone safe. Including you," Agnes said, her palms upturned in a gesture of openness. "So we'd like to lock you in the guesthouse."

"Locking me in the guesthouse of a six-million-dollar Connecticut estate is not restorative justice!" With that, Ethan kicked the ottoman out of the way and threw himself down on the ground like a child in a tantrum. "I'm not going anywhere. You're going to have to carry me."

There were no words for the shame Zoey felt at the sight of this. She had been living with this man-child for years, and she ought to have left already. But it was always the second thought that had made her stay: Who would take care of him?

Victor looked at her. He shrugged. "Do we pick him up?"

Cameron crossed the room and looked over at Ethan on the floor. "He's pretty thin."

Zoey knew Ethan was beyond reasoning with at this point. Out the window, a flash of movement caught her eye. Two white vans were pulling up to the house, silent as sharks. She ran over and peered out: people were now standing on the parking pad near the garage.

She turned back to the group, who were gathering around Ethan. He was still throwing a fit on the ground. "We have visitors," she said.

"Finally!" Victor shouted. "The police."

Chapter Sixteen

BLUE PLATE SPECIAL

Agnes felt a bolt of adrenaline course through her body as she ran outside to intercept the white vans. *Strange,* Agnes thought. *Wouldn't they send cruisers, or maybe an ambulance?* Was it the Feds? The IRS for Martin? In the minute it took to run outside, Agnes struggled to workshop her explanation: *We can explain it all. We were holding a remembering party. No, it's not like a funeral. Then we discovered a crime we had to solve. No, not to do with this body, ironically enough. Oh, its condition? Well, you see, raccoons are opportunistic omnivores. Much like my friends. You're right, officer—I know it's not funny, but do you know that Beckett quote "Nothing is funnier than unhappiness"? Of course, why would you? But it has been kind of the theme of the entire weekend.*

She expected bulletproof vests and lanyards, but once outside Agnes saw only a woman in khakis, a navy V-neck sweater, and deck shoes. She was bent down looking for a latch or release for the garage door when Agnes came within sight.

"Hey!" Agnes yelled. "No."

The woman stood up, both indignant and terrified. She must have triggered a sensor, because the garage door began to lift. "The schedule said garage load-in was okay."

Agnes looked up for a button or cord, something she could grab to stop it. She couldn't find it, and the door slowly rolled upward, exposing the Tesla, though it was parked far back in a big space. She glanced at the other employees, who were dressed the same as the woman. It was a uniform meant to look like a nonuniform. They all wore deck shoes and khakis. "Unload what?"

The door had opened on the second van, and inside Agnes could see four more khaki-clad servers and a rack of silver trays covered in tinfoil. On the door was a whimsical logo, a black square with a red scrolling banner: BON APPÉTIT FOR DESTRUCTION.

"We're the caterers. You weren't expecting us?"

Agnes homed in on the caterer's face. She had a large smile and wide hazel eyes. She sported an undercut. An undercut only ever meant one thing. Agnes stepped nervously around, trying to block the opening of the garage with her suddenly very small-seeming body. *Don't flirt with the woman discovering the dead body,* Agnes told herself.

"Is that Mr. Kroner? We need him to sign for this."

The caterer had already seen him.

"Mr. Kroner isn't going to be able to sign for anything." Agnes pointed at the clipboard that one of the guys standing on the parking pad was holding. He then handed it to her to sign.

"Look, we can pull around back if that makes you more comfortable. As long as we can get kitchen access from there?" the lead caterer asked.

Agnes was looking over their instruction sheet as Stephanie and Victor arrived to investigate as well. It appeared Martin had hired the caterers before he died. Appetizers included potato blini with caviar and sour cream, melon and prosciutto, and stuffed cherry tomatoes. Mains were grilled New York strip steak, barbecued tamarind swordfish skewers, risotto with peas and onions, and a vegetable stew with fennel, and for dessert, praline cheesecake or chocolate mousse. Agnes had not eaten all day and felt a rush of primal affection for Martin.

"I'm Lise." The caterer introduced herself while she and another team member tugged a long plastic folding table from the van and then headed with it past the Tesla and out the back door of the garage to the yard.

"It's a catering company," Agnes told Victor. "Courtesy of Martin."

"Connecticut: where the caterers show up before the police," he said. "Did she even blink at that body?"

"Not even." Agnes shook her head. "Maybe they've seen it all out here?"

Lise, the team leader of the catering crew, came back and took out a binder from the cab of the van. She withdrew an envelope and coyly handed it to Agnes with a wink. "Don't worry. We don't ever touch or move the body. We're professionals." Agnes thought she was talking with the most hardened caterer in the world before Lise whispered, "This isn't the first murder-mystery weekend we've catered. Last month we did one for a film producer up in New Milford—he had a full F/X crew, blood everywhere, and real actors playing the bodies. I think Topher Grace was one of them. But he wouldn't confirm it when I asked him."

"Right." Agnes began playing along. "And tonight we find out who the murderer is."

Lise smiled. "Maybe you'll tell me who did it later." She then moved off to direct the catering team, one of whom was carrying a large water boiler into the house through the side door.

"Did you just—?" Victor asked.

"Avoid telling the truth in favor of a flirt? I think so. I don't know what happened there," Agnes said.

She unfolded the flap of the envelope and pulled out a sheet of paper. "Dear Mia, by now my body will have been found and taken away." Agnes paused and breathed guiltily before continuing. "I probably ruined your weekend with your friends. I know they'll be there for you, more than I ever was or could be. This dinner is on me. Enjoy life. Martin."

"That settles it." Victor took the page from Agnes. "He knew what he was going to do before he did it."

"Only Martin would deliver his suicide note with the caterers," Agnes said.

Victor updated Agnes that he and Cameron had only had to carry Ethan a few feet before Zoey had screamed at him to get the hell up and walk like an adult. Zoey was out there watching him. Agnes felt a twinge of distrust at the idea of Zoey talking with Ethan. She'd lied for a whole day about where he was that night before snitching on him. But then again, Agnes had always thought that her friends put up with too much indifference and thoughtlessness from men. From Agnes's perspective, Zoey breaking away from Ethan was the healthiest thing she'd done in years.

In the kitchen Agnes sipped a beer she'd snagged from one of the ice-filled buckets that Lise's team had put out. She watched the caterers set up the water boiler on the marble island.

"I thought you were setting up outside?" she asked a male server, who gave her a confused glance.

"Have you seen the sky? Weather's turning," he said.

They first tried to fit the cistern on the back counter, but it was too tall given the cupboards overhead. Once full, the silver tower was heavy, and she watched as the caterer awkwardly transported it.

Agnes walked up to it and flicked her fingernail against its side. The cistern made a surprisingly resonant sound. She remembered Zoey had mentioned something about a kettle the night of the accident, that Mia had dropped it? Agnes's gaze flicked around the kitchen and settled on the silver kettle on top of the baker's rack. It was a strange place to put something she would regularly use. Agnes set her beer down, went over, and reached for it, but it was too high.

"If you want to wait, this'll be hot in about thirty minutes," a caterer told her.

"Sure, but can you reach that?"

The caterer turned from the island and came over. He pulled it down for her, dropping the empty dented kettle into her hands. Agnes was a coffee drinker, where Mia had loved all kinds of teas—one of those women with a preference for fragile cups and loose-leaf, ornamental pots. Even when they'd been students and couldn't spare the cupboard space. But Agnes didn't remember Martin saying anything about tea or kettles when he talked about the accident.

Steph's notebook was on the mantel, where everything had been set down in a rush after the vote. She assumed Victor and Stephanie were somewhere with Mia, updating her on Martin's note, but she couldn't hear anyone in the house. Agnes looked out the window. Lise the caterer was outside, still directing servers with trays and tables. Flipping through the book quickly, Agnes found nothing about a kettle, just the words *water on floor* and, under Martin's name, *hit head on island*—something they now knew was false because of Mia's recollection.

Agnes heard something like glass smashing from upstairs.

She dropped the notebook and bolted toward the stairway, scared for Mia. At the bottom of the stairs, she collided with Zoey, also on her way up, a silk blouse clutched in her hands. Agnes's hands wrapped around her friend's elbows. She was cold, and her skin was goose pimpled.

Zoey breathed hard. "Oh good, I wanted to ask you if we're dressing up for dinner tonight. Seems a bit weird now?"

"The police are coming for your boyfriend. So no." Agnes glanced up the stairs. "What was all that noise?"

"Just the house rattling. I think a storm's picking up."

Agnes saw the blouse that Zoey was carrying was a cobalt blue.

"Did you call the police?"

"Why do you think I didn't?"

"Is there something you want to tell me, Zoey?"

Zoey shook her head. As they left the stairway and moved into the downstairs hall, Zoey's face seemed to break. "I think if you're still the kind of person who drops her cell phone and breaks it, no way should you think you can care for another human."

"What are you talking about?" Agnes asked.

Zoey was prattling on. "I'm having second thoughts: the sperm, the cryotank. I'm supposed to do it tonight. But . . . now I don't know if I would make a good mom. I don't think I'm a good person. Lately it's all mood swings. Angry, sad. I haven't had an orgasm in a year." Zoey led her back through the house to the kitchen.

"Those fertility meds are kind of scary," Agnes said. "But how did you know Mia was making tea that night?"

Zoey moved away from Agnes. "Martin told me. That time I went to visit her at the hospital, he was on his way out."

Agnes watched as Zoey moved toward the back door.

"I should check on Ethan," Zoey said as she left. "Even if he did something horrible, I care about him still."

"Do you want me to take that?" Agnes pointed to the blue shirt, which was still clutched in Zoey's right hand. "It's Mia's. I can put it back."

Zoey looked down at it as if she'd forgotten she was holding it. "Oh yeah. I don't need it anymore."

The label on the blouse said *Dior*, just like Agnes had known it would.

Agnes had been with Mia when she'd bought the garment. Mia had met her after work for a drink, and instead they'd wound up walking and window-shopping in Soho, eventually stopping at Dior. Mia had looked at everything, and Agnes had tried not to, knowing she couldn't afford a place that had no price tags, even in her wildest fantasies. When Mia had come out of the dressing room, Agnes could see the blouse was like a dream on her; she was suddenly a blue butterfly flashing past. Mia had pivoted in front of the mirrors, wrinkling her brow and asking should she? Was it really right for her?

"Yes," Agnes had said, unequivocally. She'd been floored by her own words, because it had cost almost as much as Agnes paid in rent on her apartment. Yet she'd known Mia should buy it—she could afford it, and the item was perfectly suited to her.

"I don't even know when I'll wear it," Mia had said, after changing back into her street clothes. She'd stood cradling the shirt, debating.

"Let's crash a party tonight," Agnes had said jokingly. "And you can return the blouse tomorrow."

Agnes had expected a laugh out of Mia, but instead her friend's gaze had looked sad and distant, as if Agnes had mentioned a favorite dive long since torn down and condo'd up. "I'm going to buy this blouse," Mia had said. "So I don't forget those days." Then she'd hugged Agnes in the way that someone does when they're going away for a long time.

Agnes knew there was no way Mia would have given that blouse to Zoey.

———◄┼———

Victor was lounging in the Eames chair in the sunroom, a small room off the hall between the guest rooms, facing the back of the property. A plate of hors d'oeuvres was spilling its crackers onto his lap. He'd fallen asleep holding it.

Out the three windows, evening was coming early, with dark clouds touching the edge of the sky. Inside they were surrounded by potted geraniums and pansies.

"Victor," Agnes said. When he didn't answer, she nudged his shoulder. "Hey."

He startled awake, sat up, and put his plate on the side table.

"That red-eye caught up to me," he said, blinking.

Victor saw what Agnes was holding, and he sat up straighter. His hand seemed to reach involuntarily for the blouse hem, but he stopped.

"You recognize it?"

His expression told her he did, even before he said it. "It's Mia's."

"Zoey was trying to hide this. When did you last see Mia wearing it?" Agnes asked.

Victor popped open the camera app on his phone and flipped through some images. He showed Agnes a photo: Mia with her back to the camera, the blouse draped off her shoulders—a shade like the darkening blue sky of evening. "Was that the day of her accident?"

Victor nodded, and Agnes could see in his eyes that he realized as well that sometime between that moment in the photo and when Mia was found on the country road, she and Zoey must have met.

"Did we pick the wrong person?" he asked, looking out at the guesthouse.

"Or maybe people?" Agnes had one more party to crash to find out.

Victor squinted again at the guesthouse outside. "Wait, we put a padlock on the door."

Agnes followed his gaze. The guesthouse was just as it had been that morning when Ethan had come out of it and they'd walked around the grounds. But the door was swinging open and closed as the wind picked up.

"No one's found Mia yet," Agnes said, her voice wavering.

"I'll check the front. You take the back," he said, springing up.

⸻

Outside, Agnes checked the guesthouse, but no one was there. In the backyard and into the edge of the woods, she saw nothing.

As Agnes raced around the side of the garage, she nearly crashed into Lise, who was rolling a cart against the wind. The first drops of a cold slanting rain hit them.

"You guys go hard," Lise said with an approving thumbs-up. "The new body out front. Nice twist."

Agnes felt her mouth go dry, and she couldn't respond. She dodged around Lise, but the caterer stopped her with a touch on her back. "I found this out in the garage."

Agnes's hand closed around the rose-gold cell phone. "Thanks," she said without thinking too much about what was in her palm. She caught up to Victor at the house corner by the vans. He looked frightened.

"Mia!" Agnes shouted as she saw a body on the ground, wrapped in a torn white curtain. One of the feet still wore a Blundstone boot, the other shoeless, showing her striped sock.

"It's Stephanie," Victor said. "Looks like she fell out of that french window on the second floor."

"She's dead?"

"She's breathing. Normally I'd say don't move her, but with this storm coming, we'd better carry her in until we can get an ambulance."

Agnes felt her heart hammering in her chest and blood surging, ringing in her ears as she and Victor lifted up the top half of Stephanie and carefully tugged her toward the house, her feet dragging.

After they got her in and lay her on the sofa, Agnes peeked out the back door. Her head whipped around as she surveyed the landscape. But there was no one. The trees waved wildly as the wind blasted rain into her face. Everyone had disappeared: Mia, Ethan, Cameron, Zoey. The storm was upon them.

Chapter Seventeen

Swag Bag

Mia realized her mules weren't cut out for the terrain as she hopped over knotty roots and nearly lost one shoe. Ethan trotted after her. They were both focused on getting away from the house and the others, but the deeper they went into the woods, the more apprehensive Mia became about her decision. The sky was beginning to crease into dark welts of clouds.

She looked around for someplace to sit. Twenty more yards down the seldom-trod path, a fallen tree provided a resting place.

Ethan, also out of breath, sat beside her. He didn't sound as grateful as she would've expected—more guarded, inquisitive. "Why did you let me out?"

"What they said felt wrong," Mia told him.

"You remembered something? Something else?"

"It's not that I remembered. It's that I know how I felt when I saw you. You didn't hurt me that night."

"Thank you. You can trust me." Ethan reached out to take her hand, but when she didn't immediately grasp it, he changed the movement up and pulled a small new leaf off a skinny tree. He uncurled it with his fingers. "When we were texting the night of your accident, you said it was because I'm so good at inconsistencies. Because of *Movie Fail*, you knew that I spot the plot holes, and you thought I would see the gaps in what Martin was telling you about his business." Ethan looked at the tiny leaf, then dropped it on the ground. "You didn't tell me about the subpoena, just that you thought he was a fraud and liar with debts, and you were thinking of leaving."

"That makes sense." Mia brushed her hair out of her face and glanced at the clouds overhead. She thought she could hear the deep sigh of drops starting to fall. She had a chill suddenly. What if she shouldn't have trusted Ethan after all? "We better go."

"We go start our new lives now, right? I think that's how this works."

Mia bit her lip. "I already did that out here. I don't think it turned out too well."

Ethan moved to sit beside her, persisting. She didn't fear him, she realized, but why did he always have to persist?

"We have to go back. Confront them," Ethan said, his voice rising, strident. "Agnes is the one you should be worried about. If someone put an AirTag on your car, it was Agnes."

"No, don't go there. She's always been there for me. That I do know."

"And she's always been as in love with you."

Beside her, Mia felt Ethan stiffen, and she knew it was the first time he'd ever said it out loud—that he was in love with her—even if he hadn't said it directly. That little word, *as*, implying that, like Agnes, he was too.

Mia suddenly had a flash of what it had been like to be with him. It had happened in junior year several times. She remembered he had been good at some of it, how cradled and special he had made her feel. *Maybe it could be real,* she'd thought. "Woman," he'd said, breathing in her ear, sexily experimenting with a word none of them felt old enough to deserve yet. Their two faces close on a pillow. But she hadn't known how to be with him if they weren't just alone in her room. The world seemed to rush at him. She recalled the shape Ethan had made one night on her and Agnes's couch, immobile, curled like a child. He didn't want to go out with them but also refused to go home. She hadn't been able to properly care for him, she'd realized. His mental health was like a spider's web, immaculately built, a routine of thin wires. It was too easy to smash it down just by moving around. Maybe she'd been too selfish, or just too immature still. They'd only been twenty-one; kids, really. Perhaps these were skills they'd never been taught that they still had to learn.

"We got close making your student films, didn't we? That's why you brought them?" Mia asked, reaching down and rubbing her calf muscle. She was surprised at how she ached, but she supposed she'd already walked a mile or two with Victor that morning after lying in a bed for weeks.

Ethan inhaled a long breath through his nostrils. "You know, Agnes could have easily erased them last night."

"Why not your wife?" Mia said. "She kept going into the living room to change the music when your knapsack was there and we were in the kitchen."

"Partner. Zoey swore she'd never get married after—" Ethan stopped.

"After what?"

He sighed and gave Zoey up. "After your wedding. There were definitely some prescriptions filled after that event."

Mia raised an eyebrow. She could tell he wanted to lead her back to the topic of Agnes. Another friend with a theory to push.

As she looked down at the mulch underfoot, she had a recollection of Cary Elwes and Robin Wright in the Fire Swamp. She suddenly recalled Agnes phoning her late at night. She felt her brow furrowing, and Ethan asked her what it was.

"I remember I told Agnes I just wanted to put pajamas on . . . and watch a movie? Could that be something from the night of?"

Before Ethan could answer, Mia remembered her phone call with Agnes, standing on her patio that March night, the phone warm against her ear.

"Why were you texting about Gatsby?" Agnes had said. "That was years ago."

"I don't know what's happening. I feel like I fail everyone all the time. I'm usually the glue, and right now I don't know how to be."

"Do you want to talk about it?"

"Honestly, no. I just want to curl up on the couch."

"As you wish," Agnes had said.

"We never got to see that together, did we?"

"You want me to come out? Watch some *PB*?"

There had been a long pause as Mia had considered. "No, I'm okay. I don't want to make you do that."

Ethan waved his hand in front of Mia, as if to summon her back. "I think Agnes wanted more than a movie from you," he said, circling back to his pet subject.

"Did we—did we have a threesome, you and Agnes and me?" Mia asked.

Ethan's eyes stopped moving, like a fish.

"In Mexico. And that's why you two don't get along anymore."

"I've never been to Mexico," he said. "I don't believe in tourism."

"We were looking for a beach . . . Heaven's Mouth?"

Ethan laughed, relieved. "That's a different movie. *Y Tu Mamá También*. You did like Gael García Bernal—I remember that now."

"But you and I . . . in my room?"

"Yes, that part's real." He turned suddenly serious. "Agnes and I did play Spin the Bottle with you one New Year's Eve. It definitely *wasn't* a threesome, though. We weren't that cool."

"I'm reasonably sure I loved you, Ethan. In that moment. I have to believe that I did. But there's a delusion involved that we can be friends."

He reared back. "What do you mean?"

"It's different with men and women. The problem is it's always on us to call it off. With a woman, she hears you before you speak. Women are always listening, always watching. They read you in a way where you don't have to ask."

Ethan looked angry for a moment. He had an intensity to him that made it easy to see why the others had turned on him.

"You think Agnes sees you and hears you better than I do?" His tone was indignant. "You're a human *Leonard Maltin's Movie Guide.* Try to remember the plot to *Misery.* She's your number one fan, and that's what she wants to do to you."

Mia shook her head. "She knows when to give distance. With you, I have to say no three times before you hear it once."

Ethan stood up and began pacing. He was agitated. Mia knew what she said was true even if her memories were still isolated moments, more like framed photographs of a hand or mouth than the whole scene. The Ethans of the world were relatively harmless until they yelled at you for not loving them the way they loved you. She couldn't say whether he'd actually done that, but there was a possessiveness in his every action, from the kiss in the kitchen to the fact that he'd had to say he loved her now, so many years later, when he ought to have been focused on his own relationship.

"What are you saying to me?" There was a pained tone in his voice.

The rain was beginning to come down now, through the branches.

Mia stood up. "She understands no is not some death sentence. It's not no to you as a human being. It's just no to *that.*"

Ethan stopped pacing. "Why have you never told me this before?"

"The old Mia was afraid."

"No, I didn't see that." He shook his head. "I didn't know. I'm sorry."

The wind picked up, and all the trees seemed to bend at once. "We'd better go back," Mia said.

"I think it's this way." Ethan walked farther into the woods, picking his way around brambly trees that were leaning hard in the wind.

She ran to catch up to him just as the rain began slanting harder through the mostly still-bare branches. They weren't far enough into spring for the trees to offer much coverage.

"This way." She tugged his arm. Mia led him farther along the path, then looked to the right.

Sitting above the branches was the tree house: a small white house on stilts, real glass in the windows, tiny navy-blue shutters and door, a deck with a railing, a staircase in the front and spiderweb rope up the back. An old tree went up through the middle of it, but that seemed almost an afterthought to the structure. It was large enough to be another guesthouse, even though it was a small-scale replica of the main house, a renovated colonial in the details, down to its turret.

"This is Cameron's tree house? Must have been a hell of a divorce."

"Forty thousand dollars," Mia said. "I remember Martin complaining that Cameron had stopped using it." She didn't know where the fact had come from. Things were coming back.

They hurriedly climbed the stairs and tried the door. It was locked. The rain was driving harder now, and lightning split the sky in a bright yellow streak that was too large and close.

"Fuck it," Ethan said, reaching up to grab a small branch. He twisted it until it snapped off the tree, then used it to bash one of the windowpanes. He broke out the glass entirely, then reached in and unlocked the door. He gestured gallantly for her to go first.

Mia rushed in, and he followed.

Inside, there was a teak bench and two wooden chairs with cushions. There were small brass oil lamps on end tables. It may have been a boy's clubhouse, but it had been designed by adults. The only clues a boy had once spent time there were a jackknife and Magic 8 Ball on the table and a crate of comic books under the bed. Mia pulled a wool blanket from the set of bunk beds and wrapped herself in it. The backyard, the pool, the tree house—these were things the city-dwelling Mia Sinclair had never had. She thought about how intoxicating the normality of it all must have been for her. Martin had charmed her not with his intellect or kindness but with real estate and a stability he'd never actually had.

She tossed the other blanket to Ethan, who rubbed his face and hair with it before wrapping it around his shoulders. Ethan opened one cupboard, then gave up. "Anything to eat or drink?" he asked. "Or do the one percent not prepare for end-times?"

"It's all they think about."

Mia imagined the others must have noticed their absence by now and were probably worried. She went to a cupboard under the replica mini-island. She threw the cupboard door open. The space where she expected to see a bag of Snyder's pretzels so old it had turned to dust or a beer can crushed into a bong was instead filled with an Under Armour duffel bag.

Mia started to lift it out but immediately dropped it to the floor. It was at least ten pounds. She knelt and tugged the zipper back slowly.

Stacks of hundred-dollar bills were rubber-banded together inside, and beside them, the matte-black handle of a gun.

Chapter Eighteen

Spilling Tea

Zoey still hadn't found her phone and, in the darkness, had to feel her way up from the basement by touch—banister, wall, carpet turning to the blackwood flooring—dragging her roller case behind her. There had been power dims with every thunderclap for the last half hour, but after one that seemed to hit the house directly, the power went off.

In the living room her eyes were just adjusting to the dark when she ran into Victor, his concerned face lit by a phone screen. Rain heaved against the living room windows.

"Stephanie's hurt. Have you seen Mia?" he asked. "I'm worried something's happened to her . . ."

In the semidark she could see Stephanie, prone, on the couch, not moving.

"I'm not responsible for Ethan!" Zoey snapped. She was out of the Ethan business and wanted to announce it to the world in any way possible short of a press release.

"I get that," Victor said in his calmest voice. He looked at the roller case beside Zoey. "But no one should be leaving in the middle of this," he said in a way meant to sound sensible, but Zoey caught the other meaning. *This* wasn't over yet.

They made their way into the kitchen to look for flashlights. The caterers had left the Sternos lit under the food trays, and the room flickered with a church-like glow. Everything had been packed up, brought in, and rearranged the minute the first bit of wind had gusted.

With the light from the burners going, Victor turned his phone flashlight off. "I think someone stole my phone," Zoey said. If she could find it, she would call an Uber. "It could have been Ethan. We should really call the police again. It's not safe with him around."

A large lightning bolt illuminated the whole kitchen with a white-blue flash. A thunderclap followed a few seconds later. "Is there someone outside?" Victor asked, peering out the rain-blurred window.

"Maybe the caterers forgot something." Zoey gripped the handle on her suitcase and wished she could leave.

The door opened, but all they could see was a man holding up something. Then Zoey heard Ethan's voice. "Glad you're here. This is all going to get a lot more interesting."

"He's got a gun!" Victor yelled.

Zoey dove onto the hard stone floor. She knew she'd pushed too far by allowing Ethan to be locked in the guesthouse, like an Airbnb Count of Monte Cristo. She covered her head with her hands.

Ethan stepped into the orange light, waving the gun. Mia was right behind him. Both looked like wet dogs. "No! It's okay," Ethan pleaded. "I don't want to use it!"

"That's comforting," Victor snapped.

"Stop waving it around, then!" Zoey shouted from her crouch behind the kitchen island.

Ethan put the gun down on the counter near the cracked corner. He had a shoulder bag as well that he set down. Victor grabbed Mia and asked if she was okay.

"It's okay. I let him out," Mia confessed.

"Why did you do that?" Victor asked politely but loudly.

Cameron ran into the kitchen. "Are you okay, Zoey?"

She felt a flush of embarrassment and hoped no one would notice in the dim light, but Mia and Victor both raised eyebrows over the teenager's concern.

The small group gathered around the gun on the kitchen island, looking at an object none of them had ever held. Mia wiped a tea towel over her face and hair while Ethan unzipped the gym bag with a dramatic flourish. "We found the gun hidden out there with this. It's at least two hundred thousand dollars in cash. And there was this." Ethan held up a burgundy-red booklet and flicked its pages. "Lithuanian passport. Martin's picture is in it, but the name is Mykolas Galvanauskas. That's probably his real name."

Zoey rolled her eyes. "No. It's fake. This is his go bag."

She could feel the pull of her roller case behind her—she could just leave, she told herself—but the go bag was too alluring, and she stepped forward with the others.

"Yes, a go bag." Ethan removed his glasses and wiped the rain off them using his T-shirt. "That means he had different plans. He meant to leave, but something stopped him."

"Or someone," Mia added.

Agnes stepped into the kitchen from the darkness. "Oh, we're not going back to that theory, are we?" she said like a bored hostess.

She was now wearing the blue blouse and moved in it with a confidence, almost as if she had become Mia. Agnes slowly walked around the room, looking at each and every one of them. She stopped in front of Zoey and lingered for a minute, their bodies almost touching. Zoey looked her in the eyes and gave her nothing. Agnes stepped over to the sink.

"It's teatime, Zoey." Agnes reached up and took the dented kettle down. It was on a lower shelf than where Zoey had left it. Agnes set it on the stove with a *clank*. "Having some?"

Zoey didn't answer.

Mia was staring at Agnes and the shirt. "That's my blouse, isn't it?"

"Do you remember when you bought it?"

"I was with . . . you. Wasn't I?"

"Yes. And you wore this when you last saw Victor. In Manhattan, the day of your fall. He has a photo of you wearing it."

"Yes, I saw that," Mia said. "He showed me."

"And the next time it's seen is one hour ago. When did you take the blouse, Zoey?"

"Here. Yesterday! I loved it, and I know it's wrong, and that's why I was going upstairs to put it back."

"Did Stephanie catch you and you pushed her out the window?" Agnes asked.

"What? No!" Zoey yelled. "What happened?"

"We'll find out," Victor said. "We called 911 for real. The ambulance is on its way."

Agnes took the floor back. "Zoey is the only one here who still has to offer up where she was that night. She already admitted that watching the four-hour Danish movie about sad orgasms was a lie. And she wasn't with Ethan, because he was out."

"Could you stop now? This is all part of your Mia thing," Ethan said to Agnes. He tossed the passport down on top of the gym bag.

Zoey felt a surge of emotion. Even after she'd voted for his banishment, he was defending her. He was loyal when it mattered. That she could say for him.

"Let her finish," Victor said. "We all have a Mia thing."

Agnes didn't look fazed. "Martin spoke to a woman on the phone that night. It was someone he knew, someone upset, but it wasn't Mia. We know that because Cameron told us. And we know you and Ethan fought that same night." Agnes glanced at Zoey as she said it.

"He and I were texting. She must have known that?" Mia said, glancing at Ethan for affirmation.

"The fight sent him out to be by himself. Walking, as he does not drive," Agnes said.

"I don't see the point of two drivers in the city." Zoey crossed her arms. She couldn't believe Mia was taking Agnes seriously while she was wearing her clothes.

Martin wasn't there to say who he'd spoken to or what had been said, so to Zoey's mind, Agnes was heading toward a brick wall as far as arguments went.

"Right. Zoey, you do drive. Did you phone Martin and Mia's home looking for Ethan in a jealous rage? Did you get a drunk Martin instead, and he let slip that Mia was alone, out here in the country? Since the AirTag had already been discovered on her car and removed, you must've learned where she was from him. Did he maybe let on that she was involved with someone . . . an old college friend? That must have sent you over the edge. You imagined they were both out here. But you presumed the wrong friend."

Agnes turned on the pilot light. With a click, a blue flame lit under the kettle. "You mentioned this kettle being dropped by Mia the night of her accident. That she dropped the kettle and slipped. I checked Stephanie's notes and Martin's Facebook post. There was water on the floor the morning they found Mia, but no mention of the kettle. We know there's a defensive bruise on Mia's arm. It was from the fire poker hidden deep in the guesthouse, a place you've stayed before."

"With Ethan," Zoey argued.

Agnes smiled, but it wasn't friendly. She raised an eyebrow. "You bragged about that. How many more times you were invited up here. You also said that all the wives out here cheat—and I quote 'Club Hedonism in culottes'—because you knew that she *was*. Before Cameron discovered it on her car a few days after our Sunday brunch, you used the AirTag to trace Mia to a hotel, didn't you?"

Zoey stared but said nothing. Her whole body felt numb.

"The last time you came here, you weren't invited. You drove up, angry, while Ethan was out walking around under the Brooklyn Bridge, doing his brooding thing. Mia couldn't have expected you—she was texting with me by then. So you surprised her, and she tried to calm you down. She went to the kitchen to put tea on. But no. The fertility meds meant you were angrier than you've ever been. Rage poured out of you. Years of resentment."

Zoey backed up a step and bumped into Cameron. She couldn't believe Agnes was confronting her like this—Agnes, of all people.

"You took the poker from the living room, surprised Mia in the kitchen, striking her in the arm. The kettle fell, spilling water—there's your first *clang*, Mia." Agnes glanced at her. "The force of the blow knocked her backward, and she fractured her skull on this floor." Agnes gestured to the stone flooring they were all standing on. "You lifted the poker for a death blow but struck the island instead."

"Two clangs," Mia whispered as her skin tone turned ashen.

"Exhausted, you left her there, thinking she was dead. Luckily you got back before Ethan did. And today, you mentioned visiting her in the hospital. Why would you do that? Risk her waking up and seeing her assailant? On the drive here you told me, explicitly, that you didn't go see her, but that Ethan did. And I know he told you something that put you at ease: 'She called me Duckie.' Mia's memory was gone. You had to go to the hospital and see it for yourself."

The kettle whistled.

"You're the director?" Mia said, staring at Zoey. "I remember you in the hospital. Sitting there in a chair at the foot of the bed. You said, 'I'm sorry. It's all my fault.'"

Zoey stiffened. She glanced at Mia, uncertain of how much she recalled. Then she stepped toward Agnes to show her she hadn't out-maneuvered her—not in the slightest.

"Well, Agatha Misery. I think you have a great story there." She watched Agnes's face contort at the new nickname. "Victor, it would make a perfect show, don't you think? But new information has come to light about Martin. Cameron, what we talked about—it's time to speak up."

"I'm not sure about my dad being in New York all night." Behind Zoey his voice was weak and unconvincing. "I smoked a joint, and I fell asleep. I don't know. Maybe nine p.m.?"

"Maybe it wasn't Ethan," Zoey offered. "Maybe it was Martin. He could have come out here. And what happened in the garage could be the result of guilt. He planned to get the bag and go on the run but, tormented over what he did to Mia . . . well, you saw."

"I don't know if Cameron is a trustworthy witness," Agnes said, her gaze skipping between Zoey and the teenager.

Ethan placed his hands on the kitchen island and leaned in. "Yeah, what's with you two?! What's going on?"

Agnes fished under the hem of the blouse and pulled something from her pocket. She held up Zoey's cell. "This is your phone. And the last Google search was: *Adult woman kissing seventeen-year-old legal?* And in answer to your question, yes. In Connecticut it is legal, but so, so gross."

Zoey watched as her friend's dislike for her mounted in arguments Agnes seemed to know well enough that she'd probably already laid them out somewhere in a spreadsheet. Only the power of Mia could ever bring them together, she realized. She and Agnes would never have been friends otherwise.

Ethan's face had turned red. "Zoey, what were you doing? This little shit? Really?"

She felt Cameron put a hand on her shoulder, claiming her. "She needed a real man for a change."

Victor reached out to the gun on the kitchen island. He pocketed it, stepping noticeably away from Ethan. "I think I'm going to hold on to this for now."

Zoey batted Cameron's hand away and turned to Agnes. "Where did you find my phone?"

"It was in the garage, probably since this morning. I'm guessing you dropped it after finding Martin."

"How did you know my password?"

Agnes smiled, almost sadly. "I'm the perfect friend. I listen to all of you. I remember everything. Of course I know your password. It's *4 Privet*—Harry Potter's address—and it's been your password for twenty years. I know your handwriting. I know why Mia bought the blouse. I know you two better than I know myself. But one thing I don't know, Zoey, is why you took the blouse."

Zoey stood absolutely still, blinking. She could feel her pulse pounding through her veins and tightness in her chest.

"I saw Zoey in that shirt!" Ethan shouted.

"Shut up, Ethan," she growled.

"That night. When I came back from walking around, I thought she had put something nice on for me. She apologized. And then we had makeup sex."

Zoey could see him shrinking back; he was disgusted by her.

"I needed a shirt because I was covered in her blood!"

Everyone fell silent.

Zoey glared at Mia and said, "You got all of them: the loyal one, the rich one, the smart one. I got *him*." Then she stared at Ethan and said, "She didn't even love you. Not like I do."

———

Zoey felt their eyes on her—and beyond the wobbling Sterno lights, she knew the caterers could hear also, from the hall and the pantry, minimum wage witnesses to her failure. It was amazing how much Agnes had gotten right. There were two things she'd gotten wrong that, of course, Zoey would never correct her on.

Agnes's first mistake was the hospital. Zoey had visited before Mia woke up. She had lived most of the two weeks of Mia's coma slowly dying every day with fear that the moment Mia woke up, Zoey's life would be over. Then Zoey realized that she really wanted it to be over.

To give herself up. She'd sneaked into Mia's room and tearfully begged her forgiveness. She'd even taken out the Bible from the nightstand and read Ruth 1:16 to Mia. "For whither thou goest, I will go; and where thou lodgest, I will lodge: thy people shall be my people, and—"

Mia's leg kicked out from under the covers.

Zoey had dropped the Bible as she fell out of her chair. She'd quickly left the hospital without telling the nurses anything. The next day the doctors had decided to call in the anesthesiologist to bring Mia out of her coma.

When Ethan had told her that Mia didn't remember anything, including who he was, Zoey was given her life back. That is, until Agnes had come up with her remembering-party idea.

Agnes was also wrong about how the counter came to be smashed instead of Mia's skull.

Mia, true to her nature, was accommodating and there for her friends on the night Zoey tried to kill her.

When Ethan had stormed out, Zoey had paced their apartment, and after there were no more dishes to angrily scrub, she'd called Mia's Brooklyn number. She'd wanted to know what exactly was going on. Because of the AirTag, she'd known Mia had been at the hotel during the afternoon only the week before. *Why did Mia reach out to Ethan that evening?* Zoey had been surprised both that Martin was the one to pick up and that he was stinking drunk.

She'd demanded to talk to Mia, but Martin had slurred back, "She's at the other house, probably fucking her jerk-off college friend."

Zoey had yelled, "What do you mean? What is she doing?!" which had caused Martin to hang up.

She'd done the hour drive to Connecticut in thirty minutes. Zoey imagined Ethan at the door in a jacquard robe, swirling a snifter of

Rémy in his hand, but instead it had been just Mia, in a basic terrycloth robe, alone and surprised to see Zoey showing up out of the blue.

Surrounded by her lovely things, Mia had seemed clueless and unappreciative of all that she owned, but Zoey, of course, could not imagine it was all about to go away. A temporary set for a role about to be finished.

Seeing how upset Zoey was, Mia had invited her into the living room. Her clothes had been tossed about as if she'd gotten undressed in a hurry. Apologizing for the place being a mess, Mia had bent and picked up her jeans and the blouse, folded them, and left them on a rocking chair. Then, as Mia had gone to put the kettle on, Zoey had let the conspiracy films run free in her mind. *Mia isn't a slob. Why are her clothes everywhere while she hangs around in a robe? Is Ethan hiding in here? Or did I beat him, and Mia's subtly texting him from the kitchen: Turn around, we're caught. She's too smart for us.*

Mia had come back from the kitchen. "I'm so glad you're here. It's been a hell day. It's been a week actually." She'd slumped on the couch beside Zoey.

Zoey hadn't heard a woman about to reveal Martin's indictment, or how Mia had reconnected with Victor, had felt alive for the first time in years, and had been ready to walk away from a bad marriage. In Zoey's mind she'd heard Mia about to say, *I'm the one who won at life. I get everything, even Ethan. You and I are going to sister this shit out over tea, and then you'll be on your way to infertility and loneliness.*

Zoey hadn't been able to hold it in anymore. "How could you do this to me?" she'd asked as the teakettle whistled. "Ethan and I are trying to have a child."

"What are you talking about?"

"The texting tonight. With Ethan."

"Texting? With a friend? Is that why you're here?" Mia launched up off the couch, offended. "Do you know the day I've had? I can't do this anymore. Try having real problems, Zoey."

Mia had turned to walk into the kitchen, leaving Zoey alone in her opulent home. How could she be so self-absorbed, talking down to Zoey about "real problems"? That's when Zoey had seen the fireplace poker gleaming on the stand.

The kettle went flying with the first strike, which had connected with Mia's arm. Mia fell back onto the floor.

Zoey had brought the poker back a second time, only to slip in the spilled hot water.

The poker cleaved a chunk from the counter with a second blow that was meant for Mia as Zoey crashed down. She'd landed next to Mia on the floor, where blood had been leaching out into the water. Zoey was down only for a minute, but when she collected herself, she saw Mia's eyes were glazed, and she'd thought it was over. Everything that Zoey had kept inside—the anger, the jealousy—left her body at that moment. Mia was the ghost—an unremarkable, what-exactly-is-the-appeal ghost—that had haunted Zoey's relationship, and, at least that night, she'd thought she was exorcised.

Zoey had stood up slowly and set the two teacups and kettle back on the shelves. The poker lay on the floor. She picked it up and wondered, *What now?*

She'd noticed the crumbling closet in the guesthouse before and felt a secret thrill at that one bit of disorder in her friend's life. After all Mia had built up, it still wasn't perfect. *Renovations are a bitch, aren't they?*

In the backyard under the full moon, she'd run through anything else that might have been a record of her visit. That was when she'd seen all the blood on her shirt, much darker in the moonlight. Zoey had run back into the house. She hadn't wanted to linger any more— every second in the house was feeling like an hour. She'd grabbed the blouse from the pile of clothes in the living room and, somewhere along the turnpike, had tossed out her own bloodstained shirt from Banana Republic, purchased on sale. *It was tough,* Zoey admitted to herself, *to smell like Mia for the drive back.* Her honeysuckle sweat and Dolce & Gabbana perfume filled the entire car.

Later, when Ethan arrived home, he'd embraced Zoey and nuzzled his face in her neck, sniffing her and moaning that he was sorry.

"I could just drink you up right now," he had whispered in her ear.

It was the most passionate he'd been in months. Her revulsion with him would return, but that night Ethan had finally belonged to her, even if she'd needed to become Mia for it to happen.

Being friends with Mia had been hard, but hurting her had been as uncomplicated as hitting mud with a stick.

Chapter Nineteen

CHECK OUT

By the time the cruisers arrived, the rain had stopped, and the clouds had pushed on. As the caterers carried unused stacks of plates back to the vans, an ambulance pulled up, and Agnes watched as Lise took over trafficking, overseeing everything as if she were director of communications.

Stephanie came to and was moved onto a gurney and taken out by the medics. Before they gave her morphine for her broken legs, Stephanie confirmed Zoey hadn't done anything to cause her fall. "I was closing the windows because of the rain. I feel like an idiot," she said before drifting off again.

Agnes sat down on the couch. She still felt a buzzing in her bones—adrenaline fading. She knew she had sweated through Mia's beautiful blouse, but she had made her case as well as she could have hoped. She vacillated between ecstatic that it was finished, and exhausted.

Zoey didn't fight. Victor and Cameron stayed with her in the kitchen until the police came. Her last piece of nasty business was spitting out "Congratulations, Cagnes and Lazy!" as she passed Agnes and Ethan.

Zoey was cuffed and walked to the cruiser without incident. She was crying as they pushed her into the back seat, and Agnes didn't want to speculate whether it was self-pity or regret. She felt a vague nausea as they all stood on the front porch and watched the cruiser drive away.

"They've asked us to follow them," Victor said to Mia. "You'll need to make a statement."

"I don't even know what to say." Mia looked lost. She glanced at Agnes as if hoping she would have answers.

"Take a sweater—it's gotten cold," Agnes said. She went inside and located the leftover desserts and wrapped two slices of cheesecake in tinfoil. She tucked them in Mia's purse for her in case they were there a long time.

Back inside, Victor was scrolling through contacts in his phone and said he had a lawyer friend in New York he could wake up.

Mia nodded and nodded, but looked as though she couldn't quite believe what was happening. "Do I need a lawyer?" she asked.

"You'll need someone on your side," Victor replied.

"I'll walk you out," Agnes said to Mia as Victor made the call.

He left a voice message that began with "Amir! I'm at this party in Connecticut, and things got pretty messed up . . ."

———⸙———

Mia wrapped herself up in an oversize black cardigan, and the two women walked to Victor's BMW.

"Thank you," Mia said.

"For what?" Agnes asked.

"The memories." Mia reached out for a moment to touch the sleeve of the blouse. "I hardly ever see you in this color. You should keep it. I remember the day we bought it. There may not be that many of those."

Agnes didn't answer but held out her arms, and Mia leaned in and nestled against her. Agnes felt wet on her cheek and couldn't tell until she'd pulled back whether it was a kiss or her friend's tears. The expression on Mia's face told her it was a light kiss.

"I didn't deserve you," Mia said.

Agnes nodded and bit her lip. She understood they were saying goodbye to their tension. The friendship was finally beginning after seventeen years. "Sure you did," she said. "Everyone deserves somebody."

"I should have confided in you about Victor."

"I wouldn't have judged."

"Marriages are . . . complicated." Mia shook her head. "You know, all I see is Adam Driver punching a wall. Which is strange, as that doesn't seem like him."

Agnes smirked, getting the reference to *Marriage Story*. "That makes you Scarlett Johansson again."

The two laughed, and Agnes realized this would be easier than she could have imagined—going on.

Mia held her hand for a minute, then pulled away and got into Victor's SUV. As he trotted up the path, he said, "Good to see you again, Agnes."

As the vehicle pulled away, it felt like that moment when summer camp or the school year has ended, and you watch all your friends getting into their parents' vehicles, easing away from you as though it's nothing. Maybe it was all Mia's movie memories getting to her. Agnes took a deep breath. She would have liked to have stood there all alone for a minute, but one of the catering vans was already pulling out, and she had to get out of the way. The other white van still stood by the garage with its sliding door open, only partially loaded.

Agnes headed through the garage for the side door. The Tesla, no longer the last resting place of Martin, was being examined by two detectives. One of them was pointing to the front seat when he muttered, "Are those animal droppings?"

Agnes averted her eyes so as not to betray any knowledge and quickly squeezed past.

Lise was coming through with the silver water boiler. As they passed in the space, she said she'd poured a few cups of coffee on the island. "Thought you might have a long night ahead of you."

Agnes shook her head. "Thanks, but I think I'm done here."

Lise said, "Sure," not understanding that Agnes wasn't just leaving but tendering her resignation from The Group. From here on, Agnes's relationships would be built individually. How she related to Mia, for instance, was different from how she related to Ethan. Also, maybe it was time to tend other relationships—the ones she hadn't found yet.

Lise moved past her, her hips angled toward Agnes for just a second. She noticed she was quick, athletic—the kind of person who wasn't waiting for anyone else's approval. Ethan appeared at the end of the hall, but Agnes let herself watch Lise walk outside.

"I can't believe this," Ethan said, clutching one of the mugs Lise had mentioned. "I've lost everything. I've lost Zoey. I've lost Mia—it's not going to be like it was."

Agnes picked up a coffee from the counter. She tried to find a bright side for him. "Your show will be really famous. You know, 'YouTuber arrested for murder.'"

Ethan's head bobbed on his shoulders, and he appeared annoyed with her comment, but then after a second, an inquisitive look crossed his face. "You don't think Zoey was right, do you? That Mia never loved me?"

At that moment Agnes felt some empathy for Zoey, for how alone Ethan must have made her feel. Zoey had been driving in circles for so long, like a symbolic vehicle in a Werner Herzog movie, and in the middle was Ethan, thinking only about Mia.

"I texted Zoey's mom. I couldn't bring myself to phone," he said.

"Thank God," Agnes said. "I was afraid I'd have to do it. Zoey's parents never liked me." She laughed, but she felt a band of pain behind her eyes and nose that she knew was a precursor to tears. It took her by surprise.

Ethan saw her emotion and set down his mug. But he didn't step toward her to comfort her or commiserate about how they both should have known. That wasn't going to happen. Too many barbs had been traded; sorrows and competitions that had always run under the surface had sprung up—they were not the friends they'd been upon arrival. Her understanding of Ethan now was like the movie *Election*, which they'd watched in Adaptation Studies. For years everyone had thought Matthew Broderick was the hero and Reese Witherspoon the villain, but upon rewatch Agnes realized it was the opposite.

Agnes sniffed back and gulped the black coffee.

Cameron edged into the kitchen. He said his mother's assistant was driving out to stay at the house in a bit. "It's fashion week in Paris, and my mom can't get away."

Agnes realized that neither family nor partnership was a guarantee of anything in this life.

"Are you staying here tonight, or what are you doing?" the teenager asked Ethan.

"My mom is coming in from Long Island to pick me up. She said she'll be here as soon as she finishes a Diet Coke."

Agnes thought, *Perfect. Getting picked up like a little boy who had a bad time at a sleepover.*

———

Agnes went to her room to change out of Mia's blouse. She would keep it but wanted to put on something that felt more like her. As she was changing, she wondered why Zoey had brought the shirt back to the house that weekend. It was a strangely compulsive act that directly tied her to what she'd done. Without it, Agnes might not have thought there was any more proof than she'd found against Ethan. Zoey could've wound up only locked in the guesthouse.

Zoey must have known it was hopeless. The best she could do was to stop Mia from remembering. But how did one do that, exactly? Their memories, films, and dreams were as elusive and inescapable as their bodies. *You are what you've seen,* Agnes thought.

The pictures were locked in their minds, even when they came out of order. Mia had proved that to all of them.

As Agnes did up a black shirt, she looked down at her fingers on the buttons. She thought about Zoey and the stunning holes in even a smart person's logic. *Was it all for Ethan's attention?* Maybe she'd wanted to be the picture in his eyes for just two more days.

Agnes knew that as she'd urged Mia to look at her life, she was looking at hers, too, and looking forward—for the images that might come next that would make up her future.

Agnes walked into the hall and listened. She heard Cameron ask Ethan if he wanted to go downstairs and play Fortnite while he was waiting. Ethan said yes. It was a strange pairing, but friendship could be like that. Ethan and Cameron had lost the most that weekend, and maybe it would bring them together. She heard Lise in the garage telling one of the other caterers he could take the swordfish skewers; no one wanted them. Agnes moved across the hall into Zoey's room. There, she found the cryotank, and lifted it up and carried it. It was surprisingly light.

———†———

There were bonds that only happened at the end of your thirties, after you started to accept the body aches and the wrinkles that sneaked onto your face overnight. The thirties were when you finally understood why you'd been attracted to people when you were young. It was when you knew how to speak to each other and say what you really thought. It was when you learned to let others go a little, let people *be,* and let yourself be too. You learned to hold people accountable, and you learned to forgive.

Mia was no one's wife now. And neither was Agnes. There was no duty holding her to one place or time, one job, or even The Group. She could choose it, or not, she realized, slamming the hatch of her old Ford Focus. She could choose any future she wanted.

"Hey there," Agnes said when she spotted Lise.

Lise smiled and nodded. She had pulled off the navy V-neck of the uniform and was wearing a black T-shirt and leather jacket. Lise approached the car, holding something out. It was a business card. "In case you ever need anyone to cater a murder again. I mean, hopefully it's a fake murder next time."

Agnes glanced at the card, the woman's full name and number. *Lise Varda.*

"That's so funny," Agnes said.

Lise looked nervous. "What's funny?"

"My name's Agnes. Your last name is Varda. Like Agnès Varda."

"Who's that?"

"She's a director. From the French New Wave."

"Cool. I love old movies too," Lise said, her eyes brightening again. "I've seen all the Twilight movies, like, twenty times."

Agnes nodded her head and thought, *We can work on that,* as Lise walked away. She tucked the card above the visor, turned the key in the ignition, and waited. She tried again. Nothing caught. The Ford wouldn't start. In the rearview she watched Lise load the final trays. Agnes tried the engine one more time. She got out of the broken-down Focus.

Lise was already in the front seat of the van, its engine thrumming. She rolled down the window. "You need a jump, or a lift?"

"Do you have room for a cooler back there?" Agnes asked.

"We have lots of room. Is it food? We got our own fridge back there, too, if you want to use it."

Agnes pulled open the hatch of her Ford and took out the cryotank she'd stolen from Zoey's room. Options felt like a good thing. She carried it across the parking pad and slung it into the back of Lise's van.

"I can chip in for gas," Agnes said as they rolled down the circular drive. She opened her purse and slid a hand in, peeling a fifty from a bundle taken from Martin's go bag. Victor had most of it, to keep safe for Mia—from the sound of Martin's finances, she'd need it—but they'd made Agnes take some as well. She had enough now to get on her feet, pay down her debts, and buy a few months of certainty, which was all she needed. She didn't want to be the perfect friend anymore—Agnes wanted her own life, wherever that took her.

The van bumped and rattled past the gate. Lise put her window down, and Agnes breathed in the cold rainy air—pine and petrichor. They left the estate and zoomed through the trees under countless stars.

Chapter Twenty

AFTER PARTY

God's-eye view:

Mia emerges from a subway stop, climbs the stairs, and rounds the corner of the green rail. She doesn't hesitate or need to locate herself. She heads south.

Cut to low angle:

She wears sandals and a camisole dress, a silk neck scarf tied to one side. There is a light jacket tucked in her shopping bag purse, in case it gets chilly. But it is mid-May and late-afternoon hot. The scene is well lit as pedestrians weave around her and cabs surge and honk in the street.

Mia imagined watching herself on screen often now. It was her way of being in the world, and she accepted it.

She imagined the crane shot hovering slightly above her as she continued on her way: the view looking down at office facades and redbrick apartment buildings, water towers on roofs, or, if they decided to shoot from a window, maybe the steel lace of fire escape bars between Mia and the camera. If there were music for this scene, it would be something popular but unexpected, like the opening to *Jackie Brown* when Pam Grier moves through the airport. Mia continued down the street. Maybe "Ain't No Sunshine," by Bill Withers, or "Tiny Dancer," by Elton John, some hit from before she was born, deployed with a bit of irony. She could never have Pam Grier's poise, but she was the same height as Dustin Hoffman, and *The Graduate* also opened with the same shot. At least Mia felt like she'd finally become the main character in her own film, rather than the wife character. *How did that even happen?* she wondered before realizing the answer: as she'd gotten older, the good parts had stopped being offered to her.

It's easy to have iconic beginnings, Mia thought. *What about iconic middles, though?* Although maybe she was still at her beginning because of how things had gone. Ever since the remembering party, it felt as though she'd moved into a new story. It could be a sequel, only she was that one person in the audience who hadn't seen the first movie.

What she'd been thinking about since that weekend, especially as she got out more and people asked her frequently about her "thing," was this: *Art doesn't change the world. It's a record of the world changing.* With her "thing" she was able to recall all the details around an event of her past, from the fashion to the music to the political mood. The specifics of her own time and place were there, painted in 4K inside the four corners of the screen. But it was hard to tell people all that.

As she'd begun doing job interviews, she'd learned to smile widely and say, "I have some gaps in my long-term memory, but my short-term is excellent."

She was beginning to think of her memory as something that couldn't be recovered. Parts of her life still hung like blackout curtains on a window. She told herself that she lived in New York, and maybe the view out that particular window of her mind was just a brick wall anyway. Having a sense of humor helped with the frustration. Her neurologist said she needed to rethink what disability means—to understand her body had taken a different path than most people and to not give a damn if they didn't understand.

She'd been living in the vacant apartment of an aunt who'd been a professor at NYU. Mia didn't know if it was more beautiful than any place she'd ever lived before or if it just felt that way to someone who'd nearly died. It was across the street from Washington Square and was on the fifteenth floor with a view of the Village, just like the cyclorama in Hitchcock's *Rope*. Sometimes she had to double-check the clouds outside weren't tufts of spun glass stuck on blue canvas.

It was one of those rumored apartments given to retired tenured professors, complete with an old-fashioned elevator and operator, and every time she rode up or down in it, she pretended she was a young Shirley MacLaine in *The Apartment*. The familiarity was helpful—the surroundings of a place she'd visited as a child—even if she hadn't immediately remembered details about Aunt Debra. The 1970s decor suggested she was fond of tasteful Avedon nudes and Joan Didion hardcovers.

Everyone had been helpful. It was a reminder to Mia of how many truly good people she had known in her life, people she suspected she'd largely taken for granted before the accident.

Mia began to hurry now, as she realized she was late. She picked up her pace until she was nearly running. Her sandals danced over the sidewalk cracks.

Just before she came to the bakery where she was to meet Victor, she slowed and let herself have a self-conscious moment. She paused on the corner to pull out a compact. She touched up her makeup and flicked strands of her hair back, then forward until she was satisfied with them. They were supposed to see a film, a digital restoration of *In the Mood for Love*. She hoped they would have time to catch up enough before heading to the theater.

Victor had gone back to LA, and it was the first time they'd be together since that weekend in Connecticut. Learning how broke

Martin had left her—even the homes were taken back by his ex-wife—and all the secrets he'd been juggling made her understand why she'd been driven toward the affair with Victor. The old Mia had been left with no other option. She'd had to connect with someone. She felt lucky now, though, that it had been him.

Victor was at a table just inside the door. Mia saw him through the glass, and he saw her. "Cut to close-up," she whispered.

Mia stared at him so long he raised his eyebrow, a flickered expression of concern, but it was just that she wanted to look at him a beat longer through the glass, as if it were in fact her opening scene. She wanted to memorize him. Up and down her arms, she felt her hairs rise, and goose bumps appeared, like pale stars when they first show in the sky. Victor's T-shirt fit well, but his eyes were tired. There was something delicate around his eyes that she loved, but she reminded herself she didn't want to go too quickly. Maybe she should suggest they just sit and talk. Was the movie even actually necessary?

Life was so fast; it was nice to take some things slow. *What a sublime thing to experience,* she thought, *meeting someone for the first time twice.* She smiled back at him and walked through the open door.

Post-Credits Scene

When Agnes went to buy the *New York Post* for the first time in her life, she had to gently lift up a comatose bodega cat from the pile of newspapers. She saw a headline declaring Martin the "Mini-Madoff," and inside there were angry quotes from DAs talking about how he had evaded both justice and the oligarchs he had ripped off. There was no mention of the party, Mia, or Zoey.

Agnes understood—Martin's story was easy to tell. Her friends' story, less so.

Later, without asking Agnes, Lise had posted a tweet rundown of the weekend to right the wrongs of the article. She started with, "Folks, you're not going to believe this insane job I worked one weekend. Let me tell you about it . . . 1/40."

Goddamn Gen Z, Agnes had sworn to herself. She had texted Lise: Not everything is public! But now it was definitely public: the body, the vote, Agnes's confrontation of Zoey.

Next thing Agnes knew, a friend of a friend who worked at *New York Magazine* began sliding into Agnes's DMs with terrifyingly chirpy messages like "Your name is coming up a lot!" and "Would love to chat with you!"

"Can you tell me how the hell you solved it?" Hannah Schrager Yung asked. They were sitting in Déjà Brew, a café in Agnes's neighborhood. Hannah flicked on the recorder.

In a way, Zoey was the one to solve it with her mistakes. The blouse was something that still haunted Agnes. Its return was Zoey's undoing, and Agnes had chosen to believe that it was Zoey trying to right at least one thing—rewind her actions in the only way she knew how. She felt sorry for Zoey but couldn't absolve her. The deception had run too deep.

"'Solve,' though? I don't think I really 'solved' it."

"That's not what this tweet says, and it has thirty thousand retweets."

Hannah quoted one of Lise's tweets back to Agnes. You know the moment when Batman realizes he's Batman and embraces his destiny? SHE was like that!

Her new girlfriend had less-than-subtly spitballed Agnes into the role of Hipster Detective, the hero New York needed.

"Who is Mia to you?" Hannah shifted the cup and saucer over so she could position the recorder a little closer to Agnes.

Mia Sinclair was the most sincere and generous person she'd ever met—so smart, so beautiful, with a sense of humor that could wilt anyone who underestimated her. Agnes had loved her romantically, put her on a pedestal, and then learned to accept her—her flaws and falterings—and eventually let her go, just enough that they could both find their way forward.

For now, Mia was getting her bearings in Manhattan, and Agnes called once a week to check on her, on Fridays. They kept it to a regular schedule so that Mia wouldn't forget.

Mia's fortitude amazed Agnes, although often Mia surprised her with something she'd thought was unforgettable that had somehow disappeared into Mia's consciousness like a stone sinking below the water.

—⸙—

Agnes realized that Hannah was still waiting for an answer.

"Mia? She's my friend. She'll always be my friend."

ACKNOWLEDGMENTS

Thank you to my agent, Chris Bucci, and everyone at Aevitas Creative Management. I am so grateful to my editor Jessica Tribble Wells, for fully embracing this book and giving it a wonderful home at Thomas & Mercer. Thank you to Tara Rayers, for encouraging me to find ways these characters could grow. Thanks to Anna North for the supportive words.

I did much of the first draft during the early part of the pandemic. This meant my support network became a close circle here in Brooklyn. I'm grateful to Roberta Colindrez, for friendship and lending me a place to write. Thank you, Jenny Grace Makholm, for your strength and community. And to my hair twin, Athalie Paynting, your laughter and affinity is appreciated. Where would I be without Faye Guenther, always ready to talk fiction? For artistic collaborations and the occasional protest, thanks to Cecilia Corrigan.

Thank you to everyone in my family, especially my mother, for sharing her coma experiences from many years ago, and my partner, Brian J. Davis, who doesn't hold it against me when I fall asleep during movies. (And for your support, lending your many skills to my career, and your constant sense of humor.) Love to my son, Henry, for being patient with me. You are the best friend I've ever had.

And finally, thank you to all the filmmakers referenced here, especially Ted Kotcheff, who, over dinner a few years ago, taught me the most valuable rule of the business: "No script, no deal!"

[Cue playoff music.]

ABOUT THE AUTHOR

Photo © 2022 Roberta Colindrez

Emily Schultz is the cofounder of *Joyland Magazine*. Her most recent novel, *Little Threats*, was published by GP Putnam's Sons and was named an Apple Books Best of November 2020 pick. Her novel *The Blondes* released in the United States with St. Martin's Press and Picador, in France with Asphalte Éditions, and in Canada with Doubleday. It was named a Best Book of 2015 by NPR and *Kirkus Reviews*. *The Blondes* was produced as a scripted podcast starring Madeline Zima (*Twin Peaks*), created by Schultz and Brian J. Davis. Her writing has appeared in *Elle*, *Slate*, *Evergreen Review*, *Vice*, *Today's Parent*, Hazlitt, the *Hopkins Review*, and *Prairie Schooner*. She lives in Brooklyn, where she is a producer with the indie media company Heroic Collective.

Her next novel will be *Brooklyn Kills Me*, also from Thomas & Mercer.

www.emilyschultz.com